SPIDER
WOMAN'S DAUGHTER

SPIDER WOMAN'S DAUGHTER

ANNE HILLERMAN

HARPER

www.harpercollins.com

SPIDER WOMAN'S DAUGHTER. Copyright © 2013 by Anne Hillerman. All rights reserved. Printed in the United States of America. No part of this book may be used or reproduced in any manner whatsoever without written permission except in the case of brief quotations embodied in critical articles and reviews. For information, address HarperCollins Publishers, 10 East 53rd Street, New York, NY 10022.

HarperCollins books may be purchased for educational, business, or sales promotional use. For information, please e-mail the Special Markets Department at SPsales@harpercollins.com.

FIRST EDITION

Library of Congress Cataloging-in-Publication Data has been applied for.

ISBN: 978-0-06-227048-1 (Hardcover)
ISBN: 978-0-06-229277-3 (International Edition)

13 14 15 16 17   OV/RRD   10 9 8 7 6 5 4 3 2 1

To Don, my inspiration

For my mom, and in memory of my dear dad

SPIDER
WOMAN'S DAUGHTER

1

"I get this call, out of the blue. A woman. First, she reminds me that I saved her life. Then says she wants me to do her a favor . . ."

Navajo Police lieutenant Joe Leaphorn, retired, paused for effect, pushing away the plate of toast crumbs and empty packets of grape jelly so he could rest his forearms on the table. "Wouldn't you think she'd be offering to do me a favor?"

A couple of the cops sharing the table chuckled. "Musta been one of those rich white ladies you've been doing insurance work for," Officer Harold Bigman said. "You better not tell your Louisa."

Officer Bernadette Manuelito said, "What was the favor?"

Leaphorn smiled. "I don't know, Bernie. She set up a lunch date so she could ask me, and stood me up."

More chuckles. "Maybe she wanted to find out how good a PI you really are," someone tossed in.

"It turned out all right," Leaphorn said. "While I was waiting I ate an excellent BLT, enjoyed the quiet. And she gave me a reason not to drive in to Santa Fe that day on another case. I'm getting too old for all this stuff."

The waitress refilled coffee cups. The Navajo Inn had been a favorite meeting place for cops long before Bernie joined the force, back when Leaphorn worked full-time as a detective. Back when he first earned his reputation as one of the brightest minds in the extended, tightly knit community of the Navajo Nation police force.

Captain Howard Largo said, "Okay, folks, let's get to business. Leaphorn, you're welcome to stay as always."

Leaphorn had a standing invitation to join these Monday breakfast sessions, ostensibly to brainstorm about unsolved cases before the meeting switched to routine matters of budget and staffing. Sometimes they just shared jokes and coffee. Leaphorn and Largo went way back.

In addition to his leadership team, Largo rotated a younger officer into the group each week. Today would have been her day off, but Bernie had put on her uniform and driven an hour from her home in Shiprock, honored to be included. The brainstorming hadn't generated any warm ideas on cold cases, but it had been fun. She'd watched Leaphorn pull out the little brown notebook that lived in his jacket pocket, jot down a few things. In a day or two, if he stuck with his standard pattern, he'd call in with a good lead, a clue to follow.

Bernie felt her cell phone vibrate. Jim Chee, fellow cop and husband who had been annoyed with her that morning, calling from his office at Shiprock.

"Gotta take this. I'll be right back." She stood, all five foot two of her, and headed to the lobby. Leaphorn scooted his chair back. "You guys have boring bureaucracy to deal with. I'll get out of your hair. Thanks for the breakfast."

Leaphorn strolled into the lobby, nodding to Bernie, cell phone at her ear. "Say hi to Chee for me," he said. She watched him head toward the parking lot, noticing that he was limping a bit. She knew he had a touch of arthritis in his knee. She should have asked him about that. And about Louisa.

"Hello, beautiful," Chee said. "Done with the meeting?"

"Not quite. The lieutenant had some good stories. Now the humdrum stuff looms on the horizon. Your timing was perfect."

Through the lobby window, she saw someone climb out of the blue sedan backed in next to Leaphorn's white truck. She watched Leaphorn walk toward the truck, extract the keys from his pants pocket.

"You still grumpy?" Chee asked. "I got off to a bad start this morning."

The person extended an arm toward the lieutenant. Bernie saw a gun. Heard the unmistakable crack of the shot. Saw Leaphorn stagger back, falling against his pickup. Crumple to the asphalt.

She dropped her phone as if it were on fire, Chee still talking, and ran. Pushing the restaurant's heavy glass doors open, she raced toward Leaphorn, reaching for her gun. She watched the shooter scramble into the car and heard the sedan's tires on the asphalt as it sped away, keeping the car in her peripheral vision as she reached the lieutenant. Squatting down, Bernie pressed her fingers beneath his jaw, feeling for the thread of a pulse against her fingertips.

His beautiful dark eyes stared at her, through her. Blood flowed down his face from the hole in his forehead, onto her hands.

"Stay with me," she whispered. She spoke to him in Navajo, the language of her heart. "Don't die. Please don't die."

She heard others running up behind her, caught the blur of their brown uniforms at her eyes' margins while she kept her focus on the lieutenant. She recognized Largo's voice, taking charge, barking orders.

Bernie said, "He's alive. Two-door blue sedan. Arizona plates. Headed west on 264. Driver was the shooter. A black hoodie."

Bernie noticed the lieutenant's skin growing paler, blood pooling beneath his head. She'd never been squeamish; from the time she was old enough to walk, she'd watched her grandmother kill a chicken for their dinner and occasionally slaughter an old sheep. But if Leaphorn died, she knew his *chindi* would be restless, looking to cause trouble as they all did, as was their nature. It wouldn't matter that she loved him and he, in his gruff, official way, loved her.

She spoke in Navajo. "Help is coming. Hang in there, my uncle." She moved closer to him on the asphalt, the side of her body now against his prone shape, held his hand. She wanted to put his head in her lap, but her training stopped her. She knew moving a head injury victim could cause more trouble.

She felt the deep rumble of police units roaring to life. A siren wailed, followed by another.

Someone asked, "You okay, Bernie?"

"Yeah."

She felt Leaphorn's body shudder. "Stay with me," she told him. "I promise I'll find out why this happened and who did this to you." Who would try to kill such a valuable man? An old man now. Where was the blue car?

Then she heard a different siren, the howl growing louder as it approached. She looked up from his closed eyes as the ambulance parked and the attendants ran to her.

"One bullet hit him," she said before they asked. "A head wound. I saw him collapse. I haven't moved him."

An EMT lowered himself next to them. She smelled the sweat from his uniform.

"You hit?"

"No. Nothing."

"Who is he?"

"Leaphorn. Lieutenant Joe Leaphorn."

"No kidding? I've heard of him," the man said. "I need you to move, Officer, so we can get to work here."

She squeezed the lieutenant's hand and stood. The EMT spoke to Leaphorn as he felt for a pulse, watched for signs of a reaction to his questions. The other man rolled the gurney out with portable oxygen, a neck brace, more.

"Are you all right?" the second EMT asked her.

She nodded. "Just focus on him." She noticed a flash of metal on the ground. Leaphorn's keys. She wiped the blood from her hands onto her pants, then put the keys in her pocket.

They loaded the gurney into the ambulance. She thought about the blue car. Everything was different now. She saw Largo at his unit, radio in one hand. He noticed her, put the radio down and walked to her, put his hand on her shoulder. They watched the ambulance drive away, lights flashing.

"I didn't get much of a look at the shooter," she said. "Small. Dark clothes. A single shot. I didn't get the plate number, but it was Arizona."

"The FBI is on the way. They will need a statement from you. You know how these things work."

She knew how it worked. In any serious crime in Indian Country, including attempted murder of a law enforcement officer, investigation fell to the FBI. Leaphorn was still deputized, even though he was retired. The Navajo Police worked in conjunction with the feds, which usually meant they took the role of stepchild. But every cop hated a wannabe cop killer. When it was personal, the rules could bend, meaning the Navajo Police could have a bigger role. She knew Largo would make sure of that.

"Stay put, help Bigman secure the crime scene until whoever's coming gets here. When you're done with that, come talk to me."

"Yes, sir," she said. "This stinks." She reached in her pocket and handed Leaphorn's key ring, with a woven leather fob on the end, to Largo. "I picked these up over there. I should have just left them at the crime scene. I'll let the guys know where they were."

Largo said, "I'm glad nothing happened to you." He turned his broad back toward his car, then faced her again. "Chee called. I told him what happened. He wants you to call him."

The town of Window Rock, the capital city of the Navajo Nation, gets its American name from the red sandstone arch, a low eye in the sky, a graceful portal from heaven to the earth. Formed by wind and rain, it's known as Tséghahoodzání in Navajo. Beneath the arch, a natural spring bubbles up, a source of healing water and a tangible blessing in desert country. The spring gives the site its other Navajo name, Ni' 'Alníi'gi.

Bernie couldn't see the arch from the parking lot of the Navajo Inn. Instead, she looked at the white pickups and SUVs of the Navajo Police Department, more officers than she'd ever seen at a crime scene. But there had never been a shooting of one of the Navajo Nation's best-known policemen in broad daylight outside a busy restaurant, with a table full of other cops just a heartbeat away.

The assemblage of officers and chorus of sirens alerted the peaceful people of this largely Navajo town of about three thousand to the fact that something serious had happened. Restaurant patrons left bacon and eggs in the dining room to watch the commotion; travelers heading west from Gallup, New Mexico, or east from Ganado, Arizona, slowed down to gawk. No doubt they talked about it as they drove—probably good for at least ten miles' worth of conversation.

She watched Largo fold himself into his unit and head to police headquarters to coordinate the search for Leaphorn's attacker. Other officers, she noticed, had cordoned off the place where he had lain bleeding, along with the rest of the parking lot. It was still early, but the day promised to continue the hot, dry June. Typical early summer weather waiting to be broken by the start of the thunderstorm season was still weeks away.

In addition to curious locals, the growing crowd included the *bilagaana* tourists, visitors from California, Texas, and elsewhere who parked at the Navajo Inn for a bite to eat and a cruise through the gift shop. The crime scene meant a change in their schedules.

Officer Bigman stood next to a white man poured into a T-shirt that hugged tight to his beefy shoulders. "Phoenix . . . a flight tonight . . . ," Bernie heard, and she noticed that the tourist's face was an unnatural shade of pink. Even before he took that step toward Bigman, she'd sized him up: belligerent and obnoxious, personality characteristics amplified by being told no.

"We had nothing to do with any of this. I won't stand for it." Pink Face was yelling now, staring at her as she walked closer. "This is police harassment."

She saw Bigman's shoulders stiffen and felt her own blood spike with adrenaline.

"You need to calm down, sir," Bernie said. Her voice was louder than she'd intended. Good. She stared hard at Pink Face. "We'll have your car to you as soon as we can."

She saw him look at her hands and arms. He opened his mouth. Closed it. She kept her gaze on him, steady as an eagle.

"The one who got shot was a fellow officer," she said. "A friend of ours, too. We're doing this right. You don't want to get in the way of that. Trust me."

"How long before my wife and I can get our car?"

"As long as it takes," Bernie said.

"We'll let you know," Bigman added.

Bernie noticed the man staring at her again. "There's blood on you."

"Why don't you go inside, sir, get out of the sun."

The man opened his mouth to speak. Closed it. Headed for the air-conditioned restaurant.

Bigman exhaled loudly. "Largo says you got to him first."

"Yeah. He was still alive in the ambulance."

"It's tough being first," he said.

She remembered that Bigman had happened on the scene when an officer from Fort Defiance, a friend he'd gone to high school with, took a bullet in the chest from a drug-crazed gangbanger.

"I've got an exciting job for you," Bigman said. "Help us search the parking lot for shell casings, cigarette butts, whatever else we can find."

"Sure," she said. "I need to hang here until the feds come. I'll be back as soon as I wash off."

She walked through the lobby, now crowded with customers waiting for their cars and Navajo Inn staff watching the excitement. In the restroom, she ran cool water over her hands and arms, watched as it flowed pink down the drain, then, finally, clear. She added soap. Noticed she was shaking. Examined herself in the mirror as she washed her face with a damp paper towel. Smoothed her hair. Then went back outside to work.

The day had grown from warm to hot when the sleek black Crown Victoria with tinted windows pulled up to the Navajo Inn's front door and parked in the loading zone. Unlike most cars in Window Rock, it had a dust-free car-wash shine.

A man in a gray suit, pale blue shirt, and deep blue necktie climbed out, moving like a person sure of himself. Bernie recognized him before he said a word.

"Officer Manuelito?"

"That's me."

"Agent Jerry Cordova." He showed her his shield. "Anything interesting out here?"

"Not unless you're interested in fast food wrappers. Some cigarette butts, but nothing around where the shooter parked," Bernie said. "No shell casings."

"Let's go inside where we can talk."

He steered her to a quiet table in the rear of the restaurant. In his early thirties, she thought. Younger than the typical FBI guy who came to the rez. The FBIs stationed in Gallup were either on their way out or on their way up. Thick black hair, clear skin, a nice smile. Something about him told her he understood how the federal system worked and how to make the most of it.

"You want something?" Cordova asked.

Bernie smiled at the waitress. "A Coke would be great."

Cordova ordered iced tea.

They sat quietly a minute.

"You know him?" Cordova asked.

"Yes. I met him when I first started here." She'd left home and police work for a stint with the Border Patrol, missed Dinetah, the Navajo motherland, and rejoined the Navajo force.

The waitress brought the drinks, a plate of sizzling French fries, and a red squeeze bottle of ketchup. The round-faced, big-bellied Navajo woman had been at the restaurant ever since Bernie had been coming here. Nellie Roanhorse, Bernie remembered.

"I thought you could use something to eat," Nellie said to Bernie. "The one who got shot, he liked our fries." Bernie realized Nellie thought Leaphorn had died and was using the custom of not saying the name of the deceased so the malevolent spirit left behind, the *chindi*, wouldn't think you were calling it.

"That man was alive when he left in the ambulance," Bernie said. She saw the waitress's face relax.

"Someone picked up your phone," Nellie said. "They have it for you there at registration."

Cordova said, "We're going to be talking privately a few minutes. I'll wave at you if we need anything."

After Nellie left, Bernie sipped her Coke. "I wasn't expecting the FBI to be here so quickly."

"Luck. I had some interviews in St. Michael's. Otherwise, I would have been in Flagstaff." Cordova carefully tore the corner off a white packet of sugar and sprinkled it into his tea. "Have you ever been to that old mission? It's really interesting."

"Did you notice the typewriter they've got over there?" Bernie said. "It was the first one to be keyed for the Navajo language."

"Impressive. A beautiful spot, too." She watched Cordova empty three more packets of sugar into his tea and stir. She noticed his well-tended nails and gold wedding band.

"I heard Lieutenant Leaphorn could look at evidence and read it to discover stuff no one else saw," he said. "I heard he could make a few phone calls to his contacts and shake things up. That he could take an investigation that had been long stalled and move it forward."

"He's special. We worked together on a cold case involving a missing woman," Bernie said. "He found her body locked in one of those Quonset huts at Fort Wingate years after she'd disappeared. He has an amazing mind for detail. The lieutenant and my husband worked together on a bunch of cases a few years ago, so I knew him that way, too. He's good at what he does, and he loves it."

"That's why Largo kept him in the loop even after he retired?"

Bernie nodded. "That why we call him lieutenant, not just Leaphorn."

"I wondered about that." Cordova took out a fancy tape recorder. "We'd better get on with this. Are you ready?"

"Let's do it." Bernie felt anxiety clutch her stomach, squeezing.

"Take a deep breath," he said. She did.

"I'm not going woo-woo on you, but let your brain relax. Let your thoughts float. As I ask questions, see if any images come up. Don't push, don't hurry. Take your time to revisit the scene and study what's there. You can close your eyes if that helps."

She kept her eyes open.

She started in the lobby, watching the shooter open the door of the car.

"Tell me about the person," he said. "Every detail."

"Small," she said. "Maybe five foot three. Hundred and twenty pounds. A black hoodie pulled up. Dark pants, dark hand on the gun. I remember a glint of something silver on the wrist." She shook her head. "If only I'd moved faster, I could have had a real description. I never should have stopped my morning run."

Cordova said, "Life is full of if-onlys. You look fit to me. Better than average." He smiled at her. "But don't let me discourage you from running.

"Take another breath. Don't judge yourself, just tell me what happened. That's all." He asked about the car again, taking her over the same territory from a slightly different angle, searching for details. She remembered a glimpse of a red bumper sticker.

He asked about the gun.

A pistol, she said. Black. Too quick to see much else about it.

"Did Lieutenant Leaphorn mention getting death threats?"

She shrugged. "Not to me. He's a private man. Keeps his thoughts to himself."

"Any jealous husbands, angry neighbors, crazy kids, family feuds, stuff like that, on his plate?"

She shook her head. "He never talked about neighbors. Or about relatives. He shares his house with a lady friend, Louisa."

Cordova raised his eyebrows.

"Louisa Bourebonette."

"Bourebonette? A French Navajo?"

"Not Navajo," Bernie said. "She's a white woman, an anthropologist." Bernie thought of the old joke from Anthro 101: Every Navajo family includes Mom, Dad, four kids, and an anthropologist.

Cordova made a note.

"She's taller than I am, gray hair. Drives a white Jeep."

Cordova sipped his sweet tea, glanced out the window that faced the restaurant's back courtyard. "Is Leaphorn married? Any children?"

"No, and no kids. I can see where you're going with this.

Leaphorn's wife Emma died about ten years ago." Bernie picked up a fry, dipped it in ketchup, ate it.

"At this morning's meeting, did Leaphorn seem worried about anything?" Cordova asked.

"No. Not that I noticed."

"Sometimes shootings like this are random. Guys who hate cops, all cops, go berserk. Some poor officer ends up in the wrong place at the wrong time. This might be one of those, and Leaphorn just happened to be the first guy out. But it doesn't smell like one of those anticop cases. For one thing, Leaphorn wasn't in uniform." Cordova tried a fry. No ketchup. "Seems like the guy who did it parked out there, waiting especially for Leaphorn. "

"That's how I see it," Bernie said. "And the guy could be a *she.* Our job is to find out who."

"Cops make enemies," Cordova said. "Comes with the territory."

She knew he waited for her to say something else. "After he retired, Leaphorn started a PI business specializing in insurance fraud cases. He might have a disgruntled client."

Bernie finished her Coke. Thought about asking Nellie for a box for the fries. Decided against it.

Cordova stood up. "I'll be talking to you again." He gave her his card. "Call me if you think of anything else, no matter how insignificant it might seem."

"Whatever I can do," Bernie said.

"Pleasure meeting you, even under these circumstances. I'm sorry about your friend."

By the time she got back to the parking lot, the Arizona State Police crime team, called in by Agent Cordova and Captain Largo, was at work beside the Navajo officers. The looky-loos were still there, too.

"How's it going?" she asked Bigman. "Any news?"

He rose from where he'd been examining the asphalt. "Nothing. The shooter didn't leave a stray business card."

Bigman stretched his neck, rolling it side to side. "We talked to the staff, and a tourist couple checking out about the time the lieutenant was hit. So far, you're the only witness."

Bernie nodded. "The FBI man, Cordova, had a lot of good questions."

"I hear he's sharp," Bigman said. "Won't be long until he moves up the food chain."

"Did you learn anything about the lieutenant? How he's doing?" She pictured Leaphorn as they waited for the ambulance. Remembered the pool of blood on the blacktop.

"Nothing yet." Bigman took off his hat, rubbed his scalp. Put it back on. "This ticks me off big-time. The legendary lieutenant who wrote the primer on how to solve crimes on the rez. Taught a lot of us how to think like a crook, how to figure out why one and one don't always make two. Now we get to use what we learned to solve his own case, figure out why someone would shoot a good man."

"We'll get whoever did this," she said. "I promised the lieutenant."

Bernie climbed into her Toyota, rolled down the windows to let the hot air out. She was glad the car didn't have a thermometer. Seeing how hot it was would have only made her warmer. It was probably ninety outside, she reasoned, and warmer than that in the Tercel. She would have switched on the air-conditioning if she'd had any.

She pulled out her phone and hit recent calls.

Chee answered after the first ring. "Honey. Are you all right?"

"I'm fine."

"Largo told me what happened," he said. "Did you get a look at the shooter?"

"Just a glance. He walked right up to the lieutenant. Fired one shot at point-blank range. The bullet hit Leaphorn in the head. He never had a chance. Then the shooter drove away." She felt emotion welling up now. Shoved it down.

"It was awful." Her words came faster now, tumbling out. "If I'd gone out there with him, things might have been different."

"Things might have been different," Chee said. "You might be dead now, Officer Manuelito."

She heard the tension in his voice. She waited, partly out of ingrained Navajo politeness and partly because she knew the man. When he spoke again, his tone had a smoother edge.

"I could have lost you today. I was scared, sweetheart."

She said, "I need to go. I have to meet with Largo. I can't talk anymore."

She hung up just as the damn tears forced their way out, rushing through the hairline cracks in her willpower.

Window Rock lives on government: offices for the Navajo Nation's president, legislators, and their staffs, the court system and its support team, fish and wildlife, archaeology, fire and rescue, veterans' affairs, tourism, and economic development. The state of Arizona's bureaucracy provides jobs with departments for drivers' licenses and social services. Federal offices perch along Navajo Route 3 and Arizona 264—the highway to St. Michael's and Ganado, home of the historic Hubble Trading Post.

The Navajo Division of Public Safety headquarters occupies an assembly of low buildings on the edge of the mesa country that frames the town. The compound has a 1960s utilitarian, strictly-business feel to it. Most of the officers who serve are Diné—the Navajo word loosely meaning "The People." Related or not, they treat each other like relatives, occasionally engaging in family feuds but, in times of stress, working together with a single focus. In addition to following police procedure, for the officers on the force, serving effectively means understanding relationships among and between the Navajo Nation's extended families. The officers need to know who has a grudge against whom, who has problems with drugs or drinking, who might be a little crazy, born mean, or both. They need to understand who respects the Navajo Way and who is estranged from it. The roughly 230 men and women commissioned as officers work out of seven home-base locations, responding each year to an average of more than 289,000 calls for service spread out over the 17.2 million acres of the reservation.

Inside the police building, Bernie noticed an eerie quiet, the absence of the usual joking and carrying on, a stillness befitting he who had been ambushed. News travels fast in a place like this, and word that a famous old policeman had been shot down in cold blood moved like lightning.

Captain Largo paced in his office, door open. Bernie had never seen Largo agitated. She tapped on the door frame, saw him glance up, and walked in.

"How is the lieutenant?" she asked.

"The ambulance just got to Gallup. He made it that far."

Bernie looked at her hands, discovering dried blood beneath her nails.

"You did just right out there. Good description of the car," Largo said. "Sit down."

She felt the cool metal of the straight-backed chair through her shirt. It was the only furniture in the office except for Largo's roller chair and desk. He sat, too, looking across the piles of paper on the flat metal desktop. "No trace of the shooter yet."

"I thought of some other details," she said. "I told the FBI. Damage to the rear right fender. Whining sound, like a bad fan belt. The shooter was wearing gloves or had dark hands."

"Cordova filled me in. He said you were a good witness." Largo moved to the window. She glanced past him at the view of the parking lot, the sun glinting off the windshields. He said, "We're having coffee, joking, and then, bang. It could have been you, me, any of us in that room, any week over the past whatever many years we've been meeting there. Any wacko with a grudge could have taken a shot."

She felt the current of anger in his voice and noticed the lines of stress in his forehead. Largo seemed noticeably older than at breakfast.

"We'll catch him," Bernie said. "And we'll find out why. I promised the lieutenant before he left with the EMTs."

Largo sighed, sat down again. "I want you to take the next couple of days off. I've been involved in things like this before. They take a toll."

"Sir, I have to work on this case." She tried to keep her voice calm, not to let her surprise show.

Largo said, "I'm not asking you. I'm telling you."

"Put me in charge of this, Captain. I'll work my heart out."

"We're all in this together. Everyone here feels just like you do."

"You're wrong about that, sir." She didn't remember ever being so furious, so close to exploding. "I saw him fall. If I'd walked out there with him, I might have gotten a shot off. I have to do this. I promised him. Promised to—"

Largo held out his hands, palms facing her. "Enough. What is it about 'off the case' you don't understand, Officer?"

Bernie felt the room closing in on her.

Largo was standing now, speaking louder. "Not only were you the first responder at an incident where a fellow officer was seriously wounded, you may be the only eyewitness. You know the rules about this. Or if you don't, you ought to." He stepped close enough to touch her. "If you were a man, I'd treat you the same. Same as any officer who is there when a brother goes down. Don't start thinking this is sexist or something. It's normal procedure. Clear?"

The phone rang. He answered it. Nodded. "Yeah. Thanks."

Then he turned to her. "They're done at the crime scene." He picked up Leaphorn's keys and put them in Bernie's hand. "Go back to the restaurant. Get his truck and drive it to the house. Tell Louisa what happened. His records still have 'Wife, Emma' as emergency contact. We need to find some family. Do that for him. Then you're out of here."

She sat silently until she could trust herself to speak. "Emma had some brothers. I remember him talking about Emma's sister, too, when we first met. I don't know about anybody else, anybody closer." Largo knew the rest, how Emma's traditional Navajo family had assumed that Leaphorn would marry Emma's sister after Emma died from complications of brain surgery. Leaphorn's violation of that expectation had created a chasm.

"Find whoever we need to call," Largo said. "Then start your leave. Chee will be in charge on our end, our liaison with the feds, reporting to me."

"Chee?"

Largo frowned. "I know you, Manuelito. I know you'll be involved. You won't be able to stop yourself. But I don't want to hear about it unless you want me to fire you. Now get out of here."

She walked into the hallway outside Largo's office and saw Chee standing there, a little pale, clenching and unclenching his hands.

"Hey you," he said. Then he hugged her fiercely, without any more words, and she hugged back, forgetting she was in uniform, at work, with other cops around.

Finally, she raised her face from his chest.

"Largo told me to drive Leaphorn's truck back to his house, see if I could find any names or numbers of relatives for emergency contacts. And then go home, off the case. Can you pick me up at Leaphorn's place?"

"I'll meet you there. I have to talk to Largo first."

"He told me you're in charge of the investigation," Bernie said.

Chee nodded. "Yeah. That's the second reason I'm here. I hope Largo knows what he's doing."

*   *   *

The parking lot at the Navajo Inn was virtually deserted now, police vehicles gone, yellow crime scene tape removed, trapped tourists on their way. Bernie parked her old Toyota next to Leaphorn's white truck, one slot over from the spot the shooter had used. Someone, she noticed, had thrown dirt over the blood and swept it up. The dark spot baking into the asphalt beneath the Arizona sun could have been an oil leak. Bernie opened the unlocked driver's door. She climbed up into the truck cab and struggled with the lever, finally managing to force the seat forward enough for her legs. Chee joked that instead of telling people how tall she was, she should tell them how short she was.

She removed the round silver sunshade from the windshield and felt the heat seep in. The truck, an early 1990s Ford, seemed like an extension of Leaphorn himself. Nothing extraneous. Not a fast food wrapper, discarded toothpick, or empty to-go cup in sight. She noticed his well-used blue thermos on the passenger seat and, next to it, a pile of mail and an open package of new manila envelopes.

The Ford started right up. She located the gas gauge—half a tank—and noticed the odometer: 180,432. Almost as many miles as her little Toyota.

She slowed the truck in front of Leaphorn's house, parked in the empty driveway. She pushed the doorbell, waited for Louisa to answer, then rapped her knuckles against the wooden frame. When the house showed no signs of life, she tried the knob. Locked.

Returning to the truck, she picked up the thermos, the envelopes, and the mail. She propped the sunshade in the windshield and walked around the house to the back door. As she suspected, it was unlocked. She knocked and called, "Louisa?" She waited without getting an answer, opened the door, and stepped into the kitchen.

"Louisa? Are you here?"

Over the stainless steel sink, a moon-faced clock ticked loudly. Otherwise, the room was quiet and as neat as she remembered it. A water glass, a spoon, and a mug with the Arizona Wildcats logo stood in the drain rack near the sink.

The few times she'd been here, she'd come with Chee when he needed to discuss a puzzling case with the lieutenant. Louisa had served them coffee and store-bought sugar cookies at this kitchen table and offered an occasional opinion. The sessions prompted the lieutenant to question an odd fact or unlikely sequence of events, which inspired Chee to remember or reconsider something. The process left her smart, competent husband feeling like a schoolboy.

Bernie put the thermos and the mail on the table. Where was Louisa? Why was there one cup in the drain rack, not two?

The kitchen window faced the house next door. More Navajos lived like white people now, some in government houses built close to each other so they could have running water and electricity. When she was a girl, the nearest neighbors, her mother's sister and her family, lived three miles away. Sage, rocks, and welcome emptiness lay between them. Because he was so much older, Leaphorn must have grown up somewhere with even fewer neighbors. After he got well, she'd ask about that, prompt him to tell her some stories from his childhood.

Fatigue washed over her as though she'd run a marathon with thirty-pound weights on her legs. If she had sprinted faster, she would know who fired the shot that took down the lieutenant. She'd eased up on her jogging after she and Jim got married. She used to rise at sunrise, no matter what the season. Run to greet the day. She'd grown lazy, and that might have let the person who hurt him go free.

I wonder if he'll live through this, Bernie thought, but pushed the speculation aside. Her upbringing conditioned her to avoid negative thoughts, even as questions. Her Navajo name was Laughing

Girl, but she didn't feel like laughing now. She noticed the start of a headache. She thought of how the Holy People advised the Diné not to focus on conflict or sorrow. But evil surrounded her, too, some days as much as beauty. She saw the downside of humanity every day she worked as a police officer, in situations that ranged from petty arguments among clan members to four-year-olds fending for themselves while their parents cooked meth in the kitchen instead of dinner.

Why did the Holy People lead the Diné to a world with so much sorrow? Big sorrows, like a good man catching a bullet in the brain. Like her mother abandoning the loom she loved because arthritis crippled her hands. Like her sister Darleen, on the road to becoming a lost young woman.

A sound startled her, and then she recognized it: a row of ice cubes falling into the freezer box. Get on with it, she thought. Stop wasting time. She noticed the yellow phone on the wall. The missing Louisa must have a cell phone because of all the traveling she did. Bernie stood, scanned the list of numbers attached to the refrigerator with a magnet from the *Navajo Times*. Several doctors, a dentist, a car repair shop. Nothing identified as Louisa's cell. The lieutenant must have had her number memorized or programmed into his phone. He complained about how you couldn't get a reliable signal on the reservation and how cell phones interrupted the quiet, but he'd got his, he'd told her and Chee, to keep Louisa happy. He probably had the phone with him when the shooter attacked. But maybe he'd left it here. Worth a look. Find the phone, call Louisa, give her the news. And the logical place for the phone would be connected to a charger.

Bernie didn't notice a charger in the kitchen, so she walked down the hall, passing the living room on the right. The lieutenant or Louisa had closed the drapes to keep out the heat, leaving the house in soft, dim light. Prowling made her edgy, unsettled.

She noticed an open door on the left, a bathroom. Neat, almost sterile. Just the essential towels, hand soap, and a box of tissues; not a toothbrush or a vitamin bottle in sight. It reminded her of a motel, except for the cat box near the bathtub. The electrical outlets were empty; no charger.

The room across the hall held a double bed with a masculine gray spread draped over it and a colorful Teec Nos Pos blanket on top of that. She ran her hand over the weaving. Smooth, fine work. She'd ask the lieutenant to tell her about this rug, who gave it to him and why. The round-topped alarm clock on the dresser reminded Bernie of the clock her grandfather had owned. On the simple wooden table next to it sat a book with a pair of black-framed reading glasses on top of it, and a gooseneck lamp. No phone, cell or otherwise.

She found Leaphorn's office at the next doorway. Another large rug, this one woven to include deep aniline red yarn and the terraced diamond designs that marked the Ganado style, occupied part of the wooden floor. Among the books on his shelves, the lieutenant had intermixed brown-glazed Navajo pots, a small polychrome Hopi seed jar shaped like a flying saucer, an alabaster eagle, and an assembly of Zuni fetishes. A stuffed chair sat in the corner with a nearby table and a floor lamp. On the table, Bernie noticed a wedding basket and two framed photographs. She leaned down for a closer look at the smaller picture, a black-and-white shot of a Navajo woman holding the same basket, a young Leaphorn standing beside her, both of them smiling. She guessed the woman was his late wife, Emma. Next to it, the lieutenant had parked the color picture of Chee and Bernie on the white beach in Hawaii the week after their wedding, the vast deep ocean blue behind them. No photos of Louisa, his housemate, friend, and maybe something more than that for the past five years. No photos of anyone else, including those who might be relatives.

The room's focal point was the lieutenant's rolltop desk. She sat behind it, feeling like an intruder. He had piled a stack of books next to the computer monitor. She opened the top one, *From This Earth: The Ancient Art of Pueblo Pottery*, to a page Leaphorn had marked with a slip of paper and found a spread of photos of pots and potshards with geometric designs. She glanced at the other titles: *Anasazi Pottery*; *Ten Centuries of Prehistoric Ceramic Art*; *Pueblo Potters of the Four Corners Country*; *Ceramic Treasures of Chaco Canyon*. All from the Navajo Nation library. A research project, she guessed, for a client somewhere.

A dog barked, and then she heard a woman's voice and an end to the barking. She wouldn't like living so close to neighbors. She and Jim didn't have a fancy place, but she loved the silence of their spot along the San Juan River.

She scanned the lieutenant's desktop for the phone. Not there. She pulled her shirttail free and used it to open the top drawer. A neat pile of pens in one compartment. Pencils, all sharpened, in the other, along with an organized arrangement of letter-size envelopes, paper clips, and business cards wrapped in a rubber band.

She opened the large lower drawer next. She saw neatly labeled folders with old-fashioned paper tabs for alphabetizing, scores of files arranged behind pastel dividers. Nothing marked "death threats."

She heard a vehicle approach on the gravel road and pull up into the driveway. Louisa coming home, she thought. As she pushed the drawer closed, her gaze drifted to the floor. She noticed a wastebasket with some torn paper worth investigating and a white cardboard filing box on the floor next to it. On top sat the phone charger. Empty. Darn it.

She hurried out of the office into the living room. She pushed back the drape before opening the front door and saw Chee walking toward the porch.

"Hello, beautiful," he said. "Louisa here?"

"No. Not yet. I was hoping she'd show up so I could talk to her before you got here."

"Come outside and take a look at this."

She followed him, feeling the intensity of the sun through her uniform shirt. He stopped at the edge of Leaphorn's driveway and pointed at the dirt with the toe of his boot. "What do you think?"

"Wheel tracks. A dolly? Maybe the lieutenant or Louisa was moving something."

"Maybe one of those rolling suitcases," Chee said. "Maybe that's why we can't find Louisa."

"She'll turn up," Bernie said. "Hey, thanks for picking me up. I saw lots of files in the lieutenant's desk drawer. The current stuff might be relevant to the shooting. And we ought to check the information on his computer."

Chee laughed as they went inside. "I'll get right on it. Just point me in the right direction. Anything else?"

Bernie ignored him, leading the way down the hall to the office.

"Look at that." Chee examined the maze of wires dangling behind Leaphorn's desk. "That computer must be twenty years old. I remember him talking about how slow it was and about how he was going to get a new one." He shook his head. "It was one of the few things I ever heard him complain about. He didn't complain much. Except about me."

"He appreciates you, so he expects a lot from you," Bernie said. "He just didn't know how to show it. I mean, doesn't know how to show it."

"Tough as an old boot," Chee said.

Bernie noticed that she hadn't closed the large drawer completely. "The files are in there."

Chee extracted latex gloves from his pants pocket and nudged the drawer fully open. He scrutinized the folders, then pulled one out.

"Leaphorn and I collaborated on this case. It fascinated me to see how his mind worked. We discovered a crazed scientist experimenting with bubonic plague. An old lady tending her goats helped us solve the thing."

"Sounds like an adventure."

"It started when a rich grandmother hired the lieutenant to find her granddaughter. The girl had a job as a college intern, working on a public health project on the reservation near Yells Back Butte. Leaphorn's investigation overlapped a case I was on, a situation where it looked like a young Hopi had killed a Navajo cop."

"Did the lieutenant find the granddaughter?"

"Her body. We found the guy who killed her, and it turned out he'd killed the officer, too. The Hopi guy was innocent, except for eagle poaching." Chee added, "The lieutenant told me, 'Good job.' "

She heard the catch in his voice. Although he'd never say it, few things pleased Chee more than the approval of the crusty old lieutenant. "So, how's he doing?"

"We just got word that Leaphorn made it into Gallup."

She heard something in his voice that made her ask, "What else?"

Silence. Then Chee said, "He's too badly injured for treatment there. They called in a helicopter to take him to Albuquerque to the big hospital with the fancy trauma unit."

"When he comes out of this, let's help him get a new computer. A laptop he could take with him on cases, type his notes right into it. That would save him a lot of time."

"You think he'd give up his little leather notebook? No way." Chee turned back to the file drawer. "I'll thumb through these quickly, see if anything jumps out at me. Then I need to get back to the office. Bigman is on his way. He can box these up for us and deal with the computer."

"And will you look for Leaphorn's phone?" she asked. "I'm going to check the rest of the house, see if there's anything out of the ordinary. Maybe his cell will turn up, and I can call Louisa's cell."

She left Chee fanning through the folders. She noticed again how quiet the house was, how different from her cubicle at the station or the constant noise of her unit when she was on the road. The semiretired life might be nice, she thought, but kind of lonely.

She found Louisa's bedroom at the end of the hall. Unlike Leaphorn's room, it looked ransacked. Clothes tossed everywhere, drawers hanging open, shoes on the dresser top. She looked in the closet for a suitcase and saw empty hangers.

Chee's voice startled her. "Some of these folders might be worth following up on, but they're old. Bigman can look at the computer files, see what's more recent. You ready?"

"I'm coming." She told him what she'd found, and what she hadn't found.

"Maybe Louisa keeps her suitcase in the garage or in another closet. Maybe she's just naturally messy. Like your little sister."

Bernie said, "I don't think she's messy. Look how neat the rest of this house is. I think she left in a hurry. Let's go. You've got a lot to do."

On the way out, she pulled a business card from her pocket and wrote "Louisa, call ASAP" on the back. She left it in the center of the kitchen table, along with Leaphorn's truck keys.

Bernie slid into the passenger seat of Chee's police unit, feeling the heat from the upholstery and a film of sweat on her upper lip. Chee maneuvered in behind the wheel and had just started the engine when Largo's voice bellowed through on the scanner.

"Chee, is Bernie with you?"

"Yes, sir. We're heading back to the Navajo Inn for her car."

"Not yet," Largo said. "We found a vehicle that could be the shooter's. Bernie needs to give us an ID."

"We've got the car," Largo said again. "At least, we think so. At Ba-shas'. Bernie needs to verify that before it gets hauled in." An officer at the scene in the parking lot was keeping an eye on the sedan until the tow truck came to deliver it to the impoundment yard, where the Arizona police investigators could go over it for evidence.

"We'll be there in ten minutes," Chee said. "By the way, Louisa may be missing."

Largo said, "I'll put the word out."

Bashas' grocery, on the main drag near the Navajo Nation fair-grounds, was always busy. Merchandise reflected the needs of cus-tomers, most of them Diné and many of them rural. Folks could buy basic items in bulk you might not see at a neighborhood gro-cery outside the reservation: animal feed, Blue Bird flour, gran-ulated sugar in twenty-five-pound bags, gallon tubs of lard. The store stocked canned food in monster sizes, fresh meat, vegetables, and fruit. The sprawling bakery department made sheet cakes for all occasions. On any given day, a dozen women with children or grandchildren in tow populated the aisles.

The modern, well-stocked market was one of the best things

about Window Rock, Bernie thought. She loved to stand in the produce section when the sound of thunder came over the speakers, followed by the mist that sprayed the lettuce and parsley. She could pick up a loaf of bread and a bottle of aspirin for her mother and get a sandwich for those long days when she knew she'd be close to nowhere at lunchtime.

They spotted the Navajo Police car near the back of the lot. Next to it Officer Brandon Wheeler stood in the hot sun, looking at a dark blue sedan. Bernie and Chee climbed out and headed toward him into a gust of fiercely blowing June wind. Grains of sand bounced off their pant legs and swirled in the hot dry air. Air-propelled plastic bags plastered the wire fence that surrounded the lot and hung like flags from the piñon trees. Bernie didn't like the wind. It made her uneasy.

She walked around to the sedan's right rear fender. It was dented, just as she remembered, and had picked up a coating of silver paint. She noticed a red bumper sticker, "UNM Lobos." The University of New Mexico, her alma mater, a three-hour, 170-mile drive away in Albuquerque.

"This is the car," she said to Chee. "I'm sure of it."

"I saw it as I was driving in to help with the search," Wheeler said. "No one near it. I've been keeping an eye on it. No one has touched it since I got here."

Considering how old the car was—Bernie guessed the early 1980s—it was in remarkably good shape except for the dent. She looked in through the open window, noticed the wear on the driver's seat and a patch of duct tape over the upholstery on the passenger side. The backseat was empty, the floors clear. Whoever owned this car took care of it. Except for some sand on the mat beneath the gas and brake pedals, it was clean.

Chee looked at Bernie, then turned toward Bashas'. "I'm going into the store, ask some questions. I'll have the manager close it. You follow up on the Arizona plate check. When you're done on the radio, watch the car so Wheeler can come help with the interviews."

Chee had every right to tell her and Wheeler what to do, thanks to Largo putting him in charge of the investigation. Still, she bristled at taking orders from him. She climbed into his unit car, fuming but silent. She lowered the windows and tried to calm down before starting her assignment.

Wheeler said, "Let Bernie do the interviews. She's better with people. I can follow up with the radio and watch the car."

"Largo took her off the case," Chee said. "She's just here for the ID."

Chee sprinted toward the building, nearly colliding with a rotund Navajo woman rolling her grocery cart toward them.

The woman with the cart advanced. She said, "You're blocking my car."

"You own this car?" Wheeler asked.

The woman glared at him, the look one might give a small, ornery child. She wiped the sweat from her forehead with her hand.

"Yes. That's why I'm gonna put in my groceries and head for home once you get out of the way."

Wheeler said, "This car matches the description of a vehicle involved in a shooting this morning. We need to impound it and check it for evidence. The tow truck is on the way."

The woman's dark eyes widened. "Is this one of those TV shows where they play tricks on people?"

"No, ma'am."

The woman said, "Not my car."

"This is not your car?"

"This *is* my car. But my car was not involved in any funny business." She rummaged in a red purse and held out her hand with a set of keys. The wind stirred her short, cropped hair. "Look, see here?" She switched to Navajo and said, "I need to get on home now."

She pushed her grocery cart toward the car's trunk. Bernie watched from inside Chee's unit as Wheeler moved to block her.

"Because this car was involved in a serious crime, we have to check it for evidence," Wheeler said in English. "Please step away from it, ma'am."

"Lots of cars look like this. Do you think I'm a criminal?"

"I don't know," he said. "I'm asking you to cooperate with us, ma'am. Please show me your driver's license."

The woman stiffened and stared up at his name tag. "Officer Wheeler, my Fudgsicles are melting. I didn't have anything to do with anything bad, but I am not happy with you. This is what they call police harassment. If you keep talking like that, they might think you are crazy."

Bernie picked up the tone of Shopping Cart Woman's voice, sensed trouble in the making. Luckily, the license plate check was nearly done; the officer assured Bernie she would be able to retrieve the name of the car's owner in another sixty seconds.

"Ma'am, I need to see your driver's license," Wheeler repeated.

The woman said nothing, but her defiant posture spoke volumes.

Two police cars, uniformed officers, and an angry woman began to draw a crowd. Chee had succeeded in keeping anyone from entering the market, so the would-be shoppers with time on their hands walked over to investigate the commotion. Several bystanders knew Shopping Cart Woman, nodded to her.

"He wants to arrest me for buying Fudgsicles," the woman said. "That man has handcuffs. I can see his gun. He's going to take me to jail for shopping at Bashas'."

Bernie heard a low rumble of disapproval from the crowd about the same time as the name on the car registration came back. She hurried to the woman, greeting her in Navajo, introducing herself the traditional way, using maternal and paternal clans. The woman, Gloria Benally, did the same. Gloria Benally, the same name the DOT record search had given her as the car's registered owner.

Bernie turned to the dozen people who had gathered to watch. "A good man was shot this morning, and we are searching for a person involved in a shooting. We will open the store when we can. If you can buy your groceries later, I'd recommend that. "

She heard the siren of another police car. An Apache County sheriff's vehicle pulled into the lot, drove past them and up to the front door of the grocery store. Two deputies raced from the car to the back of the building.

She turned to Wheeler, feeling the wind beat against her face. "You can help Chee like he asked. Tell him the car is registered to Mrs. Gloria Benally and we have her here. Nothing on her record."

"You both get away from my car." Mrs. Benally raised her voice. "What in the world is wrong with you?"

Bernie said, "Officer Wheeler and I are so sorry to inconvenience you, but we need your help on this case. The experts will have to look at your car for evidence that could tell us who shot the policeman. That's why the tow truck is coming."

"Tow truck?"

"The one who was shot was a retired officer, a brave man who worked for the Navajo people. The bullet went into his head. The person who shot him drove away in a blue sedan that looked like yours." Bernie paused. "Exactly like this car. Exactly. Right down to the little dent on the fender and the red bumper sticker. I know this is true because I was there when that terrible thing happened. We need your help to find the person who did this before someone else gets hurt."

Mrs. Benally waited to make sure Bernie was done.

"I'm sorry about that man who got shot," she said. "But my car is innocent. I need my car to take home my groceries. What about my Fudgsicles?"

Bernie stared at Wheeler. "This officer will buy you some more when we're all done."

Wheeler looked puzzled. "I'm going to help Chee." He trotted off.

Mrs. Benally smiled for the first time.

Bernie spoke to her in Navajo. "I can tell you are a smart woman and a good observer. We have a mystery here. Is it all right if I ask you a few questions?"

Mrs. Benally, as the story revealed itself, hadn't parked the car at Bashas'. She explained that a friend had dropped her off. She told Bernie the story of how she met the friend at Window Rock Elementary when their sons were both in first grade there. Bernie listened, knowing that Mrs. Benally would eventually talk about the car.

"My son was sad when that boy went off to live with his uncle in Flagstaff," Mrs. Benally said. "My son, he's the one who drives the car here for me."

The wind gusted again, blowing dust in Bernie's eyes and grit in her teeth. It made the day seem hotter. Mrs. Benally had drifted into talking about her friend's son, who was working at the Museum of Northern Arizona and going to school at Northern Arizona University.

Bernie interrupted her. "Forgive me for not being a better listener, but I have to find out about the car so we can begin to learn who shot the policeman."

Mrs. Benally nodded. "Okay," she said. "Ask questions."

Some Navajos thought it rude to speak a person's name, but Mrs. Benally hadn't mentioned it, so Bernie had to ask.

"My son is called Jackson Benally."

"Did your son drive the car today?"

"Yes."

"Then why is the car here?" Bernie asked.

Mrs. Benally scowled. "He leaves it for me. He goes to study in Gallup with another boy who has a car. One of those littler ones that don't use much gas."

Mrs. Benally wasn't sure when Jackson met his friend, only that he left the house about eight, and when she got to Bashas' she found her car parked where he always left it. Bernie asked, "What does your son look like?"

"They say he's handsome."

"How tall is he?"

Mrs. Benally reached her hand a few inches above her own head. Maybe five-eight, Bernie guessed. The shooter hadn't seemed that tall.

"Is he muscular? Fat? Thin?"

"Just right." Mrs. Benally smiled. "Look here. I have a photo on my phone." She reached into her red purse and pulled out a cell from the inside pocket. Pushed a button and flashed the phone toward Bernie. A slim, serious-looking young man wearing a button-down shirt. Short-cropped, thick dark hair. Jackson looked about the same age as Bernie's sister.

"How old is he?"

"He's nineteen. Jackson asked if he could put that sticker on there," Mrs. Benally volunteered. " 'Go Lobos.' He's my first to go to college."

"Teenagers," Bernie said. "Sometimes some of them can make their parents worry."

"I worried about him last year. You know. Gangs. We never had that when I was growing up."

"Was he in a gang?"

Mrs. Benally shook her head. "Not my Jackson." But Bernie knew children kept secrets, and so did parents.

"Do you know the name of the friend Jackson drives with?"

"He calls him Lizard."

"Lizard?"

"Lizard."

"Does Lizard have another name?"

Mrs. Benally thought about it. "Leonard. Leonard Nez."

The wind pushed Mrs. Benally's plaid blouse tight against her ample chest. The sun beat down, cooking the asphalt. Bernie pictured the Fudgsicles melting into chocolate puddles.

"Why don't you and I sit in the car?" Bernie said. "Get some shade."

Mrs. Benally looked at the patrol unit suspiciously.

"It will be more comfortable than getting sand-blasted," Bernie said. "We can put your groceries in there, too."

Mrs. Benally said, "Okay, if you roll down the windows."

Bernie did better than that. She activated the air-conditioning.

She hadn't been able to stop the shooter or return fire, but with the sedan found so quickly, Bernie thought, the puzzle of Leaphorn's attack would be solved and the person who hurt him arrested. The idea that she'd helped made her feel a little lighter.

After Mrs. Benally had settled in, Bernie radioed Largo about Jackson and Leonard Nez.

"Manuelito," Largo said. "You are off the case. Remember?"

"Chee assigned me to wait with the shooter's car until the tow truck got here. Mrs. Benally and I were just talking, and I knew this was important." Bernie watched an Arizona State Police SUV pull up next to Wheeler's unit and then two groups of Apache County deputies arrive in pickups with horse trailers.

She updated Largo while the state cops parked at the McDonald's that adjoined the Bashas' lot. The vehicles outside the restaurant included rez cars and a tourist's rental RV with advertising on the side. She heard deputies unloading the horses. If the suspect had taken off on foot through open country, he'd better have a good hiding place, or they'd find him.

Largo said, "Good work. But remember—"

"I know. This isn't my case. When we're done, I'm taking the day off," she said. "Going to see my mother."

In Bashas', Chee learned that none of the twelve adult grocery store customers, six children, three clerks, and four stockers had seen anything or anyone unusual that morning. At least, not until Officer Wheeler arrived in the parking lot. The search found no one hiding. He left his card with the manager in case anyone recalled something relevant, and allowed the store to reopen, to the relief of the staff and a dozen potential customers baking outside.

At the front door, Chee stopped at an industrial-size trash can.

"Hold the base while I get the top off," he told Wheeler.

Chee pulled gloves from his back pocket, put them on, and hoisted the lid. He looked inside. No gun, at least not on top. But he extracted a black hoodie.

"I'm going to bag this." He looked at Wheeler. "I want you to take the rest of this trash, just in case."

By the time Chee and Wheeler got back to the suspect blue sedan, the tow truck operator had attached the hooks and begun rolling the car up on the big flatbed. Mrs. Benally stood next to the driver.

"Be careful," she said. Several times.

Chee asked Wheeler to update the captain.

"Largo says no record on Gloria Benally. Nothing on Jackson Benally. He asked the gang unit to see if the shooting might be some sort of initiation ritual or something," Wheeler said.

"What description is on Jackson's license?" Bernie asked.

Wheeler gave her the details. "Black hair, dark brown eyes. Five foot eight, one-forty."

"What about the other kid, Nez?"

"Nothing yet."

Mrs. Benally watched her car disappear down the highway, then walked over to them. Bernie introduced Chee, explaining that he was in charge of the Navajo side of the investigation.

"We need to get your fingerprints," he told her. "That way, we can make sure when the car is examined, they can sort them out from the bad person's."

Mrs. Benally made a noise, something between a laugh and a snort. "Will you take my picture, too, with a number underneath?"

Chee said, "I'm sorry for the trouble."

Bernie said, "Remember that we need your help to solve the crime. You are important to us."

Mrs. Benally sighed. "Let's hurry up with all this. I want to get home."

While a technician took Mrs. Benally's prints, Chee met with Captain Largo. Bernie came along.

"There's something odd about that car sitting there," Largo said. "That guy should have been on the way to wherever—not parked outside Bashas'. The New Mexico State Police are looking for Jackson at UNM Gallup, where Mrs. Benally said he should be."

Largo turned to Bernie. "Gallup, right? Not the main campus?"

"Right," Bernie said. "From what Mrs. Benally told me, I don't think Jackson did it. He enrolled at UNM on a Native Scholarship. Good grades, good recommendations. That doesn't fit the mold for a guy in a gang."

"What mother doesn't think her son is a little angel?" He looked at her again. "Did you find Louisa? Did you ask about the lieutenant's relatives?"

Bernie paused. "No. No Louisa yet. I could use some help finding her cell number. I left her a note and a voice mail on her home phone to call me."

Largo nodded.

Chee said, "If Benally isn't a gangbanger, what motive would he have for the shooting? Seems to me whoever did it must have had an accomplice with a second car. Or he's hiding somewhere he could get to fast on foot."

Largo stood, walked to the window. Bernie noticed that the blowing dust had bruised the blue sky into a pale gray.

"If it's not a gang deal and not these guys, then we have more work." Largo motioned toward a computer disc in his in-box. "Motive? These are Leaphorn's last cases as a full-time detective with us, the ones he handled after the department was computerized. And a few on there are from after he retired, where we used him as a consultant. Some of these guys might have a motive."

Bernie knew what the "some" meant. Revenge was a *bila-gaana* value, but some of these criminals had torn themselves away from the fabric of Diné life, lost their direction. Anger consumed them.

Largo moved back to his deck, ran his fingers over the case that held the disc. "I need someone to go through these in case Benally isn't our boy."

Bernie started to say something, and Largo silenced her with a look. He turned to Chee. "That someone will be you."

"Yes, sir," Chee said.

"You know what to look for. First of all, a link between Jackson, or a friend or family member of Jackson, someone in the Benallys' circle, and Leaphorn. A reason for a college boy to want Leaphorn dead. Or someone who might have threatened, coerced, blackmailed Benally into this situation. Then, look for cons Leaphorn helped send to prison who might be out now."

"Want me to work from Window Rock?"

"No. Take this back to the Shiprock office. Less hectic there." Largo sighed. "It ought to take a long day to come up with a list, but let me know sooner if any names jump out at you. Maybe we won't even need the list of cons. Maybe Jackson is our man."

"Anything else?" Chee asked. "What about the lieutenant's condition?"

"I haven't heard anything new," Largo said.

Chee took the disc, rose to leave. Bernie stood, too.

"When I picked up Bernie at Leaphorn's house, we realized he has a home office there. More files. We'll need those, too."

Largo nodded. "Have Bigman get them."

"I don't think Jackson did it," Bernie said.

"Really?" Largo's voice was sharp with ridicule. "The mother, she's about the right size, owns the car? Do you like her for the shooter?"

"She's got an alibi. Shopping." Bernie worked to keep the edge out of her voice.

"You know you'll have to testify when this all goes to trial." Largo frowned. "You need to be a credible, untainted witness, Manuelito. We don't want anybody saying Navajo Police screwed this up by not following the rules. We don't want whoever hurt the lieutenant to get off on some sort of oversight or a damn technicality. You may have already done some damage, talking with Mrs. Benally. You should have left every bit of that to Chee and Wheeler."

Bernie felt her face grow hot, anger rising. "What was I supposed to do, sit on my thumbs?"

"Exactly. And keep your mouth shut."

Largo pressed his hands together, looked grim. "The way I see it, this is the most important case we've ever handled. Your not being involved is routine procedure. Routine. It's not personal. It's not punishment. It's the way we do things. I am not saying this again. Clear?"

Bernie said, "This case *is* personal. I saw him fall. I promised I'd find whoever shot him."

Largo stood and leaned toward her. "Get out of here, Manuelito. Cool down. Your only, I repeat *only*, job is to find Louisa and

Leaphorn's kinfolks. Period. I don't want to see you here again. Or talk to you until I invite you back to work."

Bernie rose, standing next to Chee.

"I don't want to have to fire you," Largo said. "But I will if you can't follow orders."

4

Bernie walked to the parking lot in silence, heading to her car. Chee followed.

"You've been through a lot today," he said. "It wouldn't hurt you to—"

"Don't start. I don't need you or Largo to protect me. Largo thinks I should have done more for the lieutenant. No matter what he says, he is punishing me by taking me off the case."

She felt Chee's hands on her shoulders, shrugged him away.

"You're wrong," Chee said. "Largo doesn't operate like that and never has. He's been tough on me, too. Tough but fair. Stop beating yourself up. It's totally routine for an officer involved in a shooting to—"

"I didn't act like an officer out there. If I'd been faster, I could have gotten a real description, maybe even gotten off a shot."

"Stop, honey. It's over."

She noticed his look of concern and surprise. She rarely showed her anger. And she couldn't remember ever being this furious.

"We're all in this together," Chee said. "We all want to solve this case. Cut yourself some slack. You're a great officer. You did your best."

A wave of grief swept away her anger, grief not only for the lieutenant but for her own expectations of Officer Bernadette Manuelito, now proven to be an incompetent fraud.

She turned away from him, climbed into her car.

"Where are you going?"

"To see Mama and Darleen," Bernie said. "That's what I always do on my day off."

"Good," he said. "Don't forget to get something to eat. I'll call you later."

Bernie put her key in the ignition, rolled down the windows. Pulled out of the police parking lot. Tried the radio and turned it off again. Took a sip from her water bottle. Warm, of course. The problem with the Toyota's air-conditioning, an expensive problem, couldn't be tackled until she got the older bills paid off. By then it would be at least October. Cool again. Problem solved.

As she headed toward Fort Defiance, she realized she should swing back by Leaphorn's house. See if Louisa was there now, tell her what happened, get that job out of the way. Bernie made the detour, feeling the hot wind in her hair, thinking about the lieutenant. How few family photos he had in his house. No nieces or nephews, brothers or sisters. Leaphorn, she thought, never spoke of family except for Emma.

Her own family was different. She had been wrapped in love by her grandmother, her mother, mother's sisters, and maternal uncles. Her father's family, too, had taken an interest in her. Her grandfather on that side had been a Code Talker, and there were plenty of marines in the mix, a modern incarnation of the warrior spirit. When she had decided to become a police officer, they understood and wished her well.

She felt her cell phone vibrate, flipped it on.

"We just got word that Leaphorn made it into Albuquerque."

She heard something in Chee's voice that made her ask, "What else?"

Silence. Then Chee said, "The neurology unit there is full. They may have to transfer him again, I'll let you know."

"Bring the files home, and I'll help you go through them."

"Thanks, honey. I'll fix dinner."

She pulled in front of Leaphorn's house and parked on the street in a patch of shade provided by a straggly Siberian elm. Officer Bigman's department-issued pickup occupied the driveway, the only other vehicle in sight except for Leaphorn's truck. Where was Louisa?

She walked inside through the kitchen, calling to Bigman.

"In here," he yelled. "In the office." The detective sat at Leaphorn's desk, wearing latex gloves. The lights on Leaphorn's computer blinked like Christmas. He pressed a cell phone to his ear.

"No, that didn't work either," he said. "What if I just bring the hard drive down there?"

Bernie looked at the big sunflower on the computer screen and a little box that read "Password."

"I'll try that," Bigman said into the phone. He typed something else, waited. "Nope."

A pause. Bigman laughed. Then he sneezed.

"Not quite. It's one of those big old-fashioned towers," he said. "I'll have to put it on the seat next to me with the seat belt around it. I wouldn't trust it in the trunk bed. It would probably plot a revolution from back there."

He hung up, still smiling. Bernie noticed another light, red and flashing on a flat box beside the phone. Leaphorn must be one of the last few people in the universe who still used an honest-to-goodness answering machine.

"Did you see that message machine?"

"Yeah," Bigman said. "I noticed it when I sat down here. Little cassette tapes and everything. Leaphorn isn't exactly a high-tech guy, is he? That and this monster of a computer could be in a museum somewhere."

Bernie said, "He never gave anybody his cell number because he didn't want to answer it." She realized she'd used the wrong verb. The lieutenant, as far as anyone knew, was still breathing.

"I mean, he never gives it out."

Bigman said, "Have you heard how he's doing?" Sneeze.

"Hanging in there." She changed the subject. "I'll check the messages. Maybe there's one from Louisa."

"Or one from someone threatening to shoot him. Isn't that how it works on TV?"

Bernie pushed a button labeled "Listen." She heard Bigman sneeze again. The tape in the old machine was scratchy, used and erased many times. When the talking started, she recognized Louisa's voice, noted the lack of a simple hello.

"I've been thinking about what we discussed." Bernie heard emotion in her voice. Anger? Sadness? *"I would have liked the chance to change your mind, but I guess we're past that now. I don't know what else to tell you—"* The message clicked off. No good-bye.

She studied the machine. It didn't have a screen to display the caller's name and number.

"Was that Louisa?" Bigman asked. "Did she and Leaphorn get along?"

"Whenever I was around them, they seemed fine."

"A lover's quarrel?" he asked. Sneeze.

"I don't know if they are lovers," Bernie said. "But I know they are friends. Or maybe were friends. What's with the sneezing? Are you sick or something?"

"It's the cat," he said. "I'm allergic. If I left a message like that, it would mean I wasn't happy." He removed the tape that held the messages with his gloved hands. Put it in a little bag.

"What are you doing here, Bernie? I heard you were supposed to take some time off."

"Largo asked me to talk to Louisa. I was hoping she'd be here."

"I thought she'd be here when I came, and that I'd have to tell her what happened," he said. "I was glad she wasn't home."

"Did you see Leaphorn's cell phone around here?" Bernie asked. "I'm sure her cell number is in it. I really need to call her, give her the news."

Bigman sneezed, shook his head. "Not in his truck?"

"No."

"Then he probably had it with him." Bigman leaned toward the floor, his ample belly limiting his flexibility. Sneezed again.

"I've got to climb down under there, disconnect the computer so I can take it in and the techies can figure out how to access the data." He motioned to the two cardboard boxes. "Those are ancient police cases he worked before the computer system went in. Most of those guys are probably gone now. I boxed his PI stuff, too. You never know."

Bigman sat up straight. Another sneeze. Grinned up at Bernie, "Hey, you wanna help? I won't tell Largo."

Bernie crawled under the desk. "It's an amazing mess down here. Cords everywhere." She heard him sneeze.

"Unplug everything," Bigman said. "I bet Leaphorn found somebody to set this up, and never looked down here again."

The dark tight space beneath the desk and the patterns of the cords made her think of Spider Woman, for some reason. Spider Woman, the Holy Person who taught the Navajo to weave and gave the Hero Twins the weapons they needed to begin their quest to find their father the Sun and to rid the world of monsters. She looked at the way the cords came together. "I bet a woman set this up. Whoever did it must have been Spider Woman's daughter," Bernie said.

"Who? I never heard Grandma talk about that one," Bigman said.

Bernie said, "She's the one my mother always joked about when she had to redo a section of a rug. Mama told me she helps with life's unexpected complications, untangling messy situations. When I start to tell her about some hairy case, Mama says, 'Oh, you'll figure out how to weave it all together. You're like Spider Woman's daughter.'"

Bigman sneezed. Again. Again. Again.

"Blasted cat," he said. "I need to get out of here."

Bernie stood up, rolled her shoulders back. "All done. What cat?"

Bigman used his lips to indicate the stuffed chair. "It was over there when I came in." The chair was empty. "They know when you don't like them. That one came up, rubbed against me. I'm starting to itch. I'm gonna sit in the unit and finish the paperwork."

He looked at Bernie hopefully. "Someone ought to put it outside, since we don't know when Louisa will be back. It could make a mess in here."

"I'll do it," she said. "Largo put me in charge of rounding up the kinfolks."

Dealing with the cat was easier said than done. She called, "Kitty, kitty," to no avail and looked under the furniture, in the office closet. She walked through the house, searching beneath the beds, in the bathroom. The cat had vanished.

Then, inspired by commercials she'd seen on TV, she went into the kitchen. She found a sack of kibble and some canned cat food in the pantry. Louisa or the lieutenant had stored a gray plastic cat-size cage on the pantry floor. Leaphorn's—or was it Louisa's?—blue electric can opener sat on the counter. Bernie opened the Friskies and, like four-legged magic, a small orange-and-white feline with big green eyes appeared at her feet. She picked up the cat's dish and spooned in the soft food. While it ate, she brought out the cage. The cat finished, looked at her for more. Bernie reached for it, and it backed away. The cat moved close again when she walked to the counter where the Friskies sat.

Bernie grabbed a kitchen towel. At the opportune moment, she tossed a towel over the cat and, while it was confused, snatched it up and wrapped it like a wiggly, yowling burrito.

"Cat, I don't like this any more than you do, but you can't stay here alone."

Unlike useful cats who supported themselves by catching mice, bugs, and whatever else came on the premises uninvited, this one was obviously a house pet. Probably Louisa's furry darling. Chee liked cats, for some reason. Bernie decided to take the cat home. He could care for it until they figured out what was going on with Louisa, or until they knew the lieutenant's status. She gently pushed cat and towel into the cat carrier, closed the door, and deposited the noisy package in the backseat of her car. The shade helped keep it cool.

She went back in and wrote another note to Louisa, explaining why Leaphorn's computer and the cat were gone and asking Louisa to call her immediately. She left it next to the business card she'd put on the table.

She picked up the dry cat food and sealed the open can in a plastic bag she found in the pantry. She noticed the mail she'd brought in from Leaphorn's truck and thumbed through it. A payment to an insurance company and a white envelope, the kind that come with solicitation campaigns, addressed to Little Sisters of the Poor in Gallup, both stamped and ready for the post office. On the large brown envelope the lieutenant had written in small, precise script "Dr. John Collingsworth, AIRC" and a Santa Fe address. She thought for a second, then reached for a table knife to open it. If it wasn't important to the case, she'd tape it closed and send it on.

From inside the larger envelope, she pulled out a set of letter-size white pages and a second smaller sealed envelope. She opened the smaller envelope and removed a single sheet of paper precisely folded in thirds. She unfolded it to read Leaphorn's bill for services to the AIRC, dated yesterday. She looked at the white sheets. Photocopies of listings from auction catalogs and textbooks. Old Indian pots. Nothing exciting. This doctor must be an art collector, and AIRC was probably his clinic or something. She'd take it all to the post office and use their tape to reseal the brown envelope.

Bernie took the cat food, locked the back door, waved to Bigman, who looked up from his paperwork in the front seat of his truck. With the cat's protests as background noise, she headed toward the enchanted landscape of Two Grey Hills and her mother's house in Toadlena.

She went to Mama's at least twice a week, usually driving from Shiprock south on NM 491. The trip began on a wide paved highway, the main route for trucks hauling cargo up to Cortez or south to Gallup. Then she turned onto a decent dirt road, and finally onto the Navajo Nation route that led to the house where her mother now lived.

Today, since she was starting from Window Rock, she took the quieter scenic route, which hugged the New Mexico–Arizona border, climbed over Narbona Pass, and then dropped into the open landscape of the reservation. Normally she loved the panorama of scenery, the play of shadows along Black Creek Valley a bit west of the sprawling town and the vast, empty country that stretched east—shades of brown, gold, and red meeting the dome of blue sky. The cool ascent into the Chuska Mountains brought the vanilla fragrance of the ponderosas through her open windows and, on a clear day, climaxed with a view of Dinetah from the top of the pass.

Today, though, instead of the beauty around her, she noticed how her old Tercel struggled with the climb to the summit. Her brain replayed the lieutenant's shooting, her conversation with Mrs. Benally, the last turbulent confrontation with her sister Darleen.

Bernie hadn't felt sleepy when she left Window Rock, but now she could hardly keep her eyes open. She pulled over near the top of the pass, where the road widened. The wind had stirred up so much dust and haze that she could barely see Tsoodzil, known as Mount Taylor in English, rising into the clouds. It was the home of Black God, Turquoise Boy, and Turquoise Girl, a sacred marker of her homeland.

The sun shone in through the windshield, sweet as honey. Bernie pushed her seat as close to horizontal as it would go. Enjoyed a deep breath of the fresh mountain air. Closed her eyes—just for a minute, she told herself. Beyond here the route snaked down out of the mountains to connect with 491 at Sheep Springs. She'd head north another twenty minutes or so to her mother's house. Almost there.

She gave in to sleep before even unbuckling her seat belt.

The vibration of the phone in the vest pocket of her uniform shirt woke her. She looked at the caller ID. Darleen.

"You were supposed to be here hours ago. I texted you, and you didn't even answer. What happened? Where are you?"

"Sister. Hi. I got delayed. Long story. I'll be there in about half an hour. "

"You always do this to me. It smells." Darleen hung up.

Bernie climbed out of the car with that tight feeling in her belly she noticed more and more now when she talked to Darleen. She walked to the edge of the overlook, shaking the cobwebs from her brain. She saw ravens circling, heard the deep purr of a truck in the distance. Then she remembered Louisa's cat.

She looked in the backseat. The cat carrier, door open, was empty except for the towel. She peered under the seat. No cat. The front windows were wide open, easy enough for a cat to climb out. She searched around the car, checked underneath. No cat resting in the shade. And lots of places for a cat to hide. Too many for her to search. Her gaze swept the highway, east and west. At least no dead cat on the road.

Good luck to you, Louisa's cat, she thought. Watch out for the owls and coyote. I'm sorry I didn't take better care of you. She'd failed the cat, just as she'd failed Leaphorn.

She started the car and headed on to her mother's house, wondering if the day could get any worse.

Bernie smelled greasy smoke as soon as she opened the front door. Mama sat on the couch, wrapped in her favorite blanket despite the heat. A nature show blared on TV.

"It's me, Mama." She spoke in Navajo.

Mama looked up and smiled. "Sit down here with me, sweet daughter. You look tired."

"I will in a moment," Bernie said. "Is Sister here?"

"Not right now," Mama said. "That one said she'll be back soon."

Mama never called her Bernie, only the more formal Bernadette. But she rarely used anyone's English name, preferring the traditional way of identifying people in terms of their relation to you or by the name that had developed from the person's personality, a life event, or a character trait. Chee's Navajo name, for instance, translated in English to "Long Thinker."

Bernie rushed to the kitchen. She clicked off the burner beneath the frying pan, grabbed a towel to wrap around the handle, and took the skillet out the back door, set it on the ground. She started the vent fan and opened the window. Where was Sister? Keeping Mama safe was her job. If Mama had left the skillet on, if Mama had been cooking her own lunch, that raised one issue. If Darleen had walked off with the stove on, that was something else again.

The kitchen looked as if a dust devil had blown through. An egg carton, sitting open like a cardboard prayer book, had six eggs left. A half-empty bottle of Pepsi and discarded Styrofoam carry-out food containers added to the clutter. Something sticky had spilled and run to the floor. Dirty plates, cups, and silverware sat untended.

When Mama had first moved into the house, when Bernie was in high school and Darleen a baby, she allowed nothing out of place. She organized her home as precisely as a rug in progress, as neat as their grandmother's old hogan. But because of her arthritis, her heart problems, and the other debilitations of aging—they'd even worried about Alzheimer's disease—Mama couldn't do the work herself, so Darleen had promised to pitch in and help. For a while, the plan worked. But lately, Bernie thought, chaos had begun to replace order. Every week she found more to clean and straighten, more mess Sister seemed to expect her to handle.

Bernie and Darleen had agreed that Darleen could leave Mama alone for bits and pieces when she was feeling well. Bernie explained that one fall might mean a broken hip, a trip to the hospital, pneumonia. She had heard too many stories of mothers and grand-mothers gone down that road.

Bernie went back to the living room, navigating around piles of clothes and Mama's walker, on which hung Darleen's purple base-ball cap. Mama looked up at her and patted the couch. Bernie sat, picked up the remote control from the dusty coffee table, and muted the sound.

Mama spoke in Navajo. "You are here now to stay awhile."

"I'm glad to see you, Mama. What's new?" She held her mother's gnarled hand, noticing the coolness of her bony fingers despite the warm day.

Mama talked about a conversation she'd had with her sister, who lived near Crownpoint, recalling every detail. As she told the story, Mama ran her fingertips over the blanket on her lap, a fine rug she had made years before. Mama had been one of the best weavers anywhere. Her mind had relished the geometry of the loom and the interplay of color translated into warp and weft. She had created symphonies of design in gray, white, black, and brown, using wool sheared and spun from sheep they raised and tended at the old place.

Bernie loved the rug Mama had made to warm her and Chee's bed. It was a gift for their wedding, and the last her mother had completed. Because of the aching and stiffness in her hands, it had taken her more than a year, but Mama kept at it without complaint. Chee teased that Bernie had her mother's tenacity when it came to working on a police case. "You're just like her," he said. "You work on a case, bit by bit, line by line, and you keep going until you figure out what's what. Spider Woman's daughter, weaving together the threads of the crime."

When she'd finished her story about Bernie's aunt, Mama said, "Tell me what you've been doing, my daughter."

"Oh, busy at work." Bernie mentioned a call she'd handled, a lost three-year-old she eventually discovered asleep in the back of an uncle's firewood trailer, how relieved his family was to have him back safely.

"Good," Mama said. "But something makes your heart heavy."

Bernie squeezed her hand. She wasn't ready to talk about it.

Mama squeezed back, then gave Bernie news of her niece, a sweet girl Mama actually considered another daughter. She was expecting a baby later that summer. Mama never directly brought up the idea of Bernie becoming a mother, but Bernie felt the unasked question lurking in the corners of their conversations.

When Mama said she had to use the bathroom, Bernie took her arm and eased her from the couch. She was as light as old bones baked in the sun. Mama shuffled along in her socks, using Bernie to keep her balance. Bernie had asked Darleen to make sure Mama put on her shoes to reduce the risk of falling. Where was Darleen?

Bernie helped Mama with her pants and left her to her privacy. Down the hall, the door to Darleen's room stood open. Bernie noticed empty beer cans in a corner.

It looked as though a crew of burglars had rummaged everywhere, except for Darleen's desk, on which she'd neatly stacked papers, drawings that reminded Bernie of the art you'd see in comic books. She looked at the one on top, a nice sketch of a young man and young woman. Funny that her sister was so messy, but her artwork so meticulous.

Bernie heard the crunch of a car's tires on their gravel road. She walked back to the living room just as Darleen came in.

Darleen looked pale, puffy in the face. She frowned at Bernie. "I see you finally made it."

"Sister," Bernie said. "I thought you'd be here with Mama."

When Darleen walked closer, Bernie smelled alcohol.

"I thought *you'd* be here," Darleen countered. "You told me you'd drive up right after breakfast. I had things to do. I was counting on you."

"We almost had a fire on the stove." Bernie glared at Darleen. "I think Mama was cooking and forgot to turn off the heat."

"You told me you'd be here sooner."

"Something happened at work," Bernie said. "I had to—"

Bernie noticed a stoop-shouldered young man standing in the doorway, watching them. She looked at him, back at Darleen.

"He's my friend." Bernie waited for more. When nothing came, she turned to the man, probably in his midtwenties. "I'm Bernie, Darleen's sister. Please come in."

"Charley Zah." He stayed on the porch, staring at her uniform.

"I drove from work," Bernie said. She heard the toilet flush.

"Darleen told me you were a cop," he said. "Cool."

"Mama's in the bathroom," Bernie said. "I need to see if she can use some help."

"I just came back for my hat," Darleen said. "And, uh, to make sure you got here okay." She grabbed her cap from the walker.

"Stay awhile," Bernie said. "We need to talk."

"It's my day off, remember?" Darleen glanced at Stoop Boy. "We made plans."

"We have to talk, Sister." Bernie leaned on the *have to*.

"You already cheated me out of some of my day," Darleen said. "If you wanna talk, text me."

The toilet flushed again. "Quality time with Mama. See you later." Darleen stomped out the door. Stoop Boy followed.

Bernie wanted to run after her, shake some sense into her. Instead, she went to assist their mother.

"I've been thinking about the old days." Mama told wonderful stories, enriched by the complicated rhythms of her Navajo words. Bernie felt honored to have Mama all to herself. It was a rare gift, and she was grateful. "I've been thinking about this special rug. I don't think I ever told you about it." She described the weaving, the white background with the vivid figures. "It was made a long time ago. I never saw anything so beautiful. I wish you could have seen it, my daughter."

Outside, the wind rattled against the windows, trying to blow the last bits of moisture from the struggling landscape. If the weather followed normal patters, rain might come in July. Until then, hot dust.

"I was a small girl then," Mama said. "He came to the trading post at Newcomb, and my family was there. They say he made other rugs with other stories of the Holy People. But I haven't seen those rugs."

Bernie said, "He? In the old days? I thought women did all the weaving back then."

"This man was a *hataalii*. He worked at a huge loom. And the dyes for his yarn? All from plants."

Mama grew quiet. She closed her eyes. Gradually, her head slumped against the back of the couch. Bernie got up slowly and went to the kitchen to get to work. When the wall phone rang, she caught it at first jingle.

"Hey you. I left a message on your cell an hour ago. I guess you made it safely." She heard the worry in Chee's voice. Her cell, left in the car with her backpack and the cat carrier. What kind of an officer was she?

"Anything more on the lieutenant?"

"The hospital in Albuquerque couldn't take him. Full or something. So they flew him into Santa Fe," Chee said.

"Gosh, what an ordeal. What about the shooter?"

"Nothing yet. Everyone is looking for Jackson Benally. Mrs. Benally certainly did not enjoy being fingerprinted. She told me more about her angel of a son when I drove her home."

She heard Chee take a deep breath, exhale into the receiver. "How are you doing, honey? Don't change the subject this time."

"Well, Darleen is off with some boyfriend. Stoop Boy. The house is a disaster. It makes me furious that she's so irresponsible."

"Let it go for today," Chee said. "Try to relax and enjoy being with your mom."

She heard noise in the background, then Chee said, "Gotta run. I'll call you later."

While Mama napped, she focused on cleaning, taking out her frustration on the greasy stovetop. She reimagined the crime as she scrubbed, worrying over the details, wondering what she'd missed. When she heard the TV click on, she left the rest of the kitchen project for Darleen.

Mama put a bony finger on Bernie's khaki pants. "What happened here? Did you get hurt?"

Bernie looked down at her legs. Noticed the bloodstains.

"Someone I work with got shot this morning. They took him to the hospital in Santa Fe."

"Is this his blood?"

Bernie nodded. The cold breath of sadness swept over her.

"Something else happened, Mama," she said. "I had his cat in my car, and it ran away. I left the window open, and next thing I knew, the cat . . ." She felt the tears welling.

Mama looked at her. "So, you like those bird killers all of a sudden?"

"Well, no, not especially."

"The one that got lost, was it your friend?"

She had to laugh. "Not exactly. It scratched me when I tried to catch it. It made a terrible noise from the backseat. Yikes. What a racket!"

"So, you're crying about a cat, and you don't like cats? And this cat hurt you, and it wasn't even your cat?" Mama patted her hand. "I don't think that cat made you cry."

"It's been a hard day."

"Maybe you needed to cry."

Then Bernie felt Mama's cool hand on her back, rubbing between the shoulder blades the way she used to when Bernie was a little girl. It was as if that gentle pressure pushed away the strength of her resistance and let the grief and weariness flow out.

"In my room are some clean pants," Mama said after a while. "When you put them on, roll up the waist a little so they won't be too long." Mama had been taller, but now Bernie and Mama stood almost eye to eye.

Bernie took off her uniform and put on Mama's pants and one of her blouses. She washed her face and combed her hair. She felt better.

They took a little stroll, with Mama pushing the metal frame of her walker. Then she sorted Mama's laundry for Darleen to take to the Laundromat. Helped Mama take a shower and shampooed her hair. After that, she fixed scrambled eggs, toast, and applesauce. The food smelled good, and she realized that she hadn't eaten since breakfast. Thinking of breakfast brought back the shooting, and then she wasn't hungry.

"Elsie gave us the eggs," Mama said. "I don't know about the applesauce."

"Little Sister probably got it at the store."

"That one is a good girl," Mama said. "She helps me."

Bernie started to say something. Remembered Chee's advice. Didn't.

Time to head home, Bernie thought. She'd promised Chee she'd help review files of the lieutenant's old cases tonight. Where was Sister? She sent Darleen a text.

After the meal, Bernie called Darleen, but her phone went immediately to voice mail. She left a message. She mopped the kitchen floor. Vacuumed the living room carpet and Mama's bedroom. Waited for Darleen to call or text back or, better yet, to come home.

Mama protested, as she always did, when Bernie told her she had to leave.

"Stay here. You sleep in my bed. I'll sleep on the couch."

"No, Mama. I have to go home to my husband."

"Cheeseburger? You still with that guy? You not tired of him yet?"

Bernie smiled. Mama liked Chee, his traditional, respectful ways, his courtesy toward her and his sense of humor.

"I'm not tired of him yet," Bernie said. "I'm crazy about him."

Finally, Bernie called Stella Darkwater next door to come and sit with Mama. Mrs. Darkwater and Mama had become friends from the first day Mama moved in. Stella was a little off but in a happy way, sane enough to call for help if she had to. Best of all, Mama liked her.

"The house looks good today," Mrs. Darkwater said. "When Darleen asks me for help, I bring your mother over to my house."

"Darleen's young," Mama said. "It's hard for her."

"She's not that young," Mrs. Darkwater said. She put her purse on the table. "I heard somebody got shot where you work. Bad business. You be careful, girl. The one who did that is out there somewhere."

"I am careful. Where did you hear about it?"

"On the radio. They say it will be on the TV tonight."

Mrs. Darkwater took Mama's arm and helped her out of the kitchen chair. "Come on, dearie," she said. "It's almost time for *Wheel of Fortune*."

Bernie left what she'd written for Darleen in the middle of the kitchen table. She knew Mrs. Darkwater would read it, but so what? She gave Mama a kiss and headed for home.

She took BIA 310, watching for animals, watching the summer's fading light paint the rock hills red with a golden afterglow, reassuring herself that she had said what she needed to say in the note. Darleen would contact her, and they'd get this worked out. If Darleen wouldn't live up to her agreement to keep the house clean and take care of Mama, she ought to find someplace else to waste her lazy life. But Mama would never tell her that.

Bernie's car bounced along the dirt road, past an occasional lean Hereford. White people identify this part of Navajoland as Two Grey Hills. She wondered, not for the first time, what hills they counted and how they defined gray. A coyote dashed in front of the car, and she tapped the brakes. The animal trotted away, unconcerned, waving its tail with a touch of arrogance. An omen of bad luck, and this was already the worst day of her life. Bring it on, she thought, and then she forced herself to focus on the rough road.

Her car found the pavement of NM 491 at the convenience store, and she headed north into the stream of traffic moving toward Shiprock. She wondered if the missing cat had enough savvy to avoid becoming a coyote's dinner. She remembered the pan of water waiting in the shade at the lieutenant's house. She pictured the lieutenant deathly pale on the gurney as it rolled toward the ambulance. She tried to recall the shooter's face but remembered only the black hood. She thought of Cordova and the interview. He was smart, professional. Good-looking, too. About her age, maybe a touch older. She wondered if he was married to another officer or a civilian. What was his wife like?

As she pushed the car to accelerate, Tsé Bit'a'í rose in the dusk. She feasted on the sight of the rock with wings—maps call it Shiprock—rising out of the desert. Its stone bulk reassured her. Her anger with Darleen seemed trivial now, a minor irritation in a world filled with more important things. Shiprock belonged to the long history of the Diné, to the deep roots that tied her to a sacred and beautiful landscape and to generations of strong people. She marveled at the *bilagaana* imagination, foreigners seeing the rock as a big boat. Did they envision the countryside around it as an ocean of sand?

She parked the Toyota next to Chee's truck, next to the loom he had built for her. Built it himself in the traditional way outside their trailer as a wedding present two years ago. A loom she hadn't used yet.

Bernie smelled something delicious wafting out of the trailer into the warm evening air. She walked up to Chee standing on the new deck he had constructed that spring, watched him load charcoal into the grill.

"Hi. Heard anything more about the lieutenant?"

"Hey, beautiful. Glad you're home. First things first." And he kissed her.

5

After dinner, Chee put his arms around her. His warmth felt good; the night air cooled quickly at 6,000 feet. Bernie looked up. The stars shone brilliantly. As a child, she'd always wondered where the colors went when dusk faded—red and yellow to gray and black. Did they sink into the earth to reemerge with first light?

Chee said, "Bigman told me he put you in charge of Leaphorn's cat. I can't imagine him having a cat. He doesn't seem like a cat kind of guy."

She really didn't want to talk about the cat, but she told him the story.

"Don't feel bad," Chee said. "The Gallup Police couldn't track down Benally on the UNM Gallup campus. Or his friend, either, and they had more to go on than you did. They figure neither of those guys made it to school today."

Bernie asked, "Did you find out anything about Leonard Nez? I don't like Jackson Benally for it, but maybe Nez was involved."

"Nez has never been in trouble as far as we could find from a records search." Chee shrugged. "Tomorrow I'll work on tracking him down. We've got plenty of options for people with motives to hurt the lieutenant. But so far only three suspects."

"Three?"

"The boys and the mysterious missing Louisa."

"Louisa wouldn't have shot him," Bernie said.

Chee said, "Think objectively. They argued. She's missing."

"You're starting to sound like an FBI," Bernie said. "She couldn't have done it. We know the woman. She gave us a wedding present."

"Well, if you don't like any of them, we have the gallery of convicts on the disc Largo made. You busy tonight?"

"Yikes. Let's get started." She walked into the house, and he followed. "I need some brain work. All I did today was clean Mama's house and argue with Darleen."

"That, and almost getting killed and dealing with grumpy old Mrs. Benally." Chee looked sheepish. "I forgot to tell you. Darleen called. She asked me to let you know that she sent Mrs. Darkwater home, and your mom was watching TV."

"When?"

"Just before you drove in. She sounded like she'd been crying or something, but she said everything was fine. Didn't want to talk about it. You think she's okay?"

"I don't know," Bernie said. "She smelled like beer today. She's picked up a new boyfriend, a skinny guy a lot older. I'm calling him Stoop Boy because of his bad posture."

"Maybe she's in love with the guy," Chee said. "Love makes people do strange things. Look at me, for example, transformed from a bachelor eating Spam from the can to a budding gourmet chef, a Navajo Julia Child."

Bernie laughed. "You're not at Julia's level yet, but you do grill a good burger."

He hugged her. "Some girls will say anything for a meal."

She loved the way his skin smelled like summer. She turned her face toward his, and he leaned in . . .

The phone rang. Chee reached for it, picked it up automatically.

"Hi. It's Louisa."

"Hold on a second," Chee said. "I'm putting you on speaker so Bernie can hear, too."

The voice on the other end sounded tired and anxious. "I just saw the news. How is he? Where is he? This is unthinkable. Poor, poor Joe." Louisa was the only person they knew who called Lieutenant Leaphorn by his first name. "It's bad, isn't it? Tell me what happened. Joe was always so careful."

"Bernie was there," Chee said. "She's been looking for you."

Bernie stuck to the facts. She could almost see Louisa listening, stopping herself from interrupting to ask questions. As she retold the story, Bernie noticed that she had grown more detached from the scene, as if she had been an observer rather than a first responder, as if she'd watched it on television.

Louisa said, "After all those years, for this to happen when he's retired. How awful. Is he conscious? Is he in pain?"

"I don't know," Bernie said. "Where are you?"

They heard her sigh over the phone. "I'm in Albuquerque, leaving for Houston, flying out for . . . for a conference." If you lived in northwestern New Mexico, your best option for commercial air travel included a drive to Albuquerque and, if you could afford it, a night in a hotel.

"The FBI wants to talk to you about the lieutenant," Bernie said. "Where are you staying down there?"

"It's near the airport. A Holiday Inn Express."

Bernie said, "I'm sorry you had to learn about this from TV. I went to the house looking for you so I could tell you. Officer Bigman took the computer and files from the lieutenant's office as evidence, as well as the tape of your message on the answering machine. I listened to it."

The phone fell silent for a few beats, and then Louisa said, "I was angry with Joe, but I didn't shoot him."

"I thought the lieutenant usually drove you to Albuquerque so you didn't have to leave your car there."

"That right, usually he does. But, as you know, we had an argument." Louisa spoke faster now. "That man could be so rigid, so sure he was right. And he was preoccupied with a big project. I didn't think he'd even miss me. And now this."

"Did he mention any death threats?" Chee asked. "Anything out of the ordinary? Anything bothering him?"

"He wasn't one to talk about his problems. You know that. But he said something last week about a ghost from the past. I'd never heard him talk about ghosts. You know how he felt about that superstition business." Leaphorn was a skeptic when it came to Navajo witchcraft and the supernatural in all its forms and often lectured fellow officers about how superstition harmed the Navajo people.

"A ghost from the past?" Bernie asked. "Did he say anything else about it?"

"Not that I remember, and I didn't ask him. I was distracted by the, um, conference."

"When did you leave for Albuquerque?" Chee asked.

"Early. Before Joe headed off for that police breakfast."

"What kind of a conference is it?" Bernie asked.

"Oh, never mind that." Louisa's words came in a rush. "A boring one. Bernie, it must have been awful for you, watching Joe get shot like that."

Bernie said, "I'm off work for a few days, but Largo says that's just routine. He asked me to track down the lieutenant's closest relatives, just in case. Can you give me any names, contact info?"

"Joe didn't have any brothers or sisters left. His parents, that whole generation of his family, had either died or he was out of touch with them. He has the addresses of a few cousins—I guess they are cousins—in his little notebook. He'd send checks now and then."

"The brown book he kept in his pocket?" Chee asked.

"Always. Are you going to see him?" Louisa said.

"Tomorrow, if he's allowed to have visitors," Bernie said.

Chee raised his eyebrows. Bernie hated hospitals.

"What conference is it you're going to in Houston, in case we need to reach you?" he asked.

"Just call my cell. You've got the number now. Give Joe my love and stay safe out there, both of you. Gotta go."

Louisa hung up.

"What do you think?" Chee asked.

"She's lying about something. But not about caring for the lieutenant."

"Did you notice that she denied shooting him before we even had a chance to ask her?"

"That must have been some argument," Bernie said. "Louisa is in Albuquerque, just an hour from Santa Fe and the hospital. Why would she head on to a boring conference rather than be with Leaphorn? They've shared a house for years. "

"He went with her to some of those conferences. He'd be reading in the hotel while she was at the sessions. I remembered him saying that those academic types live in their own world and how Navajos ought to plant an observer there, write a book about their unusual cultural practices."

Bernie started a pot of coffee while Chee called Cordova. Then he hooked up the laptop, powered on, and inserted the disc. Shiprock, unlike some places on the reservation, had fairly reliable Internet service, in part because of its government offices and the pressure they put on the powers that be to acknowledge that the twenty-first century had arrived, even in rural New Mexico.

She pulled a chair around so she could see the computer screen. "Louisa is hiding something. Why wouldn't she tell us what kind of a conference it was? Or where in Houston she'd be staying? If she's even going to Houston."

"I bet you the FBI goes down that trail. Looks into it as a possible murder for hire," Chee said.

Bernie laughed. "You've watched too many DVDs from that bargain bin. Louisa hires Jackson Benally or Leonard Nez?"

"Well, it's hard to find a professional assassin in Window Rock. You might have to take what you can get, settle for college kids."

Bernie said, "Even the FBIs aren't that lame."

"I'll bet you a dinner."

"Steak?"

"Shake."

He got up, poured two cups of coffee, stirred the requisite two teaspoons of sugar into Bernie's, left his as it came from the pot.

She took a sip. "What about the lieutenant's mysterious cousins?"

"Ah, now you're the one thinking like an FBI. If Leaphorn is giving them money, they want him to live as long as possible."

"I meant, I need to find some relatives to let them know what happened, like Largo asked. I'll get that notebook when I go to the hospital tomorrow."

Bernie saw him frown. Start to speak, probably to try to discourage her from making the four-hour one-way drive, then yield to studying the computer screen. She'd taught him that he couldn't talk her out of anything once she'd made up her mind. No more than she could convince him that the lieutenant would have trusted Jim Chee, the same man who wasn't always the best cop on the force, to run the Navajo end of this investigation.

"You were going to say something?"

"Tell the lieutenant hello for me."

Leaphorn, they quickly learned, had been busy until the end of his official police career and as a consultant to the force. Cases ranged from sheep and cattle rustling to domestic violence, burglary, bootlegging, and drug sales. Most of his arrests had resulted in convictions. Bernie made a second shorter list of those who had been released without charges, in case they held a grudge.

They reviewed the cases for an hour, finding nothing interesting enough to be the motive for attempted murder. Bernie got up, poured them more coffee, switched off the pot. When she sat back down, she noticed something.

"Here's a case where the bad guy seems to have vanished." She tapped the keyboard. "Looks like insurance fraud involving a rug from the Long Walk."

"I think you and I did some background work for the lieutenant on that one," Chee said.

"I recall talking to him about it. He came to the house with a basket of gifts from him and Louisa right after we got back from our honeymoon. He mentioned this guy named Delos and how people thought he might be a shape shifter and how he had stolen a bunch of money and was exploiting this man from Laos who worked for him."

"That was some story," Chee said. "We never did get a straight answer from the lieutenant on what happened to Delos."

"I don't see anything in the file about that either," Bernie said.

"I'll add it to my list of things to look into tomorrow when I start on the PI files. But we have the problem of tying him in to the Benally car."

They worked quietly awhile longer.

"This is interesting," Bernie said. "Nothing to do with the Benally family, but you were involved. This man, Randall Elliot, killed a Utah rancher, and almost killed a woman he worked with. Then he disappeared. If he's still out there . . ."

"I'll never forget that case." Chee stood, stretched. "Leaphorn rafted down the San Juan, hiked into a rugged rocky canyon, and found the missing woman barely alive after Elliot almost killed her. That Elliot guy, an archaeologist, came back in a helicopter to finish her off. I got there in time to help the lieutenant carry her out—she would have died in the next day or two if he hadn't found her. Elliot disappeared before I arrived, and Leaphorn never talked about what happened before I got there."

"And?"

"Someone found human bones in the area the next spring. DNA matched them to Elliott."

"Too bad. He would have been the perfect suspect."

They went back to work. The notion of Jackson Benally or Leonard Nez shooting a cop as part of a gang initiation didn't seem as far-fetched as it had an hour ago.

After another hour, Chee walked over to where Bernie sat, put his hands on her shoulders. She felt her tense muscle relax with his firm massage. "You know, you could have been killed today. Instead of celebrating our good fortune, here we are, still working at midnight."

"I'll feel like celebrating when we find the guy who shot the lieutenant," she said. "You ready for bed?"

He smiled. "Was that a question or an invitation?"

In the quiet afterward, she noticed the subtle change in Chee's breathing as he fell more deeply asleep. She stretched her legs against the cool sheets, wide awake. A coyote began to sing somewhere along the San Juan. She thought about Leaphorn's empty house, about the lieutenant alone in a hospital bed—if he were still alive. She rewound the day: the breakfast, the phone call, the shot, the bleeding on the sunbaked pavement, the ambulance. She tried to focus on the getaway car: Had there been a second person inside? Was it really the Benally car?

After an hour, she crept out of bed and went back to the kitchen to work on the files. By dawn she had reviewed them all, made lists of possible suspects and their connections to Leaphorn. None of the criminals in the old cases except for Delos looked especially evil, motivated to shoot a man in cold blood. In fact, they all should be grateful to Leaphorn for attempting to reboot their lives.

She put on her Nikes when the sky had changed from black to gray with hints of pale peach, and quietly opened the front door. She ran to greet the dawn.

When she came back, she smelled the sizzling bacon. She saw Chee, phone in one hand, spatula in the other. She could tell from the tension in his body that whatever news he listened to wasn't welcome.

Chee put the phone down.

"I've got to go in early. The report is back from the shooter's car."

"So, did Mrs. Benally do it?"

Chee laughed. "Well, her prints are there, along with lots of others. Some are probably Jackson's. The rest? Who knows. So Largo and Cordova, the FBI guy, want me to check the names tied to the prints. We can compare them to the suspect list we made last night. See if there's any link to the lieutenant."

"I added a few names this morning," Bernie said. "I'm surprised the FBI isn't taking the lead here. That Cordova seemed pretty sharp."

"They're leaving the Navajos to us," he said. "Largo told me the FBI seriously wants to talk to Louisa. Couldn't reach her last night."

Chee cracked eggs into the hot pan. "Four or five sets of the prints they found match prints on file, but none were names I recognized from the lieutenant's work. The feds are still searching for matches to the others."

"Wow," she said. "That car was a taxi."

"I thought of something else," Chee said. "That Delos guy? I remember that the Jicarilla cops found a body in an unmarked grave a couple years ago. Turned out to be his."

Chee left right after breakfast. She did dishes, then called the Window Rock office to learn they'd heard nothing more about Leaphorn's condition. She thought about wearing jeans, but put on a clean Navajo Police uniform out of respect for the lieutenant.

When she started her car, she noticed Leaphorn's unmailed envelopes, including the brown one addressed to the man in Santa Fe, the one that needed stamps.

Bernie drove first to the post office to send Leaphorn's envelopes on the way. She saw the empty parking lot and realized the counter didn't open until eight; she was half an hour early. She dropped the smaller ones in the mailbox and headed on, southeast to Santa Fe. She'd find a post office along the way.

She passed a Laundromat. Quik Stop stores. A big truck loaded with hay bales, horses grazing. The junction for the tribe's Flowing Water Casino. She noticed the plume of steam rising from the Four Corners Power Plant. She turned on the radio, 94.5 FM Navajo-language KYAT. She didn't mind country music, at least in small doses, but she listened for news coverage of the lieutenant's shooting. She noticed a homemade green "Tire Repair Open" sign along a fence and then the "Leaving the Navajo Reservation" notice. Circle W pawnshop. A car wash. A big American flag fluttering outside a mobile home.

She slowed as a truck hauling a trailer pulled onto the highway from a dirt road, noticing that the sedan in the left lane sped past her about ten miles faster than the limit. The radio was advertising jewelry supplies you could order online as she came to Fruitland, the little settlement west of Farmington. Traffic was heavier now, the area populated with a mixture of oil field workers and farmers,

Navajos, Mormons, and retirees looking for nirvana in the fabled Southwest. She passed a block-long wrecking yard filled with generations of cars and pickups, even some heavy equipment. Farther along, she saw lots full of new minivans and trucks, windshields shining in the summer sun, tempting drivers to take on debt in exchange for a better ride.

Finally, the view she loved, the San Juan River south of the highway, flowing between rows of towering ancient cottonwoods.

Traffic was heaviest between Shiprock and Bloomfield, with fleets of oil and gas trucks making hatchbacks like hers seem tiny. After that, the number of vehicles conveniently dropped off as the scenery grew more spectacular. Her heart soared as she saw Huerfano Mesa, one of the sacred places in the origin stories, the spot where Changing Woman gave birth to the Hero Twins who made the world safe for people. Leaphorn should be here in Dinetah, not in a hospital in Santa Fe, a rich-white-person town.

Bernie had been to Santa Fe three times before. Once when her Shiprock High School team played a basketball game at the Santa Fe Indian School gymnasium. Once to accompany her mother when she had a booth at the Indian Market. And most recently for a training session at the New Mexico State Police headquarters. The town didn't resonate with her, but she'd go where she had to for the lieutenant.

Officer Jim Chee had never been much for paperwork.

Now, as he sat at his desk half done with the tedious job of checking the names from the prints against the lieutenant's caseload, he was grumpy.

He wanted to be out finding the Benally kid, not leaving it to the Gallup Police. He wanted to ask the young man why his car had so many fingerprints, where he was at the time of the shooting. Instead, he'd spent two hours comparing names of Navajos linked to the prints in the Benally car with names in the criminal reports database, and then with the names of people Leaphorn might have arrested. Looking for someone other than suspect number one, in case, as Bernie believed, Jackson Benally lacked a motive to shoot Leaphorn. Looking, but coming up with nothing except other fingerprints for which there was no match and no obvious tie to Leaphorn.

Chee walked outside, away from the confusion, looked at the Shiprock substation parking lot and Shiprock itself, a black lava thumb against the blue sky. The wind had already started to blow, a soft breeze now, but a bad sign for more dust in the air as the day heated up.

He went back to his desk, checked his e-mail, watched a brief video of a dog on a surfboard that his friend Cowboy Dashee had sent. Just when he could think of nothing else to delay resuming the inevitable, he felt the cell phone vibrate in his pocket. Bernie. He pulled out the phone, smiling, then remembered Bernie was driving to Santa Fe, passing through lonely country not defaced by cell phone towers. He looked at the number. Darleen.

"Hello there," he said. "How are you?"

"Terrible. I can't get Bernie on the phone," Darleen said. "Did she take Mama somewhere?"

"Bernie's off to Santa Fe. There's bad reception on that road. She's by herself as far as I know. She wouldn't take your mother, because she was going to see the officer who got shot."

"Mama's gone," Darleen said. "Mama's gone."

"Gone? Did she pass away?"

"Oh my God, I didn't think of that. She could be dead. Maybe whoever kidnapped her killed her. Should I call the police? You are the police!" The words came in a torrent.

Chee said, "Calm down. Tell me what happened. Start at the beginning. But first, take a breath or two."

Darleen rushed ahead. "Mama's disappeared. Totally gone. She's like nowhere. I looked all over the house, around outside, in the closets, in the bathroom. Everywhere, dude, every stinking where. Called for her really loud, screaming my stupid head off. Then I got in my car and drove around the neighborhood, yelling out the window like a madwoman. Nothing. She's nowhere."

Chee thought about it. "Was she there when you got home last night?"

A pause. "I guess she was asleep in her room. Ah. Um. I got in kinda late and then I did some drawings." Another pause. "I didn't feel so good this morning, so I didn't get up until just now."

"Did you see her last night?"

"Not exactly. The door to her room was closed. When I looked in this morning, her bed was empty, already made. She's missing, dude. Missing. Person. Who would wanna kidnap an old lady?"

"I don't think she was kidnapped," Chee said.

"Maybe she just went for a walk and fell down somewhere," Darleen said. "You think that coulda happened? The dog packs are bad out here."

Chee had handled cases in which feral dogs had attacked cattle and horses and killed sheep and lambs. He'd dealt with some incidents of wild dogs charging and biting people, too. "Is your mother's walker there?"

"Yes."

"Darleen, I'm going to give you some suggestions, places to check. Take your phone with you. Call back when you're done."

He hung up, went back to his fingerprint files. Darleen's distraction was good luck; he uncovered something interesting—a possible suspect.

His phone vibrated ten minutes later.

"Mama's okay. I went to the Darkwaters' house, like you said. She spent the night with Mrs. Darkwater. They were eating breakfast when

I called over there earlier and had the radio on so loud they didn't hear the phone in the other room or me hollering for her."

"I'm glad it worked out," Chee said.

"Me too."

"Next time Mama goes on a sleepover, ask Mrs. Darkwater to leave you a note," Chee said.

"Um. Actually, they did. It was on the table, but I didn't see it. One from Bernie there, too. I was lucky that you answered the phone. I'm glad Bernie wasn't around for this."

"Me too," he said.

He waited for her to say "thank you" but she didn't.

Santa Fe's Christus St. Vincent hospital has numerous entrances, different doors for accessing its many services. Bernie headed for large sliding glass doors that looked like a main entrance. They led to an imposing lobby and another sign, "Information." The receptionist glanced up. "May I help you?" As she stared at Bernie's uniform, Bernie noticed the dark bags beneath her eyes.

"I'm looking for Lieutenant—I mean Mr. Joe Leaphorn. He was admitted yesterday."

The woman typed the name.

"He's in CCU."

"Is that Spanish for something?"

The woman narrowed her eyes. "Critical care unit." She told Bernie the room number.

"How do I get there?"

"Down the hall on this floor. Follow the signs."

Bernie walked past a waiting area, noticing a young blonde in tight jeans pacing back and forth and an elderly couple sitting on a couch.

The critical care unit was a short hike from the entrance around several angled corridor junctions. The confusing layout had not been designed with consideration for a person already under stress. She checked the overhead signs at each intersection to make sure she stayed on the right path.

The door to the CCU had a sign with visiting hours posted. Her timing was off, but she walked in.

"What can I do for you?"

"I'm Officer Bernadette Manuelito. I need to see Lieutenant Leaphorn."

The nurse shook her head.

"Sorry, but that's impossible. Doctor—"

"It's police business." She stood taller, steeling herself for an argument. "The lieutenant's shooting is under investigation."

"I didn't know that," the nurse said. "I came on duty this morning."

Bernie waited.

The nurse looked up from her computer screen. "Before you interrupted me, I was going to say it's impossible for anyone to see Mr. Leaphorn right now. Dr. Moxsley, the neurologist, is with him, running some tests."

"How long will that take?"

"Hard to say," the nurse said. "We have a waiting area for the CCU just down the hall. You're welcome there."

"I also need to talk to the doctor."

The nurse hesitated. "He's got a crazy schedule this morning."

"He needs to make time for me," Bernie said.

"Is this part of the investigation?"

She paused. "Not exactly. The lieutenant is my—" She used the Navajo word that means one-who-acts-as-leader or one-who-is-respected as a teacher. "He and Mrs. Leaphorn never had any children, and so now I—" She left the sentence unfinished, hoping the nurse would fill in with the assumption that Bernie was the closest thing Leaphorn had to a daughter.

The nurse gave Bernie a friendlier look. "It must be tough to investigate your relative's shooting. I'll ask Dr. Moxsley to find you in the waiting room." She handed Bernie a pile of papers from a folder on her desk. "While you wait, perhaps you can help us with some of these forms."

The CCU waiting space was tiny and crammed with furniture. A girl younger than Darleen with dark hair and a shattered complexion held an infant and walked back and forth, back and forth, in front of the windows. She glanced up when Bernie came in, then looked away. A woman with a plump, lined face and a man with a bushy mustache sat close, talked quietly in Spanish. Everyone wore worry and fatigue like a second skin.

The best thing about the waiting area was the patio. Bernie took her free cup of aged coffee out where she could see the sky. A chunky man in a black jacket sat at one patio table, a Bible in his lap. She sat at the other.

Bernie believed in science, but she also believed that human life was more than anybody could keep track of with machines and computers, or put down in equations and reduce to numbers like cholesterol ratings and blood pressure scores.

The last time she had been in the hospital was in Gallup with Jim's uncle, Hosteen Nakai. The man had a mind as clear and fast as a mountain spring and a generous heart. She remembered his kindness to her, even before she had decided that Jim Chee would be her husband. He told her, "One day my nephew will be a finer man, a better person than he can see himself being. It will be good for him to have the help of a strong woman. Of one who isn't afraid of his power or of her own power."

In the two years of their marriage, Chee had blossomed into his own gentle power. She saw his fierce sense of brotherhood with his fellow officers and his dedication to the people they all served. Some policemen grew cynical with the exposure to so much evil, but Chee became more determined to make things right. To save the good citizens of the Navajo Nation from those who had lost sight of the Beauty Way. He took the responsibility to help restore the land and its people to harmony seriously. She wished Hosteen Nakai had lived to see the man his nephew had become and was still becoming.

She remembered Nakai, the great and beloved *hataalii*, looking tiny and miserable on his hospital bed, filled with cancer. Like an animal in an experiment, not like the valued and beloved elder who knew many songs and sand paintings and had helped his people. She and Chee checked him out of the hospital against his doctor's recommendation and allowed him to die as he wished in a ramada beneath the stars at home.

Hospitals made her restless, and she stood and paced. Leaphorn was more vigorous than Nakai. The advances of science, including new knowledge of our human brain and its complexity and resilience, might save his life. But what damage had the bullet done to his mind?

She watched a cloud shadow move against the building and a pile of thunderheads begin to rise. Rain this afternoon? She went back to the table and studied the paperwork the nurse had given her. Bernie had no answers for its questions: Was the lieutenant taking any medicine? Had he ever had surgery? Did anyone in his family ever have heart disease? Immune system conditions? What was he allergic to? She put the forms down. She opened her backpack and took out a mystery. A few pages later, a man in a white coat with graying brown hair in a ponytail and a laptop walked to her table.

"Bernadette Manuelito? Grant Moxsley. I'm the one in charge of Mr. Leaphorn's case."

She offered her hand, and he touched it gently and said, "Yá'át'ééh," with an accent that sounded as though the doctor knew more than a little Navajo. He sat on the chair next to her.

"I understand you had some questions for me, and I wanted to talk to you before you saw him," he said. "The injury is very serious. I've given the FBI basic information, the type of bullet, stuff like that, as part of their investigation."

He paused. "Hospitals all have a lot of rules, and one of the rules is that I should only speak to next of kin. I know from my years with public health in Tuba City that the concept of kinship is different for us than for the Diné."

Bernie waited. When Moxsley said nothing more, she said, "I visited his house after the shooting. He had a photo of his late wife. And the wedding picture my husband and I gave him. The lieutenant had no children and he has no sisters or brothers who are still with us." She glanced toward the hospital ward where the lieutenant lay. "I was the first person to reach him after he was shot. I want to talk to him about what he saw, find out if he knows who did it. So, I would say I'm family and I'm also here on business."

Moxsley said, "Would you like me to tell you what I think is happening because of the injury?"

"Please," Bernie said.

He raised the laptop cover and called up images as he explained how the bullet had entered near the temple and progressed through the brain. The good news was that it had not damaged the lieutenant's spinal cord.

"There are many things we don't know about the human brain, but we have a good idea of where to find the control panels for various functions." Moxsley looked at her with kindness. "The bullet penetrated brain centers crucial for speech, comprehension, memory, vision, and what we commonly call personality." He showed them to her, tracing the bullet's journey with his finger.

"Can he speak? Will he be blind?"

"I don't know. For now, your uncle is in an induced coma. His brain swelled with the injury, and we removed part of his skull to reduce the pressure. He looks like he's asleep, but we think some patients like this hear what's going on around them. Some respond to touch, some to the sound of a familiar voice. He might respond to you. He might not."

"What happens next?"

"Difficult to predict." Moxsley closed his laptop. "We're taking this hour by hour now, for the next few days. I'm sorry I can't be more optimistic. We know a lot about the brain, but there's a whole lot more we don't know."

Bernie said, "The lieutenant is sharper than my husband and me put together. I've never seen him give up on a challenge."

Moxsley smiled. "That is definitely in his favor."

The doctor took his pager out of a pocket, looked at it, pushed a button. "The next forty-eight hours are the most crucial. I'll be keeping a close eye on him, and he will be continuously monitored by the nursing staff."

Monitored, Bernie thought. The word made her think of those electronic bracelets offenders wore on house arrest. In a way, Leaphorn's condition was the same. He couldn't make a move, take a breath, without a machine recording it.

"We are observing him for seizures, for signs of infection, for other complications. When the swelling goes down, we will reattach the bone. In the meantime, his brain mass has room to expand without doing harm to itself. That's why you'll see all the bandaging."

Bernie nodded.

"If he survives until the swelling subsides, we will be better able to decide what happens next in terms of treatment." Moxsley extracted a card from his white smock and gave it to her. "I'll make sure we list you and your husband as next of kin and that the staff knows you can visit whenever you like. Any other questions?"

"Do you think he knows where he is or what happened?"

"No way to tell," Moxsley said.

Bernie thought of something else. A long shot.

"Do you know a Dr. John Collingsworth? I think he has a clinic called AIRC."

Moxsley smiled. "Collingsworth isn't a medical doctor. He's a PhD, director of the American Indian Resource Center. That's a great place. They have a fabulous private museum with an amazing collection of Indian art and artifacts, the kind of stuff that people from all over the Southwest come to study. My wife volunteers as a docent there. She gets us in to the museum for free."

She'd heard about the center during a course in anthropology at the University of New Mexico, and remembered the story of its origins. A rich couple moved to Santa Fe from Delaware in the 1930s, fell in love with the town and with the Pueblo Indians who lived nearby in villages up and down the Rio Grande. The husband and wife worked to promote Indian rights at a time when Pueblo, Navajo, Apache, and other Indian people couldn't even vote for president. They also collected beautiful Indian art and used their patronage to keep quality work alive in difficult times. When they died in a car wreck, they left their home, its extensive grounds, and their collection to the AIRC. Bernie had always wanted to see the place.

"Anything else?"

She shook her head. "Thank you."

"Are you ready to see your uncle now?"

"Absolutely."

Moxsley held the door. Bernie felt cold, nervous, as she walked past the CCU desk and into the medical area. In some rooms a curtain concealed the patient and whoever else was in the tiny cubicle. In others, she could see a prone figure, tubes connecting arms and body parts beneath the sheet to machines. In one room, two people sat in hard-backed chairs by the bed. Medical staff quietly went back and forth.

They stopped at the fourth room. "Here he is. Good luck finding the creep who did this."

Bernie went in alone. Leaphorn lay on his back beneath a white sheet that came to his chin. A tube ran into his left arm from a metal stand; another tube emerged from the sheets into a bag that hung lower on the bed, and another protruded from his mouth. His eyes were closed, his head swathed in bandages. His chest moved up and down shallowly, and the lights on the machines flickered.

He looked, she thought, like a man whose spirit was deciding if it should stay or if it could go. So very different from the person she had shared breakfast with slightly more than twenty-four hours ago.

She quietly walked to the bed and put her hand on his arm that didn't have the tubes. He felt warm. When the time was right, she spoke to him in Navajo. She spoke slowly, softly, but loud enough to be heard over the machines, saying what needed to be said about how she was sorry to have disappointed him, reminding him of her promise. When she was done, she noticed his eyes moving beneath the closed lids. Then the motion stopped.

Bernie stopped at the nurse's station to ask about Leaphorn's notebook.

"I imagine it's with the rest of the belongings he arrived with. Check with security."

"Where?"

"Go back down the hall, past the ER. It's on your left. Watch for the signs."

She found a sleepy-looking guard in the office, his feet propped up on the desk.

"Excuse me," she said. "I need to collect the possessions of one of the patients here."

The guard looked up.

"Are you family?"

"I'm Officer Bernadette Manuelito, Navajo Department of Public Safety. The person involved is the victim of a shooting we are investigating in conjunction with the FBI."

The man came to life, noticed her uniform for the first time.

"Sure thing." He moved his feet and brushed dirt off the desktop. He opened a drawer and pulled out a form. Handed it to her with a pen.

"You're a long way from home, Officer. What do you think of Santa Fe?"

"All I've seen this trip is the hospital. I'd rather not be here. You know how it is."

The guard returned with a clear heavy-duty plastic bag. He gave it to her in exchange for the paperwork.

Inside, Bernie found the clothes and shoes the lieutenant had worn when he'd been shot. The smaller items in his pockets had been bagged separately. She picked out his notebook and put it in the front pocket of her backpack.

It was warm outside, but not as hot as in Window Rock. The sun felt good after the chilly hospital rooms. She walked to her car, admiring the view of the Sangre de Cristo range to the east and the blue sprawl of the Jemez Mountains to the west. Whoever built the hospital, she thought, had done visitors a favor by placing the parking lot in this spot. Bernie opened the back hatch, put the lieutenant's possessions inside. As she put on her seat belt, she noticed the envelope for the AIRC.

Next stop lunch, then a post office and home.

She followed directions the security guard had given her to the College Plaza shopping center, passing up fast food restaurants and a couple franchised places in favor of the little café he'd recommended for an inexpensive lunch. It had a cute name, Jambo, and smelled like a rainbow of spices and fresh bread. Bernie sat at a table by the window and opened the menu. She found some things she recognized: lamb stew, lamb burgers, goat stew, and salads. Also, they served dishes she'd heard of but never tasted. And then came the more exotic choices—cinnamon-dusted plantains and a jerk organic tofu sandwich. And "stuffed phyllo," whatever that was.

She'd never been an adventurous eater, but aromas from the kitchen tempted her to try something new. If she won the bet with Chee about the FBI checking into Louisa and a murder-for-hire scheme, she'd ask him to take her here. Maybe she'd try that tofu sandwich.

When the waiter asked for her order, she stuck to what she knew—goat stew and a Coke. Then she took the worn brown notebook out of her backpack.

7

Bernie turned the little book over in her hands, feeling the soft leather of its cover. The book had metal rings to hold in the pages, rings that released for refills with pressure on a clasp at the bottom. From the wear on the edges, she guessed Leaphorn had used the book for decades.

By reading what he'd written here, she would intrude into the lieutenant's private life again. This seemed more of an invasion than standing in his kitchen or rummaging through his deck. Looking inside the journal felt like snooping in his underwear drawer. Still, she had promised Largo she'd find the lieutenant's relatives, and the book might hold the key to doing that job.

She opened it. The first pages were a printed annual calendar, the year-at-a-glance and then an expansion of each month. The rest of the pages were unlined white paper, some filled with the lieutenant's precise handwriting. She fanned through, hoping for a heading that read "Contacts" or even "Friends and Relations" and finding nothing like that. Much of what she saw was incomprehensible. He'd filled several pages with doodles—zigzags, half circles with wavy lines beneath, a pattern that resembled stair steps, linked triangles.

Near the end of the notebook, she came across several lists. One short vertical row of figures:

5–20 125/85 195
5–27 140/90 197
6–5 120/80 194.5

They reminded her of something she'd seen before, but what? On the next page, the lieutenant had jotted down a column of letters with what might be phone numbers. She scanned the row, found "JC" and two sets of numbers, their home number and Chee's cell number, next to it.

She looked up when the waiter brought her Coke. "Would you like some water, too?" He stood with a pitcher in hand.

"Sure," she said. "Nobody even asks me back in Shiprock."

"Santa Fe has rules about water in restaurants. It's expensive here, so we try not to waste it."

"Good idea."

He filled her empty glass. "Your lunch will be here soon."

She returned to the little book. More cryptic notes. Numbers that could be case file notations, each with a name—"Hightower," "Yellowhorse," "Shelley"—next to it. She copied them down in her own notebook. She'd talk to Chee about all this, see what ideas he could generate.

On the next pages, more dates and more figures, all without benefit of a heading. Why would he label the pages? He knew what it all meant. She found another set of entries with possible dates. The most recent, about two weeks ago, was followed by "WR/SF 179430–655." She saw three earlier WR/SF notations with different, lower numbers, but still in the 17 series. WR equaled Window Rock, she thought, and the lieutenant had noted his truck's odometer readings for his commute to Santa Fe and home again.

The waiter brought her lunch, a big white bowl filled with broth and vegetables. The smell made her mouth water. But instead of gravy like her mother made for goat stew, this African version came with curry sauce and a side of coconut rice. She poked at it suspiciously, then took a bite. Tender slow-cooked meat. Soft carrots, onions, and bite-size chunks of potato. She put down the notebook and focused on nothing but eating for the next few minutes. Maybe the savory meal would give her insights.

Next time the waiter came by, she asked for more water, instead of splurging on a refill on her Coke. Then went back to the notebook and looked at the numbers and letters again.

She remembered the lieutenant mentioning that a broken appointment had saved him a trip to Santa Fe. The brown envelope for Dr. Collingsworth now in her car was meant for a Santa Fe address—AIRC must be shorthand for his client.

Most of the pages between the mileage log and the end of the book were blank. On the next-to-last page, she noticed a slight difference in the quality and color of the paper. Leaphorn had carefully inserted two sheets from an earlier notebook. One page had six sets of initials and numbers, beginning with "AL RR42 B50A 87401." On the next, what looked like initials were followed by more letters and numbers, with symbols, %, #, ★, scattered among them. "AZ JLLB %1934." Puzzling. Then it dawned on her. Passwords. The initials before them—AZ on the first, for example—probably indicated the sites. AZ for Amazon?

She took another bite of stew. Thought some more about the lieutenant's codes, then let her brain rest as she finished lunch.

She'd promised to contact Louisa after seeing Leaphorn. But her call went immediately to voice mail, as though Louisa's cell phone had been turned off. She left a brief message.

Then she reopened the notebook to the first page with the older paper. The grouping of five numbers could be a zip code. If it was, the 87 series meant New Mexico. "RR" could be "Rural Route," and "B50A" a box number. That left "AL." Did Leaphorn have a contact named Al? Albert? Alfonso? Or were they initials? Or was what she took for an *L* his version of the number 1? A business in Farmington called A1? Or did the *L* stand for another member of the Leaphorn family? Arnie Leaphorn? Agnes?

She called the Shiprock station and asked for Chee. Sandra, the office manager, told her Chee was out.

"Could you do a favor for me? Largo asked me to track down the lieutenant's relatives, and I'm having some trouble. Can you do some reverse directory searches?"

"Sure," Sandra said. "Is your computer down again?"

"No." Bernie sipped her water, wishing it were Coke. "I'm in Santa Fe without it." Bernie read off what she assumed was AL's address, and as much as she could decipher from the other five sets of numbers and letters.

"You want to hold on, or shall I call you back?"

"Call me back."

While she waited, Bernie turned to an earlier set of numbers, and by the time Sandra called, she'd figured out that "5–20 125/85 195" must mean that on May 20 the lieutenant's blood pressure was in the normal range, although his weight was approaching 200 pounds. It didn't help solve the crime or find the relatives, but at least her thought process tracked with the lieutenant's.

Her phone vibrated, and she answered. "No luck on most of what you gave me," Sandra said. "But the AL traces to a Farmington residence that belongs to an Austin Lee." She gave Bernie the phone number.

Bernie called, disappointed that Lee didn't answer. She left a voice mail explaining that she was a friend of Lieutenant Joe Leaphorn's and needed to talk to Austin Lee or to someone in his family as soon as she could. She left her home number, too, and the number at the Shiprock substation. "Mr. Lee isn't in any trouble,"

Bernie added. If and when Lee called back, she would explore his connection to the lieutenant. Progress? She hoped so.

The waiter brought the check. She asked where she could find the closest post office.

"The closest, that would be on Pacheco Street, but that one's closed because of a big roof leak. Well, not the leak exactly. Water shorted out the electricity in there."

"So you've already had rain?"

"Last week. Not much, but the post office roof started to fail last year."

"Where's the closest one that's open?"

"Downtown." The waiter gave her complicated directions, sprinkled with things like, "Where that business supply store that closed used to be," "I'm not sure of the name of that road," and "I forget if that street is one-way."

He ended with, "Good luck finding anyplace to park there. Downtown's a zoo this time of year because of all the tourists. I avoid that post office at all costs."

Bernie thought about taking the envelope back to Shiprock and mailing it there, but it would be after five when she arrived. Then she came up with a better plan.

"Do you know where the AIRC is?"

He shook his head. "Let me ask somebody."

He returned a few minutes later with her change and the information. "It's sort of near the big folk art museum." He gave her directions, simple directions this time. Delivering the envelope to the AIRC would be easy, and she could find out what the lieutenant was working on for them. It probably had nothing to do with Jackson Benally, Leonard Nez, or the shooting. But since she was officially on leave, why not see a bit of Santa Fe?

She picked up the notebook again and opened it to the lieutenant's June calendar. She saw penciled notations on many day-

of-the-month squares: "final contract" on one day and "pu rx"—
probably pick up a prescription—on another. She found a few
squares where Leaphorn had written what seemed to be appointments. "11:30 Largo," "2—truck aligned," "9 AIRC," and "12:30
EFB." Several squares said "PM WRL." WRL looked familiar, and
she remembered the books she'd seen on his desk. Window Rock
Library. PM must mean afternoon. AIRC and Largo she knew.
What was EFB?

Leaphorn had drawn a neat X through each June day until yesterday, the day he was shot.

Bernie found a place for her Toyota in the AIRC's gravel lot, in
the shade near a patio wall. She'd heard that lack of pavement was
a status symbol in Santa Fe, that some of the richest neighborhoods
in the older sections of town bragged about their dirt roads. But she
hadn't expected dirt parking here.

A collection of beautiful old adobe buildings connected by flag-
stone walkways sat beneath large trees. Bernie admired the way
little walls gave the flowers their own separate home, calling attention to their beauty and the mountain views beyond. She knew
enough to realize that such gorgeous gardens didn't happen by accident. The mix of native plants, hardy perennials, and blooming
annuals reflected a long history of steady effort.

A worker glanced up from his raking at the sound of her steps
on the flagstones. She noticed him looking at the Navajo Police
Department patch on her shirt. "Yá'át'ééh," he said.

She returned the greeting, surprised to run into another Navajo
even though they were the country's most populous tribe. He introduced himself, Mark Yazzie, and gave his clan affiliations. Bernie
did the same. They weren't related.

"You come all the way here to arrest me?" He pointed at the
envelope she carried. "Looks like you got my records there."

"So, you've done something?"

He laughed. "Who hasn't? But not that I talk about."

"I need to leave this envelope for a Dr. John Collingsworth. Could you tell me where I can find him?"

Yazzie said, "Go straight on. You'll see his office down there. It's the biggest one here, since he's the big boss."

The terra-cotta floors glowed as if someone had spent hours polishing them by hand. Who knows, Bernie thought, maybe someone had. A huge desk dominated both the outer office and the pale woman who sat behind it. A fan whirled between two of the massive carved wooden ceiling beams. A white pot at least three feet tall, decorated with birds and flowers, occupied the space beside the desk. Paintings filled the walls.

The woman stopped typing on her computer keyboard. "Good afternoon. May I help you?"

"I need to drop this off for John Collingsworth." Bernie handed the envelope to the woman, who set it on the desktop. "This office is beautiful. What a lot of great artwork."

The woman smiled. "I love it. It makes me happy to come to work. Have you been on campus before?"

"No. Never."

The woman pulled out a desk drawer and handed Bernie a brochure. "We host scholars from all over the world who come to study in our archives and use the pieces in our collection in their research. We have Hopi *Katsinas*—they used to call them kachinas—baskets, beautiful ancient pots, and some great contemporary ones, too. Some splendid Navajo rugs, examples of modern weaving as well as some fine older work."

Bernie noticed a pot with a spiderlike design on the shelf next to the window. She took a step toward it.

"That's a Hopi piece," the secretary said.

"I've never seen that variation on a spider," Bernie said. "What does the other side look like?"

The secretary said, "I couldn't tell you. The gal who had my job before got fired for breaking a pot. You would have thought she'd killed somebody, for all the uproar the AD made over it. I never touch any of the art."

Bernie heard footsteps behind her clicking on the hard floor and noticed the receptionist straightening up in her chair. A woman, a short, slender blonde in a dove gray suit and light blue silk blouse that matched her eyes, walked toward the desk and put down a pile of envelopes and a small box. She wore Zuni earrings with a hummingbird design and a sand-cast silver bracelet that looked as though it had been made by a Navajo jeweler. A good one at that, Bernie thought. The blonde epitomized Bernie's idea of the Santa Fe version of dressing for success.

"Mail's here," the woman said. She glanced at the envelope Bernie had brought and moved it onto the pile. Then she smiled at Bernie. "Is there some problem, Officer? I'm Dr. Maxie Davis, associate director here. AD and mail deliverer."

Bernie introduced herself. "I just stopped in to drop something off for John Collingsworth. There's no problem I know of."

"That's a relief. We're already up to our eyeballs in complications, with this huge collection coming in."

The secretary said, "Officer Manuelito was asking about the other side of the pot with the spider design. I didn't want to touch it, but—"

Davis interrupted. "Good. Never touch those pots. I never touch them without gloves." She walked over to it. "The design on the back is a mirror image. Two spiders with their legs meeting to create a web of perfect black lines. A masterpiece."

"Interesting," Bernie said.

Davis said, "Navajo Nation Police Department? You're a long way from home. Have you been to the AIRC before?"

"First time."

"You should stop in at our museum. We're famous for our Pueblo pottery collection, which has some very rare ancient pieces."

"If I come up to Santa Fe again, I'll take a look."

The big door to the interior office opened and a tall man, soft in the middle, stepped out. His gray hair had thinned, showing the pink of his scalp. He wore gold-framed glasses, a navy suit, and an eagle bolo of silver and turquoise in place of a necktie.

The receptionist said, "Dr. Collingsworth, this is Officer Manuelito. She's here with a special delivery for you. Dr. Davis and I were just encouraging her to tour the museum before she heads off."

The receptionist handed him the envelope Bernie brought. Collingsworth glanced at the precise, handwritten address, felt the weight. "Did Mr. Leaphorn ask you to drop it off?"

"No." Bernie thought for a moment. "The lieutenant is in the hospital. I found this in his truck, and as long as I was coming to see him, I decided to bring it."

"Hospital? I hope it's nothing serious."

Bernie considered how much to say. "He was shot."

"Shot?" Collingsworth's eyes widened. "How terrible."

Davis said, "I saw something on TV last night about a retired Navajo cop who was ambushed in a parking lot. Was that him?"

"Yes."

"Any suspects?" Davis asked.

"It's under investigation," Bernie said. "I can't talk about what happened to Lieutenant Leaphorn."

"Leaphorn. Unusual name. But I shouldn't talk. When they see my first name, people assume I'm a guy." She looked at Bernie. "Probably the same with you. It keeps people off guard, doesn't it?"

Collingsworth stared at the envelope. "Was this all Leaphorn had for me?" He pointed a manicured nail to the right bottom corner, where Leaphorn had noted "2 of 2," with tight little circles around the 2s.

"That's all I found," Bernie said. "I opened it, and the one you'll find inside, because his shooting is under investigation."

Collingsworth opened the envelope and carefully pulled out the smaller business-size envelope and the photocopies. He opened the smaller envelope, extracted the single sheet of paper. He read it quickly.

"Officer Manuelito, are you sure you don't have anything else for me from Mr. Leaphorn?"

"What you see is all I have."

"Can you give me his number at the hospital? I need to talk to him about this right away."

"No, sir. He's in a coma and on a breathing machine."

Collingsworth crushed the sheet of paper into a ball and hurled it toward the wastebasket. Bernie watched it bounce off the rim onto the floor. "When I hired him—and he came highly recommended—I explained exactly what the job entailed. A simple little job. We joked about how he'd find it tedious. I never expected this. I never expected him to act less than honorably."

"I don't know what the issue is here." Bernie spoke slowly, weighing each word. "But I can say that in all the years I've known the lieutenant, he has always been a man of honor. Always. Always. What was in that missing package?"

Davis looked as if she was going to say something just as the office phone rang. The secretary picked it up, then signaled Davis that the call was for her. "Nice to meet you, Bernie," she said as she walked away.

Bernie said, "Dr. Collingsworth, let's step into your office. I need to talk to you in private."

"Why?"

"I need to find out what the lieutenant was doing for you, how he betrayed your trust. We can do this here if you prefer." Bernie was used to conversations with folks who had broken the law.

Drunks. Wife beaters. Embarrassed tourists she pulled over for ignoring the reservation speed limit. She trusted her ability to defuse difficult situations, but she didn't like this angry white man.

Collingsworth hesitated. "Of course." He motioned her to walk ahead of him. "You know the man better than I. Perhaps I'm wrong about him, and you can correct my misimpression." The tone of his voice said he doubted it.

Collingsworth settled his bulk behind the large desk, an old piece that looked hand-carved. Bernie sat in a padded leather chair. She pulled a notebook and a pen from her backpack.

"What kind of work was the lieutenant doing for the AIRC?"

Collingsworth said, "Our institute has been approached by the Grove McManus Foundation. I don't suppose you've heard of it, but it's one of the largest private foundations in the world."

Bernie forced herself to ignore his arrogance. Collingsworth continued.

"The foundation, headquartered in Japan, wishes to give us their entire holdings of pottery from the American Southwest, wonderful modern examples from every Rio Grande Pueblo, including some that are extinct, and Hopi and Zuni. The gift also includes ancient pieces from Chaco Canyon and its outliers. Not only are the pots themselves significant, but the gift also includes a substantial financial endowment to assist in research and cataloging. This will make the items and information about them accessible to scholars and qualified researchers around the world. The AIRC will become an international repository for select examples of priceless pottery, some created long before European contact, including art that has never been accessible or exhibited before. And on top of that—"

Bernie's police training trumped her ingrained Navajo politeness. She interrupted. "Talk to me about the lieutenant."

Collingsworth folded his hands in front of him. "With a major donation of this kind, every institution will do some vetting. That's where Mr. Leaphorn came in. The McManus Foundation assembled its holdings from numerous private collectors over the decades. We need an accurate appraisal value for insurance purposes and tax reasons. Making sure the figures the foundation provided meshed with current values was one of Leaphorn's tasks."

She knew Leaphorn did insurance work; double-checking appraisals for accuracy probably came easy to him. "I understand."

He continued. "The AIRC's statement of governance requires that a Native American expert do the vetting whenever any additions are proposed to the collection," he said. "A board member who had previously worked with Mr. Leaphorn recommended him as our insurance consultant. When I interviewed Mr. Leaphorn, I was impressed with his knowledge and his interest in cultural issues. I thought we had found one consultant qualified for both jobs. It pleased me that Leaphorn agreed to take the assignment."

He removed his glasses, studied the lenses, put them back on. "I apologize for my outburst back there. I appreciate your bringing the envelope. I didn't mean to shoot the messenger, so to speak."

"What's missing?"

"The report I hired him to write, and a summary of findings. The deadline was yesterday. But this is my problem, not yours. "

Collingsworth stood. "I apologize again for acting like such an ill-tempered dolt." He took a step toward the door.

Bernie ignored his signal. She kept her seat, planning what to ask next. She heard the music of falling water coming in through the open window behind him. The garden must have a fountain, but she couldn't see it. Her glance swept over the priceless handmade Acoma pots on the shelves as she framed her question.

"I'm a little confused," she said. "The lieutenant knows a lot about insurance and insurance fraud, but he never claimed to be a cultural expert. Explain that part to me."

Collingsworth managed a faint smile. "As Mr. Leaphorn and

I discussed, the cultural review was a formality, and only necessary with the Chaco material. These are old pots, not ceremonial artifacts or *Katsinas* or prayer sticks. A cultural anthropologist had vetted them in the 1990s when he approached the McManus family about collaborating on a book. That expert found nothing so sensitive that it could not be featured in the book or photographed. I included his detailed report in the information I gave Mr. Leaphorn. The two of us agreed that if he discovered anything he thought might be in the least offensive or sensitive, the institution would hire an expert to vet the item."

He leaned toward Bernie. "Just so we're clear on this, nothing I asked of Mr. Leaphorn was dangerous. I'd call it bureaucratic paperwork, dotting the i's, crossing the t's. I can't imagine any of this is worth shooting someone over."

Bernie said, "When did you speak to him last?"

"He called last week with some questions, promised to mail his report that afternoon. The envelope never arrived. When I saw you, I thought you had delivered it."

"You assumed a Navajo Police officer would be delivering mail to you?"

She saw Collingsworth swallow. Let him think about it a minute. Then she said, "Knowing the lieutenant, I'm sure he sent the report as promised. He's one of the most conscientious people I know. He never does anything halfway. My guess is that he wanted time to figure out his expenses, add up his mileage, and sent the bill and the research material you'd loaned him separately. He labeled it two of two. I found a new package of envelopes in his truck. Maybe that's why this one was just not ready to mail. And we all realize the post office has its problems. Maybe the first envelope is still in the mail."

"I asked him to send it FedEx, safer that way, but he said he didn't want us to have to pay the extra shipping charge," Collingsworth said.

Bernie stood and took a business card from the front pocket of her backpack. "Call me if you think of anything that might be relevant to our investigation into the shooting."

Collingsworth put the card on his desktop. "Officer, if by chance that report turns up in the process of your investigation, I'd be grateful if you or someone on your staff could call me."

She noticed his change in attitude. "Of course."

"If you can spare another few minutes, I'll ask Marjorie to show you some pots similar to the ones we hope to receive. Mr. Leaphorn enjoyed the tour very much."

"Marjorie?"

"Marjorie Rockwell, my secretary."

Marjorie, Bernie realized, relished an opportunity to get away from her desk. They strolled from her office along a shaded gravel path. Simple signs shaped like arrows pointed the way to the museum. At the front door, Marjorie slid her ID card into the slot. The light switched from red to green, and she motioned for Bernie to go in.

A huge black pot with sensuously rounded sides stood beneath a spotlight just inside the entryway. The clay sparkled. The shape reminded Bernie of the hoodoos at the Bisti badlands. Man imitating nature, and making changes.

"Impressive, isn't it?" Marjorie said. "Mr. Leaphorn stood here for five minutes. Said he couldn't believe a single person had created something so perfect. A potter from Nambe Pueblo made this."

"It's amazing," Bernie said. "I see why the lieutenant liked it. I can understand why Dr. Davis is so passionate about this collection."

Marjorie chuckled. "Passionate? She's an absolute fanatic. The pots are her life. She's here early, late. She's always been obsessed, but now she's working herself into a frenzy over the acquisition."

They walked past the reception desk into a big room with tables in the center and long rows of shelves stretching in three directions. A woman, a Pueblo Indian, Bernie surmised, sat at one of the tables, copying images from a pot shaped like a melon. Bernie noticed she was wearing gloves. At the far end an Anglo man, also wearing gloves, examined a tiny basket with a magnifying glass. He made notes on a yellow legal pad.

Marjorie pointed out a hallway that threaded past the displays to the storage area in back of the building.

"Is that where the new collection will go?"

"Oh, no." Marjorie headed toward one section of shelves. "The McManus ceramics will be displayed here in the front. We exhibit selections on a rotating basis until we can build the new wing to showcase it all. That's driving all of us crazy. We'll have state-of-the-art temperature and humidity controls, first-rate security, and well-lit space for scholars who come to study with us."

As they strolled, Marjorie pointed out some of the collection's treasures. Painted hides. Beaded breastplates. Pueblo Indian dance kilts. Bernie stopped at what looked like a pile of gray chenille with bits of old twine interspersed.

"Is this a turkey feather blanket?"

"That's right," Marjorie said.

"I've heard of these but never seen one. It's fascinating. What a great way to stay warm."

"Since you like weaving, let me show you some of our rugs."

Past the shelves, they came to a hallway with a series of small rooms. Marjorie opened one of the doors. The lights came on automatically. Bernie saw a Two Grey Hills rug, one of the most elegantly designed she had ever encountered, spread on a table. Other rugs rolled like cigars lay stored on the shelves.

"Wow," she said. "That rug is gorgeous." She longed to touch it, to feel the weaver's energy. "Do you know who made it?"

"Unfortunately, no. Are you a weaver?"

"My mother and my grandmothers were weavers. And my aunts. A rug like this takes my breath away."

"Then let me show you something else." Marjorie punched in a code to open the door to let them out, and they continued down the hall to another little room. The lights came on. Displayed against the wall was the most spectacular Navajo rug Bernie had ever seen.

"Hosteen Klah," Marjorie said. "Eighteen eighty."

Bernie recognized elements from the sacred story of the emergence of the Holy People into the Glittering World, the earth modern Diné share with the rest of humanity. She saw the four sacred mountains, the sun, moon, and major stars. The weaver had created the Hero Twins, Child Born of Water and Monster Slayer. Bernie sucked in a deep breath. This was the holy grail of the Navajo way of life from a time when many, including Klah, thought the Diné might disappear. Klah, a respected *hataalii*, or what the *bilagaana* call a medicine man, sought to preserve the Navajo way by re-creating his intricate healing sand paintings as tapestries. The rugs also created enormous controversy.

"It's the most wonderful thing I've ever seen," she said.

"One of our treasures," Marjorie said. She punched in a code to open the door. "Come again, anytime. Stay as long as you wish."

As Bernie steered her Toyota along Santa Fe's curving downtown streets and ultimately south toward the freeway and home, she realized that the genius of Hosteen Klah had moved her thoughts away from sadness and frustration to the more beautiful space of dreams and the spirit. For the first time since the shooting, she felt light, relaxed. It was good to be in that quiet place.

She stayed in the right lane as she cruised down La Bajada, past the exit for Cochiti Pueblo and the sculptural Tent Rocks, now known as Kasha-Katuwe National Monument. She didn't see any of those black-and-white New Mexico State Police cars or other law enforcement from the numerous county and Pueblo Indian jurisdictions that I-25 crossed as it headed south. She pushed the Tercel to 80, eager to get home.

Bernie turned west toward the Rio Grande at the Bernalillo exit, crossing the edge of what was once a tiny town, now fleshed out with a growing assembly of fast food restaurants and chain motels. She climbed toward San Isidro, Cuba, and Jemez Pueblo. The engine struggled a bit with the change in elevation as she entered the tall trees and open spaces of the Jicarilla Apache reservation.

She thought about John Collingsworth. Was he the arrogant know-it-all she'd decided at first impression? Or a bright, conscientious, decent guy, the sort of client the lieutenant would have enjoyed working with because they both wanted the job done right? Surely the lieutenant had finished the report by the deadline and mailed it as promised.

She used her cell phone to call Officer Bigman at the Window Rock office and ask a favor. "Swing by the lieutenant's house on your way home and take a look in the truck for me, would you? I may have left an envelope in there that Leaphorn planned to mail."

"What kind of envelope?"

"Addressed to John Collingsworth at the AIRC in Santa Fe."

"I'll be glad to look," he said. "Want me to mail it?"

"No. Hold on to it for me."

Bernie phoned Chee and told him the two of them were now authorized Leaphorn relatives and a bit about the hospital. She mentioned the AIRC, the missing envelope, and then, in more detail, the Hosteen Klah rug. Thinking of it gave her goose bumps.

"So how was your day?" she asked. "What's happening with the Benally car and the prints? Have Jackson or Nez shown up?"

"Nope. The grandma Nez lives with says he disappears for days at a time. She's sweet, but not quite all there, if you know what I mean. The feds haven't found Louisa. She wasn't at the motel she gave us. And not on any flights to Houston. Not answering her phone. They didn't find her Jeep in the airport garage or at any of those park-and-shuttle places."

She heard him sigh into the receiver.

"Where are you now?" he asked.

She told him she was about halfway to the turnoff for Chaco Canyon.

"I hope you're in the mood for ice cream," he said.

"Ice cream?"

"I found one of those little freezers at the flea market on my way home from work. Still in the box. Never used as far as I can tell. Three dollars!"

"Did it come with recipes?"

"Recipes? My dear, I don't need a recipe. I am the Sherlock Holmes of cooking."

Bernie laughed. "Did Sherlock cook?"

"He cooked for Dr. Watson. Didn't you learn that in college?"

"I must have missed that class," she said. "I didn't realize the English were known for their cuisine. Is making ice cream cooking?"

Chee probably said something in response, but all she heard were three quick beeps and silence. Welcome to the beautiful, empty Southwest.

Bernie watched the sun set against Angel Peak, cruised through Farmington traffic without mishap, and finally saw Ship Rock, her favorite landmark, rise along the horizon.

8

She was tired and hungry when she pulled into the driveway. The thought of Chee experimenting with his new ice cream machine made her smile. But as she walked past her loom toward the front door, she heard an unsettling sound, the plaintive cry of a creature undergoing torture.

Chee greeted her with a kiss. "Guess what, honey?" He didn't give her time to ask, *What?* "Bigman went to Leaphorn's to look for that envelope, and the cat was back! Waiting at the door. He had his wife bring it by. It looks fine, as far as cats go. No harm done from its escapade."

"Why is it making that awful noise?

"Maybe it ate something bad out there." Chee looked puzzled. "A bellyache."

"You had a cat," she said. "You know more about them than I do."

"You remember that?"

"You told me how you sent a cat back east to a girlfriend of yours because you didn't think it was a survivor."

"This one is a Navajo cat," Chee said. "That's another reason it's making so much noise. It wants to go out and hunt up its dinner.

But if we put it outside, it will probably try to run back to Window Rock."

She laughed. "Well, at least let it out of the bathroom."

Chee opened the door.

The cat looked at him from its seat on the bath mat. It gave a final yowl, then started licking its right front paw.

Chee smiled. "I guess we have a cat now, until we get this sorted out."

"At least you got it to be quiet," Bernie said.

"Thanks," he said. "It was your idea."

Chee went back to finishing dinner while Bernie changed out of her uniform into shorts and a T-shirt. She walked out on the deck, enjoying the evening's symphony of crickets and the comforting sound of the nearby San Juan River. She thought about the lieutenant, listening to the buzz of machines that were keeping him alive.

After dinner Chee said, "I'm surprised you haven't asked about the envelope."

"I was waiting for you to bring out the ice cream," she said. "I thought we'd talk business after pleasure."

"I didn't have enough cream to make it. Because of the cat. Sorry."

"It must have been starved. I still have food for it in my car."

The cat was watching them from the sofa. "That one has been quiet ever since you got here. I think it likes you. Or it knew where you'd hidden its food," Chee said.

"It's a she," Bernie said. "And I think she just likes being out of the bathroom."

She smiled at him. "So, did Bigman find anything?"

Chee gave the cat a pat on the head. "No luck. He looked in the truck and then in the house. All the logical places, then the illogical ones. But after what you told me about your interview in Santa Fe, I had an idea."

Leaphorn's computer was at the Window Rock station in case they needed it for evidence. Chee had asked the technician to search the hard drive for files labeled "Indian art report," "final report," "McManus," "AIRC," or the equivalent, with a date within the last month. If he found anything, it would be e-mailed to Chee.

Bernie said, "And people think I married you just for your good looks."

"My one stroke of brilliance today," he said.

She moved to the couch. "What did the background check on Jackson come up with?"

Chee settled in beside her. "Nothing. No record, not even a traffic ticket. Same as with his mother. Mrs. Benally won a big award from the tribal government back when Joe Shirley Jr. was president."

"What else happened today?"

"Mrs. Benally has assigned herself to our investigation. She's looking for a ninja. And I found Jackson."

"You found Benally? That's huge. And you're just telling me now? You better start at the beginning."

When he got to the Shiprock substation that morning, Chee had a message to report immediately to Window Rock police headquarters and to radio Largo once he was on the way.

"Mrs. Benally showed up here." Largo sounded more out of sorts than usual. "She's furious that she can't get her car back. Said she had something important to tell us, but she won't until we give her the car. She demanded to talk to Bernie, but finally agreed to talk to you. Only you. She's as stubborn as, as . . . well, you know. Stubborn."

Chee agreed.

"See if you can calm her down, explain the car situation to her again. I figure she knows something about Jackson's whereabouts. Maybe she'll tell you where he is or where he could be, where he goes when he doesn't come home. You can talk to her about all that when you give her a ride home."

"Me? I have to go all the way to Window Rock to give a grouchy old lady a ride?"

"You," Largo said. "You're in charge of the Navajo side of this case, remember? If Bernie wasn't on leave, she could do it and probably get enough information from Mrs. Benally to record her family history."

Chee said, "Yes, sir. On my way."

He appreciated the air-conditioning in his patrol car as he sailed past the volcanic buttes that rose like ruins in the dusty landscape on both sides of the paved four-lane US 491. He recalled when this route had been US 666, nicknamed the Devil's Highway, and the controversy that came with the decision to rename it to reduce talk of the highway's curse and theft of the 666 signs. This had been one of the deadliest roads in New Mexico, marked with the carnage of traffic accidents. Widening the road and adding better shoulders and rumble strips to jar awake sleepy drivers made it safer. Chee bypassed the scenic turnoffs and stuck to the four-lane, turning west on NM 264 at Yah-Ta-Hey and cruising into the Navajo Police headquarters parking lot in a little under two hours.

Mrs. Benally's mood had not mellowed with time. Chee explained again the evidence review process, how the crime scene technicians had to search her car for hair, skin fragments, other clues to help them find the one who shot Leaphorn. He called the crime lab to learn when the car could be released, got a vague bureaucratic response. He praised her generosity and the importance of her help with such a crime. Then he offered to drive her home.

"What about the Fudgsicles?"

"I don't know about any Fudgsicles," he said.

"The other officer. Not the lady. He promised to buy me some after he let mine get all melted."

"Hmmm," Chee said. "He's not here today. What about some coffee?"

He brought her a cup of strong, stale coffee from the police break room with plenty of sugar.

"Okeydokey, then," she said. "Let's go. This time, I sit in the front seat."

Chee drove her past Bashas', past the sprawling Navajo Nation fairgrounds, down a dirt road to her place. Mrs. Benally gave Chee directions, more than he needed.

"Do you know who shot the policeman?" she asked.

"We're working on it. We'll use the evidence from your car to help with that."

"Probably a white man," Mrs. Benally said.

"How would a white man get your car?"

"Same as an Indian."

"Why do you think a *bilagaana* would steal your car?"

"He didn't steal it." She gave Chee a disgusted look. "He borrowed it."

Chee said, "We don't know if the person driving was a man or a woman, a Navajo or not. Bernie—the policewoman you met— she could only verify that whoever did it was short, wearing dark clothes."

"Like one of those ninjas in the movies. Okay, then," Mrs. Benally said. "A little blue-eyed ninja. Or Japanese. Not my Jackson."

"Where does Jackson go when he doesn't come home?" Chee asked.

"He comes home," she said.

"What about yesterday?"

Mrs. Benally stared straight ahead. Finally she said, "Jackson has a good heart. We don't worry."

Chee pulled up in front of the house and parked, noticing that Mrs. Benally's front door stood open. When they reached the front porch, Chee saw a slender young man in jeans and a white muscle shirt. An unzipped pack was next to him with some thick, serious-looking books spread out on the table. A video game beeped and flashed from the TV monitor.

"Mom!" he said. "Holy catfish! What happened to you? Where's the car?"

"Officer Chee gave me a ride home because the police have taken our car," Mrs. Benally said.

"Whoa! What did you do?"

Jackson stood close to six-foot-two in his cowboy boots, Chee figured. "Whatever trouble Mom is in, she wouldn't ever do any-body harm," Jackson said. "She might lose it once in a while, get carried away, but I never thought she'd be arrested."

"I'm not arrested, because I'm not the evil ninja."

Jackson looked confused.

Chee said, "Are you Jackson Benally?"

"Right."

"You have to come back to the police station with me."

"What? No way. You're kidding me."

Mrs. Benally said, "Son, this is because of that man with the funny name, the elderly who got hurt yesterday. Some Japanese person borrowed our car to shoot him. They made my fingerprints, and now they need yours. Like on TV. I'll go with you to make sure they treat you good. "

"Crazy," Jackson said. "No joke? A ninja dude used our car in a shooting? You're kidding me."

Chee looked at Jackson. "The case is under investigation. I can't talk about it. How old are you?"

"Almost twenty."

Chee looked at Mrs. Benally. "You'll have to stay here while I take Jackson in. He's legally an adult. Besides the fingerprints, we need to ask him some questions."

"Me? Why me? I had nothing to do with this," he said. "I was in class yesterday." Jackson held up his hands, palms forward. Chee noticed a flash of gold on his wrist. A watchband.

Chee said, "You were the last person we know of to drive the car. Let's go."

Jackson blanched. Chee noticed that he avoided looking at his mother.

Mrs. Benally put her hand on Jackson's arm. "You tell the policeman everything about yesterday so we get the car back. I'll see if I can find the ninja." Then she looked at Chee. "I'll call you when I have the clues. Bring Jackson back soon. And then tell that other policeman I need my Fudgsicles."

Chee put Jackson in the backseat of the patrol car and radioed Largo. For good measure, he told Jackson his rights. If anyone screwed up in this case, it wouldn't be him.

At the station, Largo explained that the interview would be taped, that Jackson was entitled to a lawyer if he wanted one.

"I don't need a lawyer," Jackson said. "I've got nothing to say about the ninja."

Largo looked at Chee. Raised an eyebrow.

"Long story," Chee said.

The interview room was furnished with a table and two straight-backed metal chairs. Jackson sat facing the one-way mirror where Largo would be observing. Chee, his back to the mirror, began to ask questions, starting with name, age, and address for the record. The boy was nervous, but no more agitated than Chee would expect for an average young man being interrogated in a police station.

"Jackson, where were you yesterday morning?"

"I was at school, University of New Mexico, Gallup campus. I, I don't know the exact address."

Chee smiled at Jackson. "If you tell me the truth here, it will help us solve the crime. Help us get the car back to your mom."

"You got it."

"So let's start over." Chee looked at his notes, letting the silence spread over the room. "So, where were you yesterday at ten a.m.? Where were you really?"

"In class. I've got my schedule in my computer at home if you wanna see it."

"The Gallup Police checked with the registrar, found your class schedule. They talked to the instructor for that class. He said you hadn't shown up."

Jackson shrugged. "Maybe he didn't remember."

"The Gallup Police looked for you all over campus." Chee sighed. "You could be facing some serious charges. If you don't tell me the truth, you'll end up in jail. I don't intend to warn you again."

Jackson stared at his fingernails. Chee noticed that the top of his right sneaker moved up and down. Twitching toes, a poor liar getting nervous.

"Do you know a man named Lieutenant Joe Leaphorn?"

Jackson looked up. The twitching stopped. "No, sir. Never heard of him. I swear."

Chee decided he was telling the truth.

"Did you shoot a man in the parking lot of the Navajo Inn?"

Jackson sat straighter, seemed to come to life. "No way, dude. I don't even have a gun."

"Can you tell me why your car was identified by a police officer as the vehicle the person who shot Lieutenant Leaphorn was driving?"

"No. I'm clueless." Jackson shook his head. "It's Mom's car. She just lets me drive it. Last time I saw it was when I left it for her at Bashas', like I always do when my friend takes me to school. Are you sure it was our car?"

"I'm asking the questions," Chee said. "What time did you leave the car at Bashas'?"

"It was eight in the morning. Around then, more or less."

"What's your friend's name?"

"Leonard Nez."

"How can I reach him?" Chee said.

Jackson looked at his nails again. "I'm not sure."

"Think about that question again. See if you can remember his phone number, where he lives."

"He lives with his grandma," Jackson said. "Somewhere around here. I've never been to his house. We just meet at Bashas'."

"So if you didn't shoot anybody, how about this. You meet Nez and you drive your mom's car. He shoots the officer. You two go back to Bashas'. Leave the car for your mom, drive off in his vehicle."

"Lizard wouldn't shoot anybody," Jackson said. "He doesn't even like to go hunting with us."

"Lizard?"

"I mean Leonard. We all call him Lizard."

"What does he look like?"

Jackson pondered. "Average. Black hair. Black eyes. Strong. Kinda short. Quick. Looks like one of those collard lizards a little. Not really, though."

"I'm still wondering where you were when the officer was shot," Chee said. "I know you're lying about being in school. We checked on Nez. He wasn't there either. You're lying about that, so you're probably lying about everything, about the gun, about the shooting. You are in deep, deep trouble."

Chee didn't say anything else. The room grew still.

After a while Jackson said, "Lizard and I weren't actually in class. We took his truck out toward Zuni because we were working on a, um, special project. For our geology class."

"Are you sure that's right? First you told me you were in class. Now it's a different story."

"I just forgot." Jackson worked at his nails.

Chee got up, stretched, glanced at Jackson. Sat down again. "Some people think that the shooting might have been part of a gang initiation. You know something about that?"

Jackson looked up. "There's some gangbangers near where we live. You can see graffiti on big rocks where our road meets the highway. I don't have anything to do with those guys. I swear."

"So where were you really when the policeman got shot?"

"I told you. Doing that geology stuff out near Zuni."

"A class project?" Chee waited for Jackson to elaborate. Liars got themselves in trouble by adding too many details.

Jackson paused. "Yeah. Well, sort of. An extra-credit deal. Professor Coburn, he's the teacher, he likes for us to take pictures of formations, bring back rock samples, stuff like that. For extra credit."

"You're sure?"

"Dude, I'm sure we were out by Zuni."

"Did anyone see you there besides Leonard Nez?"

Jackson shook his head. Reexamined his fingernails.

"You like that class?"

"It's cool, dude," Jackson said. "Because it's summer session, Coburn does field trips. Gets us out to see the real thing. We have a chance to learn stuff that's not from books."

"Too bad you'll have to drop out when you're in jail." Chee studied his notes, took his time. He wanted Jackson to realize this was serious.

"We haven't told your mother yet about the marijuana."

"Marijuana?"

"The crime scene investigators, you know, the team that's extracting the fingerprints, looking for fibers, hairs, other things that can lead us to the shooter. They found evidence that someone had had pot in the car," Chee said. "I wanted to talk to you first about this other crime, to see if you could help us, before I asked her about it. If you're sure this Nez guy wouldn't have tried to kill Lieutenant Leaphorn, who else? And why did Nez disappear? We know that whoever shot the lieutenant was in your car. You say it wasn't you. Your mom has a real alibi, not a string of lies."

Jackson gnawed at his lip.

"While you're thinking, think about how we can talk to Nez to verify your story."

Jackson pulled out his cell phone. "I remembered that I have his number here."

"Call him," Chee said. "Tell him I need to talk to him. Put the phone on speaker."

Jackson did so. They head the phone ring, then a mechanical voice instructing them to leave a name and number.

"Shall I leave a message?"

"No," Chee said. "He'll see that you called. Just give me the number."

Largo met Chee in the hall. "Marijuana?"

"Just a guess," Chee said. "Paid off."

"We've got a message in for that geology teacher for you," Largo said. "And we can trace Nez's mobile number."

Chee didn't make it to the vending machines before the receptionist called him back.

Over the phone, Professor Coburn described Jackson as a nice kid. But there was no special project that involved missing class to head out to the Zuni Mountains. He did encourage students to do extra-credit work, but Jackson Benally had never done any. He didn't need to, Coburn said. He was in the top tier of the class already.

"Leonard Nez? Lizard? He's a different story. I don't know why he's even in college. He has rarely come to class this summer. Good thing the session is almost over. I can't say much more about him. A phantom wasting his time and money here."

Chee put the phone down and thought about it. Why would Jackson lie about where he and Nez were, and about how to find Nez, if Nez didn't shoot Leaphorn? Time to talk to Jackson again. But first, Chee decided, he'd have a cup of coffee, check his e-mail. Give Jackson time to worry.

The interview room smelled slightly of sweat now. Jackson looked almost relieved to see him.

"I was on my way to lunch," Chee said. "I thought I'd stop just in case you had anything else to tell me."

"Did you talk to Lizard yet?"

Chee said, "Remember? I ask the questions."

Jackson shifted in the hard chair. Uneasy. More fidgety than during the first interview.

"We didn't actually go to Zuni," Jackson said. "We didn't go that far. We stayed on the highway for about twenty miles and then we drove out toward the cliffs on a road Lizard knew. His uncle has a ranch out that way."

"Hmm," Chee said.

"We went to the ranch. Lizard had something to do out there, and I, well, it was a nice day and I only had a couple classes and they're easy . . ." Jackson's voice trailed off. Embarrassed.

"Did his uncle see you?"

"No. Nobody saw us. No, sir." Chee noticed the change from "dude."

"What did you do out there?"

"Just a bunch of stuff. We didn't shoot anybody."

Chee looked at the young man. Watched Jackson fidget.

"If you didn't do it, and you say you know Nez didn't do it, who could have driven your mom's car? How did some evil stranger get in there? It puzzles me. Can you explain it?"

"It's like I told you. Lizard and I take turns driving to UNM,"

Jackson said. "On the days when he drives, I leave Mom's car there at Bashas'. Twice a week, I drive us to school. Tuesday and Thursdays. I've got class all day, all day until after five. The car would just be sitting there in the lot all day. So I loan it out to people."

Chee listened.

"They give me a little money. I didn't want to rat them out."

"Who do you loan it to?" Chee remembered his days at UNM in Albuquerque, the hassle of negotiating the city on foot or figuring out the bus routes. A buddy who would loan him a car would have been handy.

"Some of the guys are friends. Some are sort of like, um, acquaintances. People I know from the gym. None of them would shoot anybody."

Chee must have looked skeptical.

"Pickup basketball," Jackson explained. "I use the money for books. Mom is proud of me being in college, but she doesn't realize how much stuff costs. She can't help any more than she already does."

Chee said, "If you get out of here, you should stop letting other people drive your mom's car. If they wreck, you'll be in big trouble."

"I am in big trouble already," Jackson said. "Are you kidding? You met my mother."

Chee tore out an empty piece of paper from the notebook and pushed it and the pen across the tabletop. "Pull out your phone again. I need the names. Phone numbers. If you have an address, e-mail, give me that, too. I've got some other things to attend to. I'll be back for the list in a few minutes."

When Chee returned, Jackson had scribbled down fifteen names with contact information. The young man showed promise as a budding tycoon. "Is this everybody?"

Jackson said, "Mom gives rides to people sometimes, too. Mostly old ladies. I don't know all of their names."

Chee said, "I'm still confused about two things. First, where were you when Leaphorn was attacked?"

"I told you I was with Lizard over by Zuni—"

Chee shook his head, and Jackson stopped.

"Think about this, Jackson. Is whatever you're lying about worth it? Worth remaining a suspect in a serious crime, a police shooting, attempted murder?

"The second thing I'm wondering about is Nez, how he's involved in all this. You're covering up for him."

Jackson looked at the tabletop.

"It would really help your case if we could find Nez to back up your story," Chee said. "As it stands now, you are our main suspect in the shooting."

Jackson looked pale. "Check out those names I gave you, sir. Maybe one of them made a copy of the key. Used our car to pin the crime on me. I was with Lizard, I swear. Hours away from Window Rock."

Chee said, "Think about it some more. I'll be back to talk to you again."

As Chee headed to the parking lot, anticipating the drive back to Shiprock, an officer hailed him with the universal sign for a phone call. Mrs. Benally, wondering when Jackson would be home. Yelling at him for saying Jackson would spend the night in jail.

"Other than you, Leonard Nez seems to be the only one who can say for sure that it wasn't your boy," Chee said.

"Well, then, I'll bring Lizard to talk to you. Along with the ninja," Mrs. Benally said. "Officer Chee, I am on the case."

"And that was my day." Chee finished the story.

"Oh, and one more thing. When I got home, there was a message from Louisa. She said she had something important to tell us."

"And?"

"And when I called her cell, it went straight to voice mail again, and she hasn't called back."

"You know, Louisa is starting to look like a viable suspect after all," Bernie said. "Odd that the feds can't find her. That she wasn't on a flight to Houston like she told us."

Chee said, "Louisa as a would-be murderer? You're not serious, right?"

"I can't imagine her doing it, but I can't imagine anybody . . ." She shook her head. "Too bad we weren't here when she called. I don't like all this phone tag."

The phone rang. She looked at the display. "For you."

"Chee," he said. He listened. "Finally. Thanks. Let Largo know I'll be in early."

"We've got a new lead on the shooting," Chee said. "One of the prints in the car traced to a guy with a record and a motive. Garrison Tsosie. He's been arrested for fighting, DWI, disturbing the peace."

"Like a lot of young guys," Bernie said. "Some of my clan brothers."

"Let me finish. Garrison has a brother serving time in the penitentiary because of Leaphorn. Now, all I have to do is track him down at his place in Crownpoint, get him to confess to shooting the lieutenant, and explain how Jackson Benally is involved in all this. Case closed."

Bernie smiled. "You know—"

"Don't say it," Chee said. "It's never that easy."

"But it's something," she said. "What about Nez?"

"No luck finding him," Chee said. "But other than the prints in the car that might be his, no motive, no connection to Leaphorn, no criminal record. He's the invisible man and just became a low priority thanks to the Tsosie link."

"We must have Garrison's brother in the files. I'll look for Tsosies."

"That'll help. But first, my wonderful homemade dessert," he said. "An old family recipe. Jell-O with fruit cocktail."

"And cookies?"

"Tomorrow," he said. "I'll make some to go with the ice cream."

Bernie put bowls and spoons on the table. Chee dished the Jell-O, squirted on the whipped topping direct from the red spray can. The cat came to attention and strolled into the kitchen. Chee gave her some, too.

Bernie's list organized Leaphorn's police files into two groups. The first featured suspects whom Leaphorn had sent to prison for violent crimes, with those convicted of violence involving a law enforcement officer topping the list. The other group were those incarcerated for drugs sales, burglary, and the like. In the second batch, among several Tsosies, they found a Notah Tsosie with the same Crownpoint, New Mexico, address as Garrison.

"Lieutenant Leaphorn arrested Notah for stealing cars," she said. "One of the last cases he worked before he retired. Not much special here, as far as I can tell. You think he could be the ghost from the past Leaphorn mentioned to Louisa?"

Chee said, "The whole idea of Leaphorn talking about ghosts doesn't sit right with me. I remember him telling me more than once that people get into enough trouble on their own, without any supernatural help. Maybe Louisa wasn't remembering correctly."

Bernie said, "Hey, she's a researcher, always collecting stories for that book she's working on. She couldn't do her job if she didn't know how to listen."

"I'm sure she uses a tape recorder," Chee said. "And a notebook. Did Leaphorn's notebook have the info on relatives you needed?"

"Maybe," she said. "He wrote everything in funny codes, but I got a hit on a guy in Farmington. Could you take a look?"

She went into the bedroom and got the notebook out of her

backpack. The cat, she noticed, had not only decided to sleep on the bed, she'd curled up on Chee's pillow. She scooped up the cat—no resistance this time—and took it back with her to the living room. She put the cat on the couch and handed Chee the little book.

"Turn to the back, where he glued in that page," she said.

Chee glanced at it. Bernie told him her theory about the addresses.

"I called Austin Lee, left a message. So far, no word."

"I can have someone follow up, since it is part of the investigation," Chee said. "If this Tsosie guy doesn't pan out, we might need these alleged relatives as suspects or as information sources."

He sighed. "This is the point in the investigation where I would pick up the phone and make that call I dreaded making. I'd talk to him. He'd help me realize how blind I was for not seeing what was right in front of me."

"You're doing fine," Bernie said. "If I'd run a little faster, I could have gotten a better description of the shooter. Maybe gotten a shot off. Saved us all a bunch of grief."

"Don't go there," Chee said.

"You either."

Chee thumbed through the notebook. "Did you get some ideas from anything else in here? Any references to ghosts wanting to take him to lunch?"

She shook her head. "I glanced at his calendar. Some of those appointments might be worth following up on if we can figure out the who and where."

Chee turned to the calendar. "EFB, twelve-thirty. The Friday before the shooting."

"I should have made the connection," Bernie said.

Chee thumbed toward the front of the book and stopped. "Did you see this?" He held up the page of Leaphorn's sketches. "I like these. They look like linked triangles, upside-down mountains. I never knew he was an artist."

She said, "I wonder why he made those?"

"He might have just been doodling," Chee said. "Did you see anything else like this in the notebook?"

The phone rang again. "I'm sure it's for you," she said.

"Let it go," Chee said. "If it's important they'll leave a message."

"Maybe it's Louisa," Bernie said. "Calling to confess."

Chee looked at the ID screen. Picked it up.

"Agent Cordova, you're working late," he said. A pause, then Chee said, "The number we gave you for Louisa's cell is the only one we have."

Chee smiled as he listened. He said into the phone, "No, I didn't ask Benally if he knew her. I didn't explore that murder-for-hire angle."

Bernie glanced at him, and he winked. She remembered their wager about the feds suspecting Louisa of hatching up a scheme with Jackson and Lizard as hit men. She hadn't believed the feds would be that dense, but now she owed Chee a steak dinner.

"Hold on," Chee said. He handed Bernie the phone.

She listened, shifting the receiver to her other ear, used her right hand to take a bite of Jell-O. "Of course, whatever I can do. Tomorrow? Where? Okay, then. See you there."

She gave Cordova her cell phone number, then she hung up.

Chee looked at her.

"Cordova wants a hypnotist to debrief me about the shooting. Figure out if I saw more than I'm remembering."

Chee said, "You seem pretty happy about that."

"I've never been hypnotized before. It might be interesting."

Chee frowned.

"What's wrong?"

"He already said you were a good witness. Why bother with this? Are they coming out here?"

"No. I need to meet him and the hypnotist at the FBI headquarters in Santa Fe," Bernie said.

"He wants you to drive all that way? That's crazy."

"He wants to solve the case. That's why they're looking into Louisa and the murder-for-hire aspect."

Chee said, "I think he likes you."

"What's not to like?"

"He's flirting with you."

"Cordova? He's married. I saw the ring."

"That doesn't matter to some guys," Chee said.

"If you're worried, come with me tomorrow," she said. "You can see Leaphorn. Make sure his doctor isn't flirting with me, too."

"You know I've got to find Garrison Tsosie."

"Maybe I could put the trip off a day," she said. "Would that make you feel better?"

Chee said nothing.

"You know this is business. Just business," she said. "You should use Cordova as a resource instead of wasting energy like this."

"So now you're an expert on crime solving?"

"Don't be so touchy," Bernie said. "So what if he is flirting with me?"

He sighed and rose from the couch. "I'm going to take a shower. I have to go in early."

She washed the dishes and tried not to let Chee's mini tantrum bother her. She hadn't talked to her mother that day, she realized, and then her thoughts shifted to Louisa, with no daughters to care about her. Louisa alone now, so it seemed. She had never mentioned her family to Bernie and obviously didn't know much about the lieutenant's. Bernie considered Leaphorn's missing AIRC report. Maybe Louisa had seen it, mailed it, or seen Leaphorn mail it. Then she thought about Jerry Cordova, his nice smile, his well-tended hands, the hint of spicy aftershave.

She reviewed how she'd answered his questions. What if she'd remembered wrong?

When she climbed into bed Chee was asleep, or pretending to be. She snuggled next to him in the darkness. When she awoke it was past dawn. Chee's side of the bed was empty, and the phone was ringing.

By the time she bounced out of bed and answered the phone, the ringing had stopped. She noticed that the driveway was empty except for her Toyota.

The message was from Cordova, asking her to get back to him ASAP.

He answered on the first ring.

"Have you left for Santa Fe yet?"

"No," she said. "I was going to call you. I was hoping we could reschedule."

"Great minds think alike," he said. "The hypnotist has a sick kid. She can't come in today, and her backup is in Phoenix at a trial. Could you do it tomorrow?"

Bernie said, "Tomorrow is better. That way Chee might come, too, give me some company on the drive."

"I hear Chee is working with this Tsosie lead," Cordova said. "Depending on how things go with him today, maybe we won't even need the hypnosis. I thought you aced all the details, but sometimes this procedure excavates a few more tidbits."

Bernie said, "You have a good interview technique. Very professional. I might steal some ideas from you."

"Stealing, huh? I might have to take you out to lunch as a punishment and give you a lecture about that."

Bernie didn't know what to say.

Cordova didn't miss a beat. "Tomorrow at nine? I'll call you if there's any change. Thanks for being flexible."

Bernie put on her sweatpants and running shoes—the new green ones she loved. She brushed her hair and went outside into the glorious morning. Along the banks of the San Juan the air smelled fresh, alive. The day's heat hadn't settled in yet, and birds flitted in the brush. The old songs her mother had taught her rang in her head, gentle greetings for the day to ask blessings for the world and all the creatures it contained. She thought about Chee, wondered if he still had the grumps. She thought about Leaphorn and told herself that worry would do no good. She thought about her mother and Darleen and Louisa. Her thoughts drifted toward Jerry Cordova, wondering what had brought him to the FBI, if he was a southwesterner, if he flirted with every woman he met.

Then as her body found the rhythm, she just ran, feeling the breeze on her skin, listening to the serenade of the river, relishing the sturdiness of the cottonwoods and the soft gray leaves of the Russian olives. She let the new day enfold her.

When she got home, she noticed that Chee had fed the cat and emptied the cat box before he left that morning. She picked up the phone to call him, and heard the rapid tone that signaled a waiting voice mail.

"Hi. This is a guy who rents the house from Austin Lee, you know, the one you left a message for yesterday? I called him, and he said to tell you he already knows about what happened."

End of message. She'd been a cop long enough to understand why "a guy" didn't tell her his name.

She called Chee's cell. Before she could say hello, he started apologizing. "It's hard to be married to the most beautiful girl in the world. I acted like a jerk."

"Don't worry about it," she said. "I've been edgy ever since the shooting."

"I think you're perfect," he said.

"I'm even better now." She told him about the Austin Lee call.

"And Cordova called," she said. "The hypnotist couldn't make it today. We rescheduled for tomorrow, and I told him you'd come, too. Was that true?"

"Yeah, if you'll still have me," he said. "I'd like to see Leaphorn. I think I can wrap up the Tsosie lead today."

"What's up with that?"

"I'm on the road now, heading to Crownpoint to talk to him. Could you take a look at Leaphorn's notebook again, see if you find anything that could be a reference to Tsosie, initials GT, NT, anything like that?"

"Sure," Bernie said. "That will take a minute. I'll call you back. Maybe something in that little book can help us, I mean you, solve this."

"Us is right." She heard him exhale. "I worry about you pushing yourself too hard, honey. Seeing somebody you respect shot down in cold blood is a big deal."

"I'm fine," she said. "I was thinking this morning about those triangles in Leaphorn's notebook. Some of my old college texts are at Mama's house. I'm going over there to see if there's anything in them about sacred symbols. Maybe that's why Leaphorn made the sketches."

"That reminds me," he said. "Something funny happened yesterday with Darleen. She called to tell me your mom had been kidnapped."

"What?"

He relayed the story.

"There they were, the two grandmothers, happily playing cards in Mrs. Darkwater's kitchen while your sister was having a breakdown," he said. "I never heard anybody sound so relieved."

Bernie had finished her shower when the phone rang again. The ID read "AIRC," so she picked it up. It was Maxie Davis, calling on behalf of Dr. Collingsworth, asking if Bernie had news about the missing report.

"We searched his truck and his house for it," Bernie said. "Nothing." She didn't mention the copy that might be on his computer. No reason to raise Collingsworth's hope with speculation.

"I'll check with the woman who sorts the mail here to see if it could have been misplaced," Davis said. "It's hard to find good help."

"I noticed some sketches Leaphorn made of geometric designs," Bernie said. "They look to me like what you'd see on old Pueblo pottery. I was wondering if they might have been sensitive images."

"As far as I know, no sacred symbols are involved in the McManus pots. I doubt that those doodles have anything to do with us."

"When the report shows up, it will probably explain all this," Bernie said.

"It might," Davis said. "Collingsworth is giving us all grief about it."

After she hung up, Bernie called Largo's office and left a message about potential relative Austin Lee, thereby completing her assignment. If only the rest of the case would fall into place, she thought, before Chee started to beat himself up over it.

She welcomed the lack of company in her car, the wordless world of scenery and motion, the hour of driving that gave her time to switch from Officer Manuelito who promised to solve Leaphorn's shooting to Sister and Daughter. Thirty-two miles of paved highway with a steady parade of big trucks heading from Colorado to Gallup through the little berg of Shiprock. The Rock-with-Wings that gave the town its American name to the west, magnificent in its rugged beauty. Blessed landscape. Navajo homeland. How lucky she was, she knew, to be part of this world. To know where she belonged.

She passed Little Water and then Bennett Peak to the west. She thought about what she'd say to Darleen, how to start the conversation. How to tell her baby sister that she worried about her drinking, worried that she was becoming an alcoholic, worried that she didn't take care of their mother as well as she should, worried that her friend, boyfriend or not, was a bad influence. How to tell her that without also saying, "You are a failure"?

Bernie planned to go right at the convenience store at the junction of US 491 and Navajo Route 18. She noticed the police car at the store's entrance. If she'd been driving a police car herself, she would have radioed to see if there was a problem. But she wasn't on duty, didn't have a radio, and it was none of her business.

She pulled into the parking lot and went inside.

Officer Harold Bigman was listening to the store owner, Leo Crowder, a white man with a belly that hung over his belt. Bernie walked up behind Crowder, not interrupting but letting Bigman know she was there. He acknowledged her with a glance. She picked up a bag of nuts, a bottle of Coke, and a copy of *Woman's Day*, her mother's favorite, from the magazine rack. The cashier, a middle-aged woman, took her money without a word and didn't offer her a bag.

"You having a hard day?" Bernie asked.

The woman glanced toward Bigman.

"Kids. Tried to break in. Probably high on meth or something. Damaged the back door. Someone happened to be driving home past here, noticed the truck, pulled in to see if everything was okay. That musta scared them off. Makes me nervous. One of them lost some sunglasses. Maybe they'll come back for them. Kids are dumb like that. And then that old one, the policeman, getting shot in Window Rock. Too much bad news."

"I know what you mean," Bernie said. "The policeman is in a hospital in Santa Fe where they have special doctors for people with head injuries."

"Good. That makes me feel better."

Bigman had finished his interview. "Yá'át'ééh," he said. "You off to see Mama?"

"Yes," she said. "She likes to look at this."

Bigman picked up the magazine and recited the cover headlines. "'Update Your Kitchen for One Hundred Dollars.' 'Fifty Foods to Boost Your Immune System.' 'Too-Tired-to-Cook Recipes.' I like this one, 'Dance Moves for Shimmery Summer Sex Appeal.'" He handed the magazine back to her. "These sound more like you than your mama."

"Yeah, especially that last one," Bernie said.

"I heard on the scanner that Chee has a potential suspect in Crownpoint," he said. "Hope that pans out. How's the cat doing?"

"She misses you," Bernie said.

Chee felt optimistic. He found the Tsosie house without difficulty, and a green pickup truck stood in the driveway. A woman came to the door, surprised to see a uniformed officer there. The proper and expected reaction.

When they introduced themselves, Chee learned that the woman, Garrison and Notah Tsosie's mother, was a distant relative. Which meant the small bit of conversation designed to discover where Garrison was now—living with his girlfriend, Rose, in Gallup—took more than an hour. It also involved eating a Spam sandwich, a treat he'd cut back on since he married Bernie. Mrs. Tsosie added delicious slices of raw onion and tomatoes from her garden, and gave him a box with a big piece of homemade chocolate cake, making him promise to share it with Bernie. Mrs. Tsosie told him that Notah, the older of her two boys, realized he deserved to be in prison and harbored no negative feelings toward the officer who had arrested him.

"It turned out for the good," she said. "Notah got his GED in there. Now he's studying something else."

"What about your other son?" Chee asked. "Some people think he might be angry at a policeman who sent a person in his family to prison."

"I know people like that, too," she said. "But Garrison, he felt sad that his brother had come so much out of harmony, strayed away from the right way. He missed his brother when that one went to prison. Garrison even started to go around with some of Notah's friends, the ones who didn't keep out of trouble. But then, well, he met Rose."

And after some ups and down, Garrison had straightened out.

"See these?" Mrs. Tsosie put her index finger behind her earlobe, pushing her hair away so Chee could examine her large silver-and-turquoise earrings.

"Wow. Beautiful."

"Garrison made these. He's taking some classes and learning skills. My boy has talent."

Mrs. Tsosie encouraged Chee to meet her son, and gave him Garrison's address in Gallup and his home phone number.

Pleasantly stuffed and behind his self-imposed schedule, Chee called Largo.

"Thought I ought to let you know that Garrison Tsosie's mother is a clan sister," he said.

"Do you think you'll have a problem because they're kinfolk?"

"No problem with Mrs. Tsosie," Chee said. "If it looks like something with Garrison, I'll let you know. From what she says, he's now an upstanding citizen."

"What else would a mother say? Stay on top of it," Largo said.

Chee drove to Gallup. He found Rose's sister at Garrison's address, babysitting Rose's little boy and her own children. She told him Garrison and Rose had gone to Ramah to help some friends move. She didn't know the friend's last name, address, or phone number, but remembered where the house was, more or less. Garrison and Rose were in Rose's white Ford truck. Garrison was the nicest guy in the world, she volunteered, except for having a bit of a temper when he drank. And he wasn't drinking anymore.

Chee cruised the extra forty miles to Ramah, found the friend's house, learned that Garrison and Rose had left about an hour ago. The friend gave Chee Garrison's cell phone number, but when it rang, they heard music chiming in a newly relocated sofa. Bruno Mars singing from "The Lazy Song" about not wanting to answer his phone. Chee offered to take the cell to Garrison.

By the time Chee got back to Gallup, Garrison Tsosie had called his friend about the lost mobile phone and knew Chee was on the way. Garrison fit Bernie's description of the shooter, short, small-boned, dark hair and skin—but then so did about half the people on the Navajo reservation.

Unlike the average crime suspect, Garrison Tsosie invited Chee to come in and sit. Rose's sister was gone and had taken the kids to play at her house.

"It's hot in here," Garrison said. "Would you like a cold soda?"

"How about some water?" Chee said.

Rose, a buxom young woman in tight jeans with a tattoo on her ankle, brought water in a plastic Flying J cup. She didn't look Navajo; perhaps Hispanic, Chee thought. Whatever, she was pretty in an overly fussy sort of way.

Chee took a sip and started to put the cup on the coffee table.

"Wait a minute," Rose said. She hustled off to the kitchen and came back with a cardboard coaster, "Fire Rock Casino" embossed on it in bright red. Chee sat the sweaty cup on top of it. Rose perched next to Garrison on the couch.

"I made this table for Rose and me in woodworking class—that's why she's so particular about it." Garrison moved his hand over the surface. "First big project. It's good to have something to do at night rather than partying."

"Nice job," Chee said. "Your mom told me you make jewelry, too."

Garrison grinned. "My brother Notah, he taught me a little. I play around with it. My big brother, now he's an artist. You should see some of that stuff. He did this one."

Garrison pulled up his sleeve to show Chee an inch-wide band of sand-cast silver. "He got the idea for the design from a white guy when he worked construction at Chaco Canyon. You know, the big place with all those ruins?"

"Notah is one of the reasons I'm here," Chee said. "An officer got shot, and he was the one who sent Notah to prison."

"Too bad," Rose said. "I saw something about that on TV. In Window Rock, right? That officer was famous. I didn't know he was the one who got Notah."

"Me either," Garrison said, "Notah is one crafty brother. That guy must have been pretty smart."

"He was," Chee said. "I mean he is. He's still alive."

"Notah is still in prison," Garrison said. "And he's not the same guy. I mean, he's still smart, but he doesn't have so much anger now. He says he deserved what happened because of too much drinking, drugs."

Garrison got up, walked to the kitchen, turned on a fan that promised more noise than cooling. "I was going that way, too. But then I met Rose."

Chee said, "We found your fingerprints in the car that was used in the shooting."

"No. That's messed up. I don't even have a car. We only drive Rose's truck."

"And we haven't been to Window Rock since last September for the fair," Rose said.

"An eyewitness identified Jackson Benally's car as the vehicle the shooter drove," Chee said. "And Jackson confirmed that you had driven it."

Garrison eyes widened. "Somebody used Jackson's mom's car to shoot that man?"

"That's right," Chee said. He felt his phone vibrate. Ignored it.

"What happened to the car? If it got screwed up, Mrs. Benally will kill him. I'm serious, man. That lady is fierce."

"The car wasn't damaged."

"Jackson wouldn't shoot nobody," Garrison said. "He's a straight arrow."

"What about you?" Chee asked. "What about your fingerprints?"

"Whoa. Not me. No way. I didn't even know the old dude. Just because I got into a little trouble once or twice, that doesn't mean nothing."

Chee waited.

"I use Jackson's car on Tuesdays sometimes," Garrison said. "I do a deal for the car while he's in school. I used to trade him some weed, but not anymore. I give him a little money, maybe some jewelry he can sell or give to a girl. He lets lots of guys drive that car. Maybe one of them did it."

Chee shrugged.

Garrison got up. Sat down again.

"You sure Jackson's car was there at the scene?"

"Yeah."

"Maybe whoever saw it there got things wrong."

"No," Chee said. "The person who shot the policeman used that car. Where were you Monday morning?"

"At Earl's, selling stuff. Rose drops me off before she goes to work. You can ask anybody there, man. They know me."

"After that I picked him up and we went to a meeting," Rose offered. "AA. Then we went downtown to Sammy C's and got a pizza. I have the receipt somewhere. We brought it back here. My sister came over with her kids and we ate and they went home and we watched a movie and went to bed."

Chee looked at them. "Do you have a gun, Garrison?"

"A rifle my uncle gave me. I keep it locked up because of Buddy, Rose's boy. And her sister's kids are here all the time. I'll show it to you if you want."

Chee went into the bedroom with Garrison, found the gun in a locked case. A weapon for hunting deer, not a pistol for shooting a man from a car at close range. Chee relocked it. Part of him celebrated the fact that this young relative of his had refocused his life for the better. But he felt profoundly disappointed that he'd failed again to find the man who shot Leaphorn.

They went back to the living room. "Did you ever notice any kind of sparkly sand in the Benally car?" Chee asked.

"Sparkling sand?"

"Light colored. In the front seat, on the floor of the driver's side."

Garrison looked surprised. "Jackson takes perfect care of that car, man. If anybody he rented it to left anything in it, he took them off the list. So where's the car at now?"

Chee said, "The FBI has it. Still checking for evidence."

"They better be good to it," Garrison said. "Mrs. Benally will throw a fit, man, a big one."

Chee reached into his pocket and handed Garrison the phone he'd brought from the couch cushion. He gave him a Navajo Police Department card and wrote his own cell phone number on the back. "Call me if you think of something that might help us solve this."

"You got it," Garrison said. "Think you might wanna buy some jewelry or something?"

Rose opened her purse and pulled out little plastic bags, each with a set of heart-shaped earrings inside. She showed some to Chee.

"I'll keep it in mind. I might need a present for my wife."

Rose nodded. "Wives like presents. We'll make you a special deal."

Garrison said, "A buddy of mine sells my stuff down at Earl's for me when I'm not there, if you change your mind on your way out of town. I'll keep my ears open for you, cousin."

Earl's Restaurant waited for customers along Route 66, a few blocks east of the classic El Rancho Hotel. Chee remembered interviewing a woman at the hotel—an interesting assignment that involved a suitcase of missing diamonds, a plane crash over the Grand Canyon, and a young relative of his Hopi friend, Officer Cowboy Dashee. He remembered looking at the old black-and-white photos of the Hollywood stars who'd once stayed there as he waited for Dashee in the hotel lobby, and grabbing a bite at Earl's when they finished questioning the woman.

Customers loved Earl's for its ample servings, good chile, fried chicken, and Navajo tacos. And for allowing Navajos and Zunis to set up stalls outside and sell their work from table to table. Eating here was like having lunch at a craft fair, Chee thought, or a flea market, depending on who showed up selling what.

He talked to Earl's manager. Yes, Garrison Tsosie had been there every morning that week with his jewelry and wood carvings.

"He makes quality items and seems to sell pretty well," the manager said. "Especially to tourist ladies. Nice guy, especially now that he isn't drinking."

Back in the car, Chee took a deep breath and picked up the radio to call Largo with the bad news that their best lead had fizzled. But before he could, his phone vibrated. Bernie. She sounded frazzled.

"What's happening out there? I figured you were busy when you didn't pick up, but then I got worried . . ." She left the thought hanging. He knew the rest of the sentence.

Chee said, "I'm as well as can be expected for a guy who ate too many raw onions at lunch. And for a guy who just discovered that his main attempted-murder suspect has an ironclad alibi."

"You'll figure this out. You're a wonderful cop. Be careful."

He heard Bernie's mother in the background.

"I have to go," she said. "I'll see you at home. I love you." Her phone clicked off.

He got out of the car and went back to the porch at Earl's and bought a pair of Garrison Tsosie's earrings. Silver hearts with a piece of red agate in the center.

11

Bernie's mother sat in the kitchen wearing her old purple bathrobe, looking out the window at the mountains. Bernie had made a pot of coffee
for them, poured them both a cup, added sugar to hers and to Mama's.

"Do you like to sleep in the morning, Daughter? When you
were little, you always rose with the dawn. But people change."

Bernie laughed. "I still get up early. Last night we had a cat in
the house and it made noise and then it wanted to sleep on my head.
I was happy to get out of bed."

"Is this the cat that got lost?"

"Somehow it made its way back to our friend's place," Bernie
said. "The one who got hurt. So now Husband and I will take care
of it until he gets well."

Mama said, "Cats should be outside where they can work."

"I know, but I don't like it when they kill birds," Bernie said.

"It's their nature," Mama said. "Nothing to be done about that."

Mama pushed the bowl and spoon away. "I will get dressed, and
then let's take a little walk before the heat comes."

Bernie took her arm so Mama could leverage herself out of the
chair. She helped her dress, noting that the clothes hung too loosely

on her gaunt frame. They went outside. The summer sky was sprinkled with a few high clouds that could, but probably wouldn't, bring rain. They walked slow step by slow step for about half an hour, examining the new plants that had come up from seeds Bernie had gathered and the wildflowers and shrubs she had transplanted last fall and that Mama and Darleen watered for her. As they walked, Mama mentioned a weed with healing power and a plant the old ones used as a dye for yarn. Bernie tried to remember the names to jot down so she could look them up later.

"What happened to the one who got shot?" Mama asked.

"I saw him in the hospital," Bernie said. "He could not open his eyes and look at me." When they got back to the house, Bernie helped Mama lie down in the bedroom. She moved on to the living room. Her UNM texts sat on the bottom shelf of the bookcase. She'd saved the books from her favorite classes: botany and southwestern anthropology. She sat on the floor and looked at the titles on the spines. She pulled out a thick volume, *Native Arts of the Southwest: Roots and Routes*. It left a sprinkle of dust in the air.

She took the book with her to the couch, slipped off her shoes, and opened it to the table of contents. She realized that this was one of the same books the lieutenant had left on his desk. She remembered the instructor who had assigned it, Professor Stuart, her favorite teacher at the university. In addition to teaching cultural anthropology, he used art created by the Southwest's first inhabitants to explore the patterns and stories of exploration, colonization, and social disruption. The Pueblo pots pictured in the book included the simplest early work, and ceramics created during the days when Spanish conquistadors and settlers came to the Southwest looking for gold and souls to save. Other photos depicted ceramics from Mexican rule, the American period, the Indian Wars, boarding schools, World War II, and beyond. Finally, the illustrations showed work considered contemporary art as well as Indian pottery.

She remembered Professor Stuart telling her class that at Chaco Canyon's Pueblo Bonito alone, seventy thousand artifacts had been removed. Many went by the crate-load to big museums in the East or into the private holdings of collectors who looked the other way when it came to legality. Seventy thousand from just one of the cities that formed the Chaco complex. Amazing.

Now, she thought, thanks to the AIRC, a few of those pieces would be coming back to the American Southwest, shipped all the way from Japan. They would be home, or at least closer to it, available to be studied and admired. And the lieutenant had something to do with that homecoming.

She scanned the index for references to Chaco Canyon and found many, too many. She stretched out, her head resting now against the arm of the sofa. It was easy to relax at Mama's house, maybe because when she was here, she knew Mama was safe.

Bernie looked at the first sets of black-and-white photos. Ancient artists decorated the bowls, pots, plates, figurines, vases, and canteens with swirls, lightning designs, and triangles similar to the ones the lieutenant had sketched. She pictured a group of sisters sitting under a shady ramada somewhere, each with a pot in front of her and a yucca fiber brush, chatting as they painted black designs on the white surfaces. Copying from one another, perhaps, but each adding a unique flare to make her design ever so slightly individual. They probably never imagined that a thousand years later some curious Navajo would be thinking about them.

She felt her eyes growing heavy. Heavier. She'd just close them a moment, she thought. As she hovered on the groggy edge of dreams, she heard a car approaching. She was in the parking lot at the Navajo Inn. She saw the lieutenant stagger.

Bernie startled awake. A door slammed. Darleen walked in and headed straight for the bathroom as Bernie heard a car drive away.

By the time Little Sister came out, Bernie had her shoes on and her wits collected.

Darleen spoke first. "I'm glad you showed up today. I thought you'd be working. My stomach hurts. I've got a headache, too."

"I'm on leave for a while," Bernie said. She stood and walked toward Darleen. "I need to talk to you. You haven't been buying groceries or keeping the house up like you promised. And the other day, you smelled like you'd been drinking. You do now, too."

"So?"

"So I don't like it. You're not taking care of this place or of Mama."

Darleen said, "Mama's fine. Give me a break. I can't argue about this now. I need to lie down."

"You never want to talk about it."

"That's right. Why should I? You never listen. You already know everything."

"What—" Bernie stopped herself. She took a breath. Fighting never got them anywhere. "That one who was here with you that day, is he your boyfriend?"

"He's a guy I know. I don't wanna talk about him. I didn't even want to go with him that day, but he sort of made me. And I don't want to listen to you nagging me either."

"What do you mean, he made you? Does he threaten you? Hurt you?" Bernie felt her blood rise hot, ready to go to battle for her little sister. "Nobody has the right to make you do something you don't want to do."

"He's kinda like you," Darleen said. "He's got my life all figured out, like you do. You make me do what I don't want to. You think I want to be here every stinking day? Listening to Mama tell the same stories over and over? So what if I drink a beer or two?"

Darleen wobbled to the couch, stretched out on her back, pulled a pillow over her eyes.

Bernie said, "When you dropped out of high school, you promised to use the time you weren't helping Mama to study for your GED. Remember? You agreed."

"Whatever. That was then. I changed my mind. Why bother getting a piece of paper? This is now. I need to have some fun."

"Fun? You need to live up to your agreement. You need to start taking better care of Mama. And you need to get your GED before you forget what you learned in high school."

"Shut up!" Darleen wrapped her arms over the pillow. Her voice was muffled. "You come in, handle some little things, go away. I'm here day after stinking day with nothing to do except slave work. Borinnnng."

"So do something," Bernie said. "You could spend all the time you save *not* cleaning, *not* shopping, *not* cooking, studying for your test. You're living here for free, coming out fine, except you think you have to whine and feel sorry for yourself."

"I'm working on my drawings." Darleen took the pillow off her head and sat up slowly. "That's important to me. You are Mrs. Perfect Navajo Police Department, and you know everything. I'm like hired help. My life stinks, but nobody cares."

Darleen was crying. "What's the point, anyway? What's the stupid point? So I get the GED, become a second-class high school graduate. What then? Huh? What do I do? Work? Work where? There's no jobs here on the rez. Move? No money for that. I'm still stuck here, watching my life crawl by. My art is good, I know it is. But nobody cares about that. Yeah, I like to drink. It's the only vacation I get."

Bernie took another deep breath. It broke her heart to see her sister cry, even though she was still mad at her. "I didn't realize how frustrated you were."

"And I thought you were the bright one, Big Sister," Darleen said. "Frustrated? Yeah, right. You ignore my texts. I can never get you on the phone when I want to talk. Whenever I call your house, you're not there and I talk to the Cheeseburger."

Bernie said, "You know my hours are weird. Sometimes by the time I get home it's too late to call. I call back."

"Hardly ever. Lie as much as you want."

Bernie swallowed. "Okay. Sometimes I see it's you and I don't answer. I'm tired. I've dealt with too many upset people. I don't have the energy to listen to you complain about Mama and how bored you are. But fine. I'll call you every day. Even if it's late and I'm exhausted. I promise. You like that?"

Darleen leaned back against the couch. She looked pale. "Sure. Whatever."

"Your stomach hurts?" Bernie said.

"Yeah. Too much coffee on top of too much beer."

"I didn't know you drank coffee."

"I don't, but Charley Zah said I should. Maybe that's what's making me sick."

"You're not pregnant, are you?"

Darleen gave her a dark look. "I told you I don't have a boyfriend. Babies? Mama gave you that job, having the babies. You're not doing it very well."

Bernie went to the pantry and found a box of saltine crackers. Let her anger cool.

"Eat some of these," she said. "They might help settle your stomach."

"No, thanks."

Bernie found her backpack, extracted a roll of Tums. Gave them to Darleen. "You can keep them. Chew a couple. They won't hurt you."

Darleen peeled back the paper. "Thanks."

Bernie said, "I appreciate what you do for Mama. I know—"

Darleen said, "No. You don't know the first thing about what it's like here day after day."

"You want to tell me?"

"I wanna tell you that I can't do this forever," Darleen said. "I need to have a life. I need time to do my art."

"Get your GED," Bernie said. "That was what we agreed on. You have to take the first step. Then we'll figure out what's best for you and for Mama."

Darleen crunched on the antacid. "Did you know that guy, that retired cop who got killed in Window Rock?"

"He isn't dead," Bernie said. "I know him. He's a sort of friend of mine, more like an uncle or something. He and Chee worked together on some cases."

"What happened to him?"

"Somebody drove up, shot him, drove away."

"Just like that, some random freak thing?"

"The FBI doesn't think so," Bernie said. "They think the shooter was out to get him."

Darleen looked at her. "Don't let that happen to you."

"I'm off work for a few days, so you don't have to worry," Bernie said.

"I'm serious," Darleen said. "Mama needs you."

"Mama needs you, too," Bernie said. "And so do I. I'm sorry if I'm bossy."

"You've always been like this. I guess you can't help it." Darleen hugged a throw pillow to her midsection. "I'm going to sleep now."

Bernie went back to her research. She noticed, on pots from several of New Mexico's Rio Grande Pueblos, flowers, lizards, bird designs, as well as a stunning variety of geometric forms. She knew archaeologists had discovered pottery in ancient Pueblo kivas. But the book's text made no mention of research that linked any of the designs to ceremonies or sacred rituals. She found scant references to any of the pots themselves being created for special ritual use. Maybe Davis was right and Leaphorn was just doodling. Or maybe Bernie needed a reference book with better and deeper information.

In a while, Mama was awake and ready for lunch. After they ate, Bernie showed her Leaphorn's notebook with the triangle drawings. Darleen snoozed on.

"Those drawings are like the old ones made," Mama said. "The ones who lived at Chaco Canyon." She looked away from Leaphorn's pictures. "The man who drew them, was he your friend who got hurt?"

"Yes."

Mama closed the notebook. "Don't look at them too long."

"Are they sacred?"

Mama smiled. "Some say everything natural on this mother earth is sacred."

Bernie went back to the photographs. She found pictures of canteens and bird effigies, of pictographs and petroglyphs pecked and painted on the Chaco Canyon walls. She found images of centuries-old turquoise and argillite beads and beautiful gaming pieces. Interesting and frustrating. She put the book back on the shelf and took out another. This time, she turned to a page with photos of pottery cylinders.

She read, "Found in Pueblo Bonito, these rare cylindrical jars have flat bases and can stand upright. The small holes or clay loops near the opening indicate that they could hang from a cord and perhaps were used as drums. The asymmetrical geometric black-on-white designs complement the shape, rare in Anasazi pottery."

She took out her own notebook and jotted down some information, things to think about. The bold black-and-white designs looked almost identical to those the lieutenant had drawn. Why had these designs captured his attention?

Having found what she thought she needed for the AIRC pottery research, she investigated what the book had to say about the art closest to her heart, Navajo weaving. She showed Mama some of the pictures and told her about the rug at the AIRC museum. Bernie described its craftsmanship and the tale from the Navajo creation story that it told.

Mama said, "That sounds like the rug I saw as a little girl. The rug I talked to you about, except the story is different."

"I'm sure of the story, Mama. I looked at that rug a long time. I couldn't take my eyes off it, it was so striking, so well done."

Mama patted her hand. "The one who made that rug, some people thought that he shouldn't do it. Some people thought he was wrong. They said prayers used for healing should not be captured in a rug. But those were hard times. Some people wondered if the Diné would be able to continue. Many, many died from disease, from nothing to eat after the government made us kill our sheep. People died of broken hearts. Valuable old ones who knew the stories and the songs and prayers for blessings."

Bernie knew about the years of forced livestock reduction, starvation, acculturation. Sad days for the Navajo people.

"The one who made that rug, a white woman encouraged him to do the weaving. The *bilagaana* remembered everything she saw and made drawings of the sacred sand paintings the *hataalii* used for healing. They took those drawings and the rugs of the sacred stories away to a special place."

In college, Bernie had learned about the collaboration between Hosteen Klah and Franc Newcomb and Mrs. Newcomb's friend Mary Cabot Wheelwright. Their work included audio recordings of sacred chants. It all had grown from the assumption in the 1930s that the Navajo were a dying tribe.

"I think they had good hearts," Mama said. "But old things leave, new things come, that's the way it is. This world changes. Some say it can't hold everything."

Mama asked about the rug Bernie had seen at the AIRC, specific questions about the colors used and the arrangement of the designs. "I would like to see that rug," she said.

"I would love to show it to you. It's a long drive to Santa Fe."

"And a long time home again. Not today. Another time."

Bernie nodded. "We'll do it."

Mama smiled. "Darleen should come, too. Is Darleen here?"

"She had a headache. She was on the couch, but she went to her room. She's probably sleeping."

"Darleen has lots of headaches. She says drawing makes her eyes tired, but I think it's from the drinking."

"Where does she get the alcohol?" Bernie asked.

Mama shook her head. "Bootleggers don't care how old you are."

"Where does she get the money?"

Mama shook her head again. "I don't know. Don't worry so much about her."

Darleen said she felt better when she came out of the bedroom an hour later. She and Bernie drew up a grocery list. "I've been thinking," Bernie said. "If you'd like to take a GED class in the evenings, I can come and stay with Mama a couple nights a week. It would get you out of the house."

"I'll think about it," Darleen said.

Mama patted Bernie's hand. "You better get going. Cheeseburger will be wondering what happened to you. Bothering us about it."

"Yeah," Darleen said. "I'll see how the classes work. Let you know."

On the way home, Bernie called Chee's cell to tell him she was on her way. No answer. She called the home phone, no answer. Left messages at the Window Rock and Shiprock offices. Came home to a dark house. Fed the cat. Fixed dinner. Ate alone. Went to bed with apprehension and let the cat sleep with her.

It was nearly midnight when she heard Chee's footsteps on the trailer floor.

"Hey you," she said.

He bent over to kiss her. She sensed his exhaustion. "You coming to bed?" she asked.

"Not yet," he said. "I've got some thinking to do."

By the time he was out of the shower, she'd made coffee.

He kissed her. "You didn't have to do that, but I'm glad you did. I've got something to go with it. Hungry?"

"Always."

Walking back outside to retrieve the cake from his trunk somehow reminded him of the thumb drive with Leaphorn's AIRC report on it, the one he'd told Bernie he would get her. He found it in his pocket, along with the earrings.

The cake seemed to have gotten better after eight hours in a warm car.

"So we're going to Santa Fe tomorrow?" he asked.

"Today, actually. Then we can go to the hospital. Can you get off?"

"Yeah, as long as I'm reachable. I wrapped up things today as well as I could."

"Did anyone track down the Lizard boy?" Bernie asked.

"Lenny the Lizard? Still looking for him. He's our next viable suspect," Chee said. "Him and Louisa and Mrs. Benally's ninja.

"Hey," he said. "I have another surprise for you."

"A nice one?"

He extended two closed fists. She picked the one on the right. He opened it to reveal the thumb drive.

"Leaphorn's report?"

"Yes," he said. He smiled at her. "But that wasn't really the surprise."

She tapped his left fist, and he opened it to show her the earrings.

"They're beautiful. What's the occasion?"

"Just a little thank-you for putting up with me."

The cat jumped to the sofa and settled into Chee's lap.

"She missed you," Bernie said.

"She's probably homesick for the lieutenant and Louisa," Chee said. "After I interviewed Tsosie and ran out of leads, I thought, well, time to call Leaphorn. Then I remembered."

"He would have taken you back to the scene of the crime, had you review the clues, the way he always did." She wondered, for the fortieth time, about the accuracy of her description of the shooter and the car. She'd worked with enough eyewitnesses to know that their recollections often left much to be desired.

"Tomorrow I want to ask the lieutenant about a sing," Chee said. Leaphorn wasn't a traditional Navajo, but Chee had done a healing ceremony for him years ago after a particularly disturbing case. Back in the years when Chee had been studying with his uncle who had passed away. "I think I can find someone who will do it when he gets back home again."

Before Bernie went back to bed, she plugged in the laptop and inserted the thumb drive to check for Leaphorn's AIRC reports. She found more than she bargained for.

12

The row of files, all titled "AIRC" with numbers to follow, stretched to the bottom of the laptop screen. She opened the first one, the lieutenant's bill for consulting services, including photocopies and mileage. It matched the contents of the small envelope she'd delivered to the AIRC, along with the photocopied pages.

She clicked on the next heading, a larger file dated a week earlier. Research material, some sort of online auction catalog from a place in New York. She glanced it at. Indian artifacts were among the listings.

She closed both of the open files and clicked on the next one. Sure enough, it looked like the missing report. How simple was that?

She glanced at the first page, Leaphorn's cover letter addressed to Dr. Collingsworth, admiring the lieutenant's economy of language. She scrolled to the report itself.

The introductory section concerned the question of insurance valuations, the lieutenant's area of expertise.

The narrative opened with a concise explanation of how insurance appraisals worked, and how they differed from the valuations collectors might place on their holdings for an auction or a tax deduction in the case of charitable donations. Bernie skimmed Leaphorn's discussion of changes in the overall market for Native American art and artifacts. He noted that most of the values mentioned in the appraisals Collingsworth and the AIRC board had received from the McManus Foundation seemed accurate for the date they were created. He recommended that the AIRC increase the existing coverage of the McManus collection by 20 percent because of the added risk of displaying the artifacts to AIRC visitors, staff, and researchers. The report mentioned that the few exceptions to the accuracy of existing valuations would be dealt with in the appendix.

The exceptions made her curious, but she continued reading.

Part 2 focused on the appropriateness of the collection for exhibit. Leaphorn outlined reasons many American Indian tribes did not want certain items they attributed to their ancestors publicly displayed, or even viewed by scholars or museum professionals. Their rationale included, he wrote, "explanations that may not be disclosed to non-tribal members or to tribal members who are not initiated." He had read the descriptions of uncommon, nonutilitarian items provided by the appraisers. He also had paid considerable attention to the lengthy report of a cultural anthropologist who had vetted the most potentially sensitive material.

Bernie recalled Collingsworth's mention of that.

Leaphorn wrote that he had also conducted his own follow-up research on potential sacred items, using interviews and written sources that he documented at the end of the report. In conclusion, the lieutenant assured Collingsworth that the collection in its entirety "could be displayed to an audience that might include American Indians without fear of offense."

She looked up from the screen. The lieutenant was good at this. He used the same logical thinking and methodical research he had

been known for as a police detective. What she'd read proved that
Collingsworth's suspicions were off track. Too bad it was too late at
night to call him and tell him so.

Bernie skimmed through the list of sources and footnotes. She
reached the exceptions Leaphorn had noted to the pottery valuations.

The lieutenant began with a statement:

> I have concerns about the McManus collection item numbers
> 2343–2355 as specified in the EFB appraisal. The previous apprais-
> er may have dramatically undervalued these items. In my research
> to date, I have been unable to find the reason for these lower val-
> uations. These pieces are rare. Comparables may be difficult to
> locate.

The next page had twelve small black-and-white photographs of
ceramics with identification numbers and descriptions. Interesting,
Bernie thought. The pieces that had raised questions in the lieutenant's mind were tall cylinders. Some of the photos looked a bit
fuzzy.

> Dr. Maxie Davis and I discussed this discrepancy. She suggest-
> ed that, with her extensive knowledge of the pottery found in or
> created at Chaco Canyon, she could update the valuations. She
> also noted that the AIRC's collections contain at least one oth-
> er example of this ancestral Pueblo pottery style and noted that
> insurance on that piece had been purchased as part of the larger
> collection without objection.

> This anomaly in an otherwise sound earlier appraisal also raised
> questions for me about the origin of these pots. Until the prove-
> nance of these pieces can be verified, I recommend that the AIRC
> accept them on a contingency basis only.

Bernie turned on the printer and printed the report. She made a second copy of the page with the pictures and item numbers that the lieutenant was curious about.

All she knew about art and artifact valuation was what she'd learned from that show on PBS where people bring in their treasures for appraisals and information. Some learn Uncle Bob had a good eye for art; some learn the carving they bought at the flea market was worth half what they paid. Watching the experts talk about antiques had taught her the word *provenance*.

Why would the values on those pieces Leaphorn had questioned be too low? A collector might undervalue something to reduce the insurance bill, she figured, but what if he had to file a claim? Maybe the market had changed, making them more precious and expensive.

She put the report in an envelope and wrote Collingsworth's name on the outside. She left it and the single page on the kitchen table, where she'd be sure to find them in the morning.

When she fell asleep, she dreamed that she stood in line along with a group of tall, slender black-and-white pots, all waiting to be admitted to the antique show on TV.

Bernie and Chee left for Santa Fe before daylight, and the sun comes up early in June in northwestern New Mexico. Earlier, Chee had fed the cat and, even better, made coffee for them both. She put on jeans, a summer blouse, and her comfortable green athletic shoes. They took his truck because its air conditioner worked.

They drove through the beige-and-yellow landscape. Traffic stayed mercifully light even when they reached Farmington.

"Isn't this where that guy you're looking for lives?"

"Austin Lee? I'm not sure where he lives," Bernie said. "This is where he owns a house."

"I asked about him. If it's the same guy, he works with the hus-

band of the woman who comes by the office with breakfast burri-
tos," Chee said.

By the time they left Bloomfield, heading southeast toward
Cuba, Bernalillo, and ultimately on to the New Mexico State Police headquarters in Santa Fe, the sun was up. It added a warm glow
to the rocky protuberance of Angel Peak and lit the maroon, gray,
and yellow sandstone and mudstone badlands that surrounded it.
Chee pulled the truck off on the shoulder so Bernie could drive.
She moved the driver's seat closer to the steering wheel and adjusted
the mirrors.

"I'll be glad to get this hypnotism thing over with," she said.

"So that's why you've been so quiet," Chee said. "Don't worry.
Even if that hypnotist has you barking like a Chihuahua, you won't
have a big audience."

Bernie gave him The Look. "The idea of having a stranger pok-
ing around in my head makes me nervous. I don't think I got it
wrong, but what if I did? What if we've been spinning our wheels,
focusing on the Benallys and their connections?"

"Cordova said you were a great witness, remember?" Chee said.
"But if you forgot a little something or made a tiny mistake, this
guy can help. That's all. This isn't about your deep, dark secrets. It's
about the lieutenant."

"You're sure Tsosie isn't involved?" Bernie asked. "He admits
access to the car. He had a motive because of his brother. And from
what you said, he fits the description."

"He has an ironclad alibi," Chee said. "And he swears his brother
isn't poisoned by revenge. He said they follow the Navajo way."

"Yeah, they do," she said. "Especially after getting busted. Especially when he's chatting to a policeman looking for a suspect."

"I didn't get that feeling. Not because he's my cousin, but because he was telling the truth. It sounds like his brother's doing
pretty well in prison."

"His friends at Earl's or the manager there could be lying to protect him," Bernie said.

"You're suspicious this morning."

"Did you tell Largo he's your cousin?"

"Well, sure. Of course."

"If I thought a cousin of mine might be involved in something, I'd be tempted to tread lightly."

"No, you wouldn't," Chee said. "You would never do that. Do you think I would?"

"No. Of course not. I'm just talking. I'd love for you to solve this case." She glanced over at him again, took his hand. The truck swerved slightly to the right.

He said, "Watch your driving. You know what the speed limit is here?"

"Sixty-five. I'm barely doing seventy."

Chee said, "What happened to the lieutenant is every cop's nightmare. It sits on your shoulder, makes you nervous."

"Do you think about that?" Bernie said. "About some ghost from the past coming back to get you?"

"Don't worry about me, beautiful." Chee reached over and massaged her neck, felt the tension.

"Only if you promise not to worry about me," she said.

"I can't do that," he said.

"Well then . . ." She changed the subject. "I wonder what Louisa and Leaphorn argued about. It must have been something major, for her to leave him. And I wonder why the feds haven't been able to find her. Makes her look guilty."

"Or it makes them look incompetent," Chee said. "And it makes the murder-for-hire theory less outlandish. Speaking of which, you owe me a steak. I'll collect at lunch, thank you very much. I'm getting hungry already thinking about it. I'll have a baked potato, too. Or would fries be better?"

Bernie groaned.

"And what about Leonard Nez?" Chee said. "Another missing person. I don't like that we haven't been able to talk to him, even though he doesn't seem to have any connection to the lieutenant, or any reason to have shot him."

Bernie said, "So what about this? Louisa hires Nez to shoot the lieutenant. Nez subcontracts the job to Mrs. Benally's ninja. Jackson is in the backseat, doing his homework. They drop Jackson off at the Zuni site for his geology project, shoot, bring the car back to Bashas', and vanish together, ninja style."

"Good scenario," Chee said. "But make the ninja and Nez time travelers to get from Window Rock to Zuni and back to Bashas' in an hour."

"We'll have to ask them about that when Mrs. Benally brings him in."

They cruised along on the four-lane highway through oil and gas country and up into Ponderosa Pines and past the Jicarilla's Apache Nugget casino, a lonely outpost of slot machines, gas pumps, and convenience store. When they entered the Rio Puerco Valley, they called Louisa. No answer again. This time Chee left the message, saying they were on the way to visit the lieutenant. They headed into Cuba, where Bernie stopped for gas. They both got another cup of coffee, and Chee took over the driving.

They had heard some officers grumbling that the state of New Mexico put too much money into prisons and too little into improving training and facilities for law enforcement. But compared to the Navajo Police headquarters, the New Mexico State Police building on the south side of Santa Fe was a palace. Bernie checked in at the desk, and then they sat in the lobby. Chee had brought a book.

Bernie walked down the hall to the restroom, came back with fresh lipstick. She checked her phone for messages. Got up and read the bulletin board. Came back and sat next to Chee again.

"Don't worry about this," he said. "What's the worst that can happen? You'll crow like a lovesick rooster or cluck like a chicken. Some joker will put the video on YouTube. You'll be famous, and then you can support me as a full-time animal impersonator."

She stared at him with that special gaze she reserved for those rare occasions when she wondered for a split second why she'd married him.

They waited, watched a few officers come and go. It was strange to see no one they knew.

Chee said, "I've been thinking more about lunch. We should go somewhere that has both steak and sopaipillas. Somewhere nice."

"Sopaipillas? I love sopaipillas."

"I know you do. Miniature fry breads. Puffy. Served with honey or stuffed with ground meat, onions, chile."

"Stop. You're making me hungry. I can't think about food and worry at the same time."

"It's settled, then," he said. "Although you might want to go to KFC when you're done. You know, visit your sisters. Original and extra crispy."

Chee opened his book and had progressed from page 45 to page 48 when Agent Cordova walked up to them. He shook hands with them both, told them the FBI had no new leads in the Leaphorn case. They had tracked down a few parolees with distant ties to the lieutenant, finding all of them had solid alibis. Then he escorted Bernie back to the interview room.

Was Chee imagining it, or did she stand a little taller and suck in her tummy when she saw him?

Cordova guided her not to a regular interview room as she'd expected, but to an office with a desk, a couch, and a couple of large chairs, photographs of flowers on the wall. Instead of windows, it had a one-way observation mirror. He motioned her to a charcoal gray recliner. "The hypnotist will be here in a minute," Cordova said. "She's good. You'll like her." He sat down on the couch. "How's everything?"

"I'm going to the hospital to see the lieutenant after this. I'll know more then."

"I meant, how are you doing with the aftershock?"

"Aftershock? I keep thinking that there must have been something I could have done."

"Those if-onlys will kill you," he said. "Are you on leave?"

She nodded.

"You look good in civilian clothes," he said.

"Thanks. My sister thinks my fashion sense is hopeless."

"You'd look great in anything. I love those green sneakers."

The door opened, and a fit black woman entered. Cordova introduced her, Michelle Abernathy. He put his hand lightly on Bernie's arm. "I'll be observing the session in the next room. It's a pleasure to work with you."

Abernathy sat behind the desk.

"Officer Manuelito, thank you for coming to Santa Fe today. You made my life so much easier."

"Please call me Bernie."

"Bernie, have you been hypnotized before?"

"No."

Abernathy explained the procedure, stressing that the session would focus only on the shooting and the events immediately preceding it. She had reviewed the transcript of Bernie's interview with Cordova, which she had on her laptop, and also listened to his recording of their session. The theory behind this kind of hypnotism, she explained, was that in a state of profound relaxation the brain could sometimes retrieve suppressed or forgotten memories with the help of a trained therapist to guide the process.

"Will you tell me if I say something different than what's on the report?

"Yes," Abernathy said. "I can give you a copy of my tape of the session if you'd like it. Any other questions?"

"I guess not," Bernie said. "Let's do this."

Abernathy dimmed the lights. They started with simple relaxation cues. Abernethy was good—thorough, professional, unintimidating, likable. Bernie let herself unwind. After a while, Abernathy asked her to imagine that she was watching a movie of Leaphorn's shooting running in slow motion, and that she could stop the action whenever she wanted, frame by frame. Abernathy moved the process forward with a series of questions.

Bernie described the person dressed in black leaving the blue sedan, walking straight toward the lieutenant. Walking quickly. She watched the hand with the pistol extended toward him.

"What does the lieutenant do?"

"He glances up. Looks at the person."

"Does the lieutenant recognize the person?"

"I'm not sure." Bernie exhaled. "He looks surprised, like he's just about to say something."

"What do you see next?"

Bernie described the black barrel of the pistol, the sound of the gunshot, a flash of sunlight against metal on the shooter's wrist, the lieutenant sinking down onto the asphalt. Abernathy asked about the gun, but Bernie could see no more details.

"I'd like you to rewind. Please take a closer look now at the wrist. Can you see what caught your eye more clearly?"

"I see a wide metal band."

"Do you notice anything else?

"I'm looking at the front, and I don't see a watch face. I guess it's a bracelet."

"What color is it?

"Silver," Bernie said.

"Can you see anything else about it?"

Bernie let the image wash over her brain. "It has hearts, linked hearts, as a design. Looks like a sand-cast bracelet."

Chee drove them both to the Flying Tortilla for lunch—her treat to settle their bet about the FBI. She ordered the stuffed sopaipilla with ground beef and green chile. He had the steak and chile relleno combination because the menu described the chilies as "Big Jim." She told him about the session.

"The only thing that surprised me was the bracelet."

"Too bad it wasn't an ID bracelet with his name on it."

"Still, it's a new clue. Better than nothing," she said.

"We just have to find somebody who drove the Benally car and also has a silver bracelet. That's probably every Navajo who was in it. Men and women."

Bernie said, "Maybe you need to talk to Mrs. Benally again. Ask to see her jewelry." She took another forkful of her lunch.

"I guess hypnotism makes you hungry? It made me hungry, and I wasn't even the subject," Chee said.

"I was starved," she said. "I was too nervous to eat breakfast."

He used a tortilla to mop up the last of his green chile sauce. "How far is the hospital from here?"

"It's halfway across town," she said. "Maybe fifteen minutes."

"Too many people die in those places." Chee pushed his plate to the side. "And you never know if the person you're visiting just wants to be left alone."

Although he wouldn't have said it, she knew Chee's acquiescence to the hospital visit showed how much the lieutenant meant to him. She'd seen Leaphorn's brisk way of dealing with Chee, pointing out overlooked clues, unquestioned assumptions, and gaps in logic. She knew the criticism left her smart, competent husband feeling like an unworthy apprentice. Still, Chee honored the man.

The nurse in CCU remembered Bernie from her earlier visit, recognizing her even without her police uniform. "Your uncle seems more alert today," the nurse said.

"Can he talk?"

"No, he can't speak because of the breathing tube. Dr. Moxsley will be here this afternoon, and he'll do another assessment of the injury."

Bernie led the way to the lieutenant's bedside. The room was dark and cool. Leaphorn lay unmoving and looked smaller than before. His head was still swathed in bandages and the tubes and monitors still in place.

"Yá'át'ééh." Chee spoke softly and walked toward the bed.

The lieutenant's eyes fluttered open for a brief moment, seemed to search in the direction of the voice. Then closed again.

Chee spoke in Navajo. "My wife and I are here, making sure you are behaving yourself," he said. "We wanted you to know we are thinking of you."

Bernie said, "I hope you're feeling better today. We miss you."

Leaphorn had a little more color in his face, and the swelling seemed to have gone down. It gave her hope to see him like this.

She switched to English. "We talked to Louisa on the phone, and she said to tell you she wishes she could be here. That she loves you."

Leaphorn inched his hand in her direction. She reached for it.

"I'm finishing up the AIRC job for you," Bernie said. "I met Dr. Collingsworth and Dr. Davis, and I saw some of the collection. Beautiful pots. And they showed me the Hosteen Klah rug. I couldn't take my eyes off it."

Chee said, "Now I'll fill you in about the progress of the investigation into your shooting. In a word, nothing. Only dead ends."

Chee told the story of his encounters with Mrs. Benally and her enterprising son, of the cake and Garrison Tsosie. Just when Bernie had begun to worry that Chee was talking too long, he said, "We need you to get better so you can help us work this case. Then we won't have to try so hard."

Leaphorn's eyes fluttered open again. He looked toward Chee and moved his lips. The ventilator kept him from speaking.

"Do you know who shot you?" Chee asked. Leaphorn moved his head up and down ever so slightly.

Bernie found a notebook and a pen in her backpack. She offered him the pen, and his hand moved weakly toward it, then sank back onto the bed.

"Next time," Bernie said. "Rest now. Get stronger."

Chee said, "I've been wondering if you might like a singer to pray over you for healing. Just lift up a finger or something if that's right. If you don't want this, just stay still."

Leaphorn lifted the index finger of his right hand, pulsing it over the bedsheet, and moved his head almost imperceptibly. He seemed to point at Chee with his chin. The effort exhausted him. He closed his eyes, and Bernie felt his grip relax.

In the hallway she said, "He wants you to do a sing. Let's talk to the chaplain here about that."

"Me?"

"He pointed at you."

"Why talk to the chaplain? What would he know about it?"

Bernie said, "You might have to bend the rules a little to do a ceremony in the hospital, but the lieutenant can't be the first Navajo they've had here. And it's good to have Jesus and the White God on our side, too."

"I thought I could arrange something for him when he was well enough to travel," Chee said. "But I see how weak he is. We should do it soon."

13

The chaplain's office was closed. They found a plastic container fastened to the door with a slot for messages. Chee left his card with a cell number and a note.

They walked to the truck, noticing the clouds piling atop the Sangre de Cristos like a layer of soft gauze. "Leaphorn can see the mountains from his room," Chee said. "That's about the only good thing I can think of."

Bernie remembered Dr. Moxsley's concern that the bullet might have damaged the lieutenant's vision, but she didn't mention that. She said, "The staff is nice, too."

"It surprised me to see him so frail," Chee said.

Bernie nodded. "I'm worried about him."

When they climbed into the truck, she picked up the report she'd printed for the AIRC and told Chee how to get there.

They took Old Pecos Trail toward the Plaza, then Santa Fe Trail, a narrow road that followed the old wagon route of Anglo settlers who came to Santa Fe in the nineteenth century to trade with local merchants.

As he drove, Chee thought about the sing for Leaphorn. He needed to consult a *hataalii* who had experience with this kind of exceptional situation, ask if he would be willing to come to Santa Fe, and then help make the arrangements. It would take a few days and some persuasion. Perhaps the lieutenant would be well enough to come home and the ceremony could be done properly in Dinetah, the land between the sacred mountains. But according to the doctor, that was highly unlikely in the near future.

"Turn here," Bernie ordered, and they drove onto a curving road with beautiful, historic homes that resembled haciendas set behind hedges, adobe walls, and garden gates. The narrow paved street was framed with tall trees. Low ridges of brick-covered asphalt, called speed humps because they were smaller than speed bumps, slowed the traffic.

Chee parked in the dirt lot in front of the American Indian Resource Center reception building. As they headed down the path to Collingsworth's office, she pointed out the way to the museum.

Chee said, "Leaphorn upgraded when he went to work here. The Window Rock headquarters look pretty darn shabby compared to this. They even have a garden. Nice!"

Bernie stopped to look at a plant along the walk. "These are just about to bloom. This ought to be a beautiful peony."

"Peony?"

She ran her fingers along the round top of the bud. "These flowers just last a few days, but they are huge and gorgeous. I saw them for the first time on one of my botany class field trips."

Dr. Collingsworth had left campus for a meeting with a board member, but Marjorie, the secretary, told Bernie he was due back shortly. "May I get you anything while you wait? A bottle of water? A soda? How about for your companion?"

Bernie introduced Chee.

"I found that report Dr. Collingsworth wanted on the lieutenant's computer, and since I was in Santa Fe, I figured I'd drop it off. I looked through it to make sure it was the right one. I noticed that the lieutenant only had one major concern." She handed Marjorie the envelope.

"I'm sorry you went to all that trouble," Marjorie said. "I found it this morning. I haven't had a chance to show Dr. Collingsworth, but I called and told him." She indicated a manila envelope on her desk with Leaphorn's characteristic handwriting.

"I'm glad it's here," Bernie said. "I guess the mail finally came through. Now you'll have two copies."

"It wasn't in the mail," Marjorie said. "Evidently it arrived earlier and had been misdelivered to someone else's office. I looked everywhere for it after you left. Came in this morning, unlocked the office, went down the hall to start the coffee, and when I came back, I discovered it here on my desk. Somebody must have found it and dropped it off. It's funny whoever it was didn't want the credit."

"That is odd," Bernie said. "Who knew the report was missing?"

"Dr. Collingsworth sent around an e-mail to everyone. Some folks let their mail pile up. Mostly junk these days. Anyway, I'm sorry you two made the trip for nothing."

"Oh, not for nothing," Chee said. "I'd never been in this part of Santa Fe. Pretty fancy. And I'd never heard of the AIRC until Bernie got involved and starting talking about the rug you showed her the last time."

"The Hosteen Klah? Would you like to see it?"

"I would. If it's no trouble," Chee said.

Marjorie said, "No problem. The museum isn't open to the public, just to researchers and private tours, but I'll call and tell them you'll be over. That rug is one of our masterpieces." She smiled at him. "I'm sorry I can't go with you. Bernie knows we have a lovely collection of Native American pottery and baskets over there, too. Take your time. Enjoy it."

Thick adobe walls kept the AIRC's administrative offices relatively cool, but even at Santa Fe's 7,000-foot elevation, it was warm outside. They strolled to the museum, a newer building, cleverly constructed to blend in with the historic campus. As Bernie expected, Chee stopped to admire the huge black pot with its flecks of mica sitting under the spotlight in the entry corridor. They signed in at the front desk as requested. "Cold in here," Chee said.

"Climate control to protect our collections." The receptionist spoke in a voice just above a whisper. She gave them both plastic badges that read GUEST. "Don't touch anything, but enjoy looking at the collection. Let me know if you have any questions."

"May we see the big Navajo weaving, the one in the back room?"

"Of course," she said. She clicked a button on the console. "I've disabled the lock so you won't need the code to get out. The door is open for you."

Bernie marveled again at the wealth of artifacts on display, things she hadn't even noticed on her first visit. The museum housed some of the best ancient Indian art available to researchers anywhere, and a nice gallery of modern pieces inspired by these traditions.

"Wow," Chee said. "I don't see how they even have room for that new donation you told me about. This place is packed tight. Look at all this great stuff."

"Collingsworth said when the new collection comes, it arrives with enough money to build a wing to house and display it. That's a pretty nice gift."

She opened the door to the rug room, and the rheostat brought the light up slowly, automatically.

The Klah rug looked even more beautiful than she remembered, remarkable both for the way it gave form to the sacred Navajo Holy People and for the skill of its weaving. It took her breath away all over again. Standing here, she thought, is standing in the presence of greatness. This must be how white people felt when they went to the Sistine Chapel. As she absorbed its grandeur, her concern about the lieutenant dissolved like salt in warm water. She felt gratitude in the presence of such creative genius, gratitude that she lived in such an amazing world and that her mother had taught her the joy of weaving. Gratitude that she knew the lieutenant. Gratitude that she had found and married such a fine man. She looked at Chee. He seemed lost in reverie. His eyes pooled with tears.

When he noticed her gaze, he whispered, "This was the perfect time to be here. Thank you."

Bernie smiled. They stood in silence.

When they walked out of the room and down the hall to the main part of the museum, she felt lighter, as though a boulder had been lifted away from her heart.

"I wish my uncle Hosteen Nakai could have seen that rug," Chee said. "It ought to be in Dinetah, not in a museum in Santa Fe."

"I agree. But if it wasn't here, it might be hanging in some collector's living room, and we would never have been able to see it. And if it hadn't been for the lieutenant, we would never have known it was here."

Before they left, Chee stopped at the museum entrance desk.

"Wonderful collection," he said. "I imagine you have a lot of security around here."

The woman nodded. "State-of-the-art. That's right. Some of these pieces are priceless and irreplaceable."

Bernie said, "The camera in the hallway isn't working. You might check it."

The woman looked puzzled. Studied her monitor.

"Why do you say that?"

"I noticed that the light that blinks when those cameras record wasn't blinking. It was a solid green," Bernie said. "I doubt what's on your monitor is being recorded."

The woman looked skeptical. "I'll check with the company that takes care of the system. We've never had any trouble. The people who visit us are like you two. Respectful and interested."

"But you never know," Bernie countered. "And why pay for a security system that doesn't do its job?"

The woman said, "You're the police officer who was here with Dr. Collingsworth. That's why you know so much about this."

Chee said, "That, and she's just naturally nosy. That's another reason I love her."

Bernie laughed. "Curious. Say I'm naturally curious. That sounds better."

They ran into Collingsworth on the sidewalk as they headed to the parking lot, and Bernie made the introductions.

"I'm glad I caught up with you," Collingsworth said. "Sorry you had to make a trip for nothing. Marjorie told me you went to a lot of trouble to find that report. She should have called you to let you know it turned up here."

"It gave me a chance to see the museum," Chee said. "Great collection."

Collingsworth turned to Bernie. "I apologize again for acting like such a lout. I should have known that Mr. Leaphorn would do the job. I'm sure the board will support his recommendation that we add twenty percent on the insurance to cover the new pieces. Other than that, I was relieved to see that he didn't raise any major issues about potential sacredness or the valuations."

Bernie said, "I was tired when I read through it last night, but I thought his questions about those oldest pots, the cylinders from Chaco that he mentioned in that exceptions section, were interesting. I'm not an expert on this, but those concerns seemed worth following up."

"What exceptions?"

Bernie said, "I'm talking about the first and last pages, where he talked about those pieces that the McManus Foundation may have undervalued."

She saw the puzzled look on Collingsworth's face.

"You remember, the pages where he copied those blurry photos for you of the pots he had questions about. The tall, thin ones?"

Collingsworth stopped walking. "I never saw any of that. It wasn't in the envelope he mailed us."

Bernie said, "It was part of the report we found on the lieutenant's computer, and it's in the copy I left for you. Maybe he forgot—" She stopped herself. The lieutenant seldom forgot anything. He would never neglect to send something so crucial to his findings, material he wanted Collingsworth to notice.

"Forgot to send them to me?" Collingsworth asked. "He certainly seemed competent, but even the best of us can make a mistake. I'll take a look at what you so nicely delivered. But undervalued? That's as rare in this business as a gold-plated dinosaur tooth. Unscrupulous collectors have been known to inflate valuations . . ."

Collingsworth's voice trailed off, and he took a few steps back so he could stand in the shade. "If he were able to follow up on this, I'd give Mr. Leaphorn an extra day or two to solve that little puzzle. But as I understand it, that's not possible."

Bernie said, "Let me look into it, see if I can find out something about those pots."

"I'm confident those questions will prove to be nothing more than nitpicking. The references I checked said Mr. Leaphorn was an absolute stickler for details." Collingsworth took a handkerchief from his pocket, mopped the sweat from his forehead. "Why do these old pots matter to you?"

"It's not about the pots for me," she said. "This might be our friend's last job, or at least his last job for a long time. He'd want to make sure it was finished correctly. Since he can't follow up on it himself, I'd be willing to tie things up."

Collingsworth hesitated. Replaced his handkerchief. "I don't see how this can do any good, but it won't do any harm. I'm sure Leaphorn's questions are just technicalities, but we can't be too careful with a collection like this. If I don't hear from you in a couple of days, I'll assume you reached a dead end. Keep track of your hours, and I'll pay you what I would have paid him to follow up on this."

"That won't be—"

"I insist," Collingsworth said. "But I expect to hear from you in forty-eight hours or sooner. Don't pull a Leaphorn on me."

He indicated a row of low adobe buildings on the north side of the parking lot.

"Dr. Davis has the envelope of research material you returned earlier. It might come in handy. She's in her office across the way there."

Collingsworth walked toward his office, and they headed to the northern complex. Chee pointed out the shiny gray Lexus SUV with a magnetic American Indian Resource Center logo as big as a basketball on the side. "Salaries must be good here, if that's the company car."

They knocked on the door with the sign that read "Associate Director."

"Come in." Bernie introduced Chee and explained the reason for their visit. In contrast to Collingsworth's imposing space, Davis's office had an invitingly homey look, with a fireplace, bookshelves, and a couple of stuffed chairs with reading lamps and low tables. Pots sat among the books. Framed photographs hung on the walls, gallery style, one above the next.

Davis opened a drawer in her desk and handed Bernie the envelope of photocopied pages. "You're welcome to this, but why do you need it?"

Bernie told Davis about her arrangement with Collingsworth.

"I heard that Marjorie found the report on her desk," Davis said. "I thought we were good to go. As I told Leaphorn after Collingsworth hired him, I can fill in the blanks. Those pots are in my area of expertise. I'm sure you have other things to do."

"Actually, I don't," Bernie said. "It means a lot to me to finish this."

Chee said to Davis, "I think we've met before somewhere. You seem familiar."

"I hear that a lot." Davis smiled, one of those smiles that could make a husband forget he was married. "I guess I have one of those faces."

Bernie said, "The lieutenant had questions about a few of the pots in the initial appraisal, the one done by a company called EFB. Have you ever heard of them?"

"Let me check our list," Davis said. "I have a master file of appraisers we use. It will just take me a minute to see if they're in there."

Davis motioned them to the two chairs and went to her computer. Bernie noticed a sleek white jar decorated with thunderbolts, topped with a cloud-shaped lid with a ceramic lightning bolt as its handle. Contemporary, but patterned after old ceramics. It sat on the desk directly in front of Davis. "Are the pots in your office part of the AIRC's collection?"

"Some of them," Davis said.

Bernie stood to take a closer look at the white jar. "This tall one looks like those old cylinders they found at Pueblo Bonito."

Davis said, "That's right. The McManus collection has a few precious pieces like that. You'll have to come and see them when they get here."

Chee said, "I like that lightning design. It reminds me of the work they do at Zuni Pueblo."

Bernie said, "And it looks useful, like a cookie jar."

Davis glanced up from the computer screen. "It's an urn."

Bernie and Chee turned their eyes away, looked at each other.

"My boyfriend—fiancé, actually—was murdered. When they found him, all that was left were a few bones."

"Murdered? What happened?" Chee asked.

"I never found out exactly. He disappeared in a canyon along the San Juan River. He was an archaeologist. He studied old mandibles, jawbones, and developed an important theory about genetic mutation among the Pueblo ancestors at Chaco. He was exploring it as a way to track migration patterns." Davis sighed. "Randall's theory would have directly tied the Chaco civilization to contemporary Pueblo people, Hopi and the Rio Grande folks. When he died, his brilliant ideas died with him."

Davis looked back at the computer. "Sorry, I can't find a reference to EFB. Many of the McManus family appraisals were done quite a while ago. That's why Collingsworth hired Leaphorn."

Chee asked, "Did they ever find the man who killed your fiancé?"

"Some odd story floated around about a psychopathic hermit who lived in a cave above the San Juan, near Sand Island," Davis said. "No one made much of an effort to track him down. The policeman involved in the case knew more than he let on."

She turned to Bernie. "Enough of that. Good luck with your assignment. Let me know how I can help. I'll see you guys out. I've got to head off for some field work."

Chee said, "I love these photographs. Beautiful clouds."

"Thank you," Davis said. "I took them. Photography is my hobby. I see lots of beautiful country when I'm out looking for ruins."

They walked out together and watched her get into the big SUV.

Bernie unlocked the truck, slid behind the steering wheel, and rolled down the windows. Even though they had found a parking spot in the shade, the afternoon sun had done its job. The steering wheel felt like a burner left on simmer.

"I know I've seen that Davis woman before," Chee said.

"I did notice how she smiled at you," Bernie said.

"I bet she smiles at every guy like that. While you were thinking about her, I figured out how to track down EFB Appraisals." He pulled out his phone. "I know somebody who might know something. He works for the New Mexico museum system here in Santa Fe."

He put the phone on speaker and they were in luck. Chee's contact, Rocko Delbert, a former Navajo Police officer, was happy to talk, updating Chee on his grandmother, mother, aunts, wife, and each of his four children. Then he chatted about his new assignment at the Museum of Indian Arts and Culture. Chee asked Rocko about EFB.

"Funny you should mention that," Rocko said. "I saw Ellie, the one who owns EFB, a few weeks ago. She'd been teaching at Arizona State, got laid off, and now she's back here, doing what she used to do a long time ago. She came to the museum to search the archives for background information and documentation she needs for the appraisals. Last time she was here, she asked if I knew how to get in touch with Joe Leaphorn. You know, the legendary lieutenant?"

"Tell me more about this Ellie," Chee said.

"Eleanor Friedman-Bernal. She's the one who started EFB. Got divorced years ago. Dropped Mr. Bernal, but kept the company name the same. Now she goes by Ellie Friedman."

"Do you know why she wanted to contact Leaphorn?"

"Well, you understand it was none of my business," Rocko said. "But she told me a long story about how she used to work at Chaco Canyon as a ceramics researcher. Got in some trouble, she got hurt. Leaphorn helped her. Something like that. Maybe she needed a private eye."

"Do you know how to reach her?"

"I've got the address for her new office. She said she wanted to hire me this week for a couple of hours to assemble some bookcases, but she hasn't called me yet."

"That's here in Santa Fe?" Chee asked.

"Right." Rocko gave him directions.

Bernie started the truck and drove while Chee navigated and watched for street signs.

"Do you think Davis keeps the ashes of her boyfriend in that pot?"

He shrugged. "White people have strange views about death."

"It gives me the shivers thinking about it," she said.

"So stop thinking about it. Hey, that looks like the street we want," he said. "Get ready to take a left."

The small L-shaped, one-story commercial complex sat tucked in behind a building that had once been a warehouse and was now a gym of some sort. They cruised the nearly empty parking lot and among the storefronts found a sign: "Indian Art Appraisals." An aged brown Subaru was parked near the front door.

Chee sat in the truck. Bernie knocked. No answer. She tried the door. Locked. The shades were drawn.

Bernie noticed a woman emerging from the office next door. The lettering on her shirt read "Tailoring by Janelle."

"Hello," Bernie said. "Do you happen to know when Ms. Fried-man will be back?"

"No. Sorry."

"If you see her, would you ask her to call me?" Bernie wrote her cell phone number on the back of her Navajo Police business card.

Janelle looked at the card and back at Bernie. "I'm the proper-ty manager here. I wouldn't have thought you were the police. I was thinking of calling the police, actually. I'm afraid Ellie is in trouble."

The woman looked toward the truck at Chee.

"That's my husband," Bernie said. "He's a policeman, too. We drove up together. Why do you think she's in trouble?"

"He's more what I think of when I think of cop." The woman grinned, then turned serious again. "I don't know her very well.

She just moved in here a few weeks ago, but she asked me to do some alternations for her. I came by to pick up the clothes, but she didn't answer the door. Her car was here, the Subaru, so I figured she was on the phone or had just changed her mind. Or just blown me off. She's kind of prickly, ya know?"

Bernie nodded.

"But when I came to work the next day, Friday, her car was still here in the same spot. I knocked on her office door again. Nothing. Maybe some client, or a boyfriend or somebody, came by for her, and they left her car here. But it's odd. And it hasn't moved since either."

"That does sound suspicious," Bernie said.

"I'm creeped out about it, that's a fact. I'd hate to think that she'd died in there or something," Janelle said.

"Me too. We ought to check her office. Do you have a key?"

Janelle hesitated, pushed a strand of stray hair out of her eyes. "Technically, I'm not allowed to go in there or let anybody else in there."

"But this is different," Bernie said. "A matter of life and death. And I'm a police officer."

"I've watched a lot of cop shows on TV. I know how it is. If somebody is in danger or something, you guys barge on in. Right?"

"That's how it is on TV."

While Janelle went to her shop for the key, Bernie motioned to Chee. He joined her on the sidewalk outside Ellie's office.

"What's up?"

"Rocko's woman might be MIA," Bernie said.

Janelle came back with an envelope with the key inside. She looked at Chee. "I understand you're a policeman."

"That's right. An officer with the Navajo Nation."

"Where's that?"

"West of here. It's as big as New England."

"Oh," Janelle said. "I think I have heard of it. I think I saw something on *National Geographic* about that once."

Janelle put the key in the lock, tried the handle, and the door opened. She took a step inside.

The EFB office smelled of dust and unused spaces. Bernie grabbed her arm. "Wait here, ma'am. This could be a crime scene."

"There's a bathroom in the back. Better check that, too," Janelle said. "Looks like my tenant was the world's biggest slob. Or the place has been ransacked."

Other than a desk, a rolling chair, and a second upholstered chair, the room had no furniture. Every drawer in the desk stood open, most of them empty or nearly so, except for the top one, which held a collection of pens, pencils, Post-its, and the like. Papers, books, and file folders lay helter-skelter on the floor. Some boxes—all of them open—sat upside down or lay on their sides on the carpet.

In the bathroom Bernie found more empty drawers standing open, a roll of paper towels, and extra toilet paper. No Ellie.

"Hey, here are the bookshelves Rocko talked about." Chee nudged a pile of boards with the toe of his boot.

Bernie paused at an arrangement of framed photos on the walls, large color prints of masonry doorways, the famous Sun Dagger solstice marker, and towering stone ruins. They seemed out of place amid the chaos.

Chee looked over her shoulder. "Chaco Canyon. You can see those T-shaped doorway openings at Pueblo Bonito. Nice picture."

Bernie looked more closely at the desktop, noticing a thin layer of grit, a box of tissues, a blue coffee cup, an empty phone charger, and an old-fashioned, pad-style desktop calendar turned to June. Some of the numbered squares had times, names, phone numbers, addresses inside. Ellie had written "Pueblo Alto!" in one. Another read "SJ," with a phone number. Bernie made a note of the names, numbers, and days in case any appointments offered a clue to the missing woman's whereabouts. She noticed something interesting.

"Come look at this." She pointed to one of the squares: the lieutenant's home phone number written in blue pen. "I wonder why she wanted to meet with him."

"Another mystery," Chee said. He leaned over to examine the bottom desk drawer, pulled out some typed pages, and extended them to her. "Do these look familiar?"

Bernie recognized them. They were the missing section from the lieutenant's report on the McManus collection.

Janelle hadn't heard any unusual noise from the office, she said; hadn't seen anything strange except Ellie's unmoved car. She relocked the door and gave them Ellie's home address from the rental agreement in her files.

"She told me she lives by herself," Janelle said. "I'd feel terrible if she'd had a stroke or something and was just lying there."

The address was about two miles away. Bernie drove. "So why all the confusion in that office?"

"I think someone was looking for something," Chee said. "Maybe Ellie herself, maybe someone else. Hard to say. More than just your standard moving-in mess."

Chee checked Leaphorn's notebook calendar against the notes on Ellie's. The appointment dates matched.

"So Ellie stood him up. I think we've found the ghost from the past," he said. "I figured out who this Ellie is. The color photos reminded me. She's the woman who used to work at Chaco Canyon. Remember the missing researcher who was nearly killed by a coworker? The one whose life the lieutenant saved? That was Ellie. Eleanor Friedman-Bernal. What a mouthful of a name."

"Are you sure?"

"Absolutely. I remember because I was the one who tipped off the guy who almost murdered her."

"You wouldn't have done that," Bernie said.

"I did. Luckily, I realized how dumb I'd been in time to help the lieutenant get her to the hospital. She was unconscious when I got there, and I never saw her again. Ellie had been involved in some questionable digging in Pueblo Indian sites, ruins along the San Juan River. Quite a place to rescue somebody. I had to rent a helicopter."

"Odd that now she's missing again. History repeats itself."

"Except instead of being a victim, this time she might be our suspect," Chee said.

Ellie Friedman lived in a working-class neighborhood with a hodgepodge of apartment complexes and stand-alone houses that combined pseudo adobe exteriors and the impractical flat roofs that were Santa Fe's trademark. Chain-link fences, painted rocks, and miniature windmills in the front yards added to the ambience.

Ellie's address led to an unlandscaped new apartment building at the end of a block, one of the few two-story structures in the area. Bernie parked and climbed the stairs to the unit, Chee following. She rang the doorbell, heard it chiming inside. The shades were drawn. Bernie leaned down to peek through the metal mail slot in the front door, noticing a pile of full-color shopping flyers and advertising promotions on the floor.

"You could contact Cordova, let him call the local cops, have them open the door in case this is a crime scene," Bernie said.

"I guess I could." Chee tested the doorknob, and it moved in his hand. Unlocked.

He called, "Police. Welfare check. Eleanor, are you okay? Ellie, are you here?"

Bernie glanced up and down the empty concrete walkway, then followed him inside the apartment, stepping over the mail and quietly closing the door.

The hot air smelled stale at first; then a waft of aged garbage drifted toward them. The living room had a black couch, a matching chair, a poster of the Grand Canyon, and a big-screen TV. Except for the mail, the living room and adjoining dining room were relatively neat. Bernie noticed stacks of books on the floor and a drawer in the coffee table pulled open.

She walked down the hall, looked in the open doors. In the bedroom, contents from the oak dresser—lingerie, T-shirts, and other clothes—had been dumped on the double bed. A hardback thriller with a red-and-black cover sat on the nightstand. The closet door stood ajar, the hanging garments pushed to one side. No suitcase. Did Ellie have it with her, wherever she was? The yellow-walled bathroom was in similar disarray. Bernie saw a basket of cosmetics on the counter. A single towel on the rack.

She caught up with Chee in the kitchen.

"It's been a while since Ellie was here," he said. "I checked the utility room, too, and the closets. Found no body and nobody home."

"Ditto," she said. "The bedroom and the bath are a mess, just like her office. Seems like Ellie made a fast exit. Or she tore the room up looking for something."

Bernie noticed the drooping plants on the windowsill. She touched the soil in their pots. Bone-dry. "Look at those limp African violets. Poor things. Wonder why she didn't give them to a neighbor, or to Janelle, before she left?"

Bernie went back to the living room, crouched to go through the envelopes on the floor. "No one has picked up the mail since last Wednesday."

"I'll call Cordova, let him know we have another possible suspect in the Leaphorn shooting."

"How would Ellie get access to the Benally car?" Bernie asked. "And why would she shoot the man who had saved her life?"

"Good questions," Chee said. "All we need are answers."

14

After Cordova, Chee called Largo with the news of the missing
Eleanor Friedman.

"Chee, be here in Window Rock tomorrow at noon to meet
with the feds and the state police," said Largo. "Talk about where
to go from here."

"Anything new?"

"Not much. The Arizona DPT found a Leonard Nez, brought
him in for questioning. The wrong Leonard Nez, fortysomething.
Benally's still quiet about Nez's whereabouts." Largo made a little
puffing noise into the receiver. "The feds sent somebody out here to
ask Jackson some questions about Nez. Same ones we asked."

Largo chuckled. "They think Louisa might have paid him, Nez,
or maybe the two of them in a murder-for-hire scheme."

He asked Chee to give Bernie a message. "Austin Lee's ex-wife
called. Said she doesn't see Austin much, but if she does, she will
give him the news about Leaphorn. She said to tell your wife that
the lieutenant and Lee are clan brothers. Said she was sorry about
the lieutenant getting shot."

"I'll let Bernie know. Anything else?"

"Yeah," Largo said. "Remind her she's on leave. Not that it will do any good."

Chee drove south on I-25 to the outskirts of Santa Fe, past the quirky shed with the huge sculpted dinosaur and the junction for NM 14, the road to the state penitentiary. The towering cloud formations in the June sky had brought a bit of shade, but no rain. Now they hinted at the possibility of a Technicolor sunset.

Bernie watched the scenery change from the cottonwoods of the Cienega Valley to the volcanic cliffs of La Bajada, the steepest hill between Santa Fe and Albuquerque. Near the summit she glimpsed the ruts of the old road taken by horses and wagons and then by Model Ts in the days before the paved, divided highway stretched so smoothly between Albuquerque and Santa Fe.

"I read in *New Mexico Magazine* that some of those old cars had to chug up this hill backward to make it over the top," she said. "It took most of the day to get from Santa Fe to Albuquerque. Now it's an hour."

"Less if you're the one driving," Chee said. He cruised past the turnoff for Cochiti Lake and onward toward Santo Domingo Pueblo. Bernie pulled out the envelope Davis had given her, taking new interest in the material she had just scanned before, searching for answers to the lieutenant's questions about the EFB appraisal.

Chee's phone rang in the car charger.

She answered it, switching to speaker.

"Ah . . . hmm. I'd like to talk to Officer Jim Chee."

"He's driving at the moment. This is Officer Manuelito. Is there something I can do for you?"

"You're the one who almost got shot?"

"Who is this?"

"Jackson. You know, Jackson Benally. I thought of another place people might have got to the car."

"I can hear you," Chee said. "Hey, Jackson."

"Mom lets me drive to the ranch where I work on Saturdays and Sundays and when I'm not in school. We have to leave the keys in the ignition in case they have to move the cars when they bring in a big load of hay or livestock or something." He spoke fast. Nervous. "What if somebody there made a copy of my key? Then they snuck up and stole the car later? Shot that officer."

Chee shook his head, eyes on the road. "Let me sit with that idea awhile, Jackson. In the meantime, I'm still wondering what happened to Leonard Nez and thinking about that uncle and his ranch. The idea of somebody making a copy of your car key, figuring out the car is at Bashas', that's pretty far-fetched, don't you—"

He stopped when he heard "Shhhh" and saw Bernie's finger across her lips.

The phone fell silent, too, but Bernie noticed that it still had bars. Jackson must be thinking.

"What's the name of this ranch where you work?" she asked.

"The Double X. Near Cortez," the boy said. "You know where that is?"

"I know where it is. Give me the phone number."

Jackson rattled off the number from memory, and Bernie jotted it down. A good sign. Maybe he was telling the truth.

"What about Nez?" she said.

"Gosh, I can barely hear you," Jackson said. "Your signal is getting—" And then he hung up.

Bernie said, "I think we should give the ranch a call, see if Jackson's story checks out."

"Go ahead," Chee said. "Why don't you just take charge? I'll keep looking through files, tracking down dead ends, spinning my wheels. Your new pal at the FBI would rather work with you anyway."

"Sorry, I shouldn't have shushed you. I thought Jackson might come up with something important if you pretended to be interested."

"That ruffled my feathers."

She stared out the window, watched the lava-formed landscape stretch to the blue rim of mountains to the west, thinking about Ellie who'd disappeared and her involvement in all this. Thinking about her promise to Leaphorn and how far she was from fulfilling it.

"You're quiet," Chee said.

"I'm frustrated. Wrapping up this appraisal stuff for the lieutenant should have been as easy as one phone call to EFB. Instead, we get another puzzle."

Chee waited. "What else?"

Bernie sighed. "I don't like the way the lieutenant looks in that hospital bed. He's not getting any better. Seeing him that way also makes me realize I need to spend more time with Mama. And I'm worried about Darleen. I tried to call her a couple times today. No answer."

She paused so long, it seemed she was done. Then she said, "Mostly, though, it's the case. Our leads vanish or turn into complications when we examine them twice. It's so disappointing. It's driving me crazy. I can't stop thinking about it, wondering what we've missed."

She reached over and put her hand on his leg, felt the warmth of his body through the denim of his jeans. "And I'm wondering if whoever shot the lieutenant might try to kill you, or Largo, or someone else we work with next. What if the feds are wrong, and the shooter is a crazed cop hater?"

Chee took one hand off the steering wheel and put it around her shoulders. She scooted closer to him, glad that the truck had a bench seat. "You have to let it go, honey," he said. "We're doing the best we can."

"Then there's you," she said. "There's us. Not enough time for that, either. If we didn't work together, we'd hardly see each other."

"You're right," he said. "When we're done with this, let's take a little trip up to Monument Valley. We can stay with my relatives up there. Hike around. Not think about work for a day or two."

They passed the gaudy lights of Casino Hollywood, another successful Indian attempt to even the score with Spanish and Anglo usurpers and their descendants. At Bernalillo, Chee turned northwest onto US 550 toward Zia Pueblo. After about twenty minutes, he put on the turn signal, slowed, and moved toward the shoulder.

"Something wrong?"

He didn't say anything.

"Getting sleepy? Want me to drive?"

He shut off the engine. Clicked his seat belt free, then reached over to release hers, too. He climbed out and walked around to open her door. He reached for her hand.

"Mrs. Chee, would you stand here with me and savor the moment?"

The sky was majestic. The Sandia Mountains rose like a rugged blue monolith to the east, glowing in the reflected oranges, vivid reds, and brilliant sunflower hues of the sunset. He put his arm around her as they watched the light change from magenta to smoky rose and dissolve into the soft gray of summer predarkness. "I worry about you," he said. "The happy girl I married has too much to do. Too many burdens."

She snuggled in closer to him. "Sunday night, when you came home so late, I told myself everything was fine. But still. And after what happened to Leaphorn . . ."

"Life goes too fast," he said. "We don't want to live like crazy Santa Fe people."

She laughed. "Yeah. We want to live like crazy Shiprock Navajos."

As he held her, she noticed the gentle flirting light of evening's first star. So' Tsoh, "Big Star." Venus, the goddess of love.

Bernie drove through the twilight into Cuba, a speck of a town

known for its restaurant, El Bruno's, which served some of the best
New Mexican food in Sandoval County. They both ordered enchi-
ladas, Bernie's cheese with green chile and Chee's with roast beef
and Christmas chile—red and green. They had stopped here a few
times with the lieutenant after a long day of meetings in Albuquerque. Leaphorn always had a burger, Bernie remembered, with no
cheese or onion, and followed up with a piece of pie topped with a
scoop of vanilla ice cream.

They walked back to the truck, a nearly full rising moon light-
ing their way.

"How far is it from here to Chaco Canyon?" Bernie asked. "I'd
like to see the place where those darn pots came from. And since
you don't have to be at work early . . ." She let the sentence hang.

"It's a quick fifty miles to the turnoff, then another slow twenty
to the ruins."

"Do you have camping gear in here?"

"Yeah," he said. "Two sleeping bags. Even a sack of trail mix we
can have for breakfast."

"Let's spend the night at Chaco. Get up early, see some of the
park before we have to go to work."

Bernie drove the paved highway to Nageezi. Driving NM 550 after dark used to scare her, with its deadly combination of big trucks,
long distances, and occasional random crossroads. The alcoholism that
plagues Indian country added to the lethal mix, along with sleepy, inat-
tentive drivers. Then the New Mexico Highway Department widened
the road and added rumble ridges to startle drivers who drifted onto
the shoulder. Bernie passed trucks hauling cattle, semis on their way
west, and a scattering of pickups, station wagons, and SUVs. She made
a left when she saw the sign for Chaco Canyon National Historic Site,
driving first on pavement and, when it ended, on hard-packed dirt that
became washboard and sand. Not another car in sight.

Chee said, "I haven't been here since the lieutenant and I handled that case where Ellie disappeared the first time. She worked here."

Bernie nodded. "That the time you rented a helicopter? Did you just put it on your credit card?"

Chee laughed. "That's a long story. Actually, there were two helicopters. The guy who hurt Ellie was a pilot as well as an archaeologist. He had been digging in the graves of the old ones, and Ellie found out. It was a fascinating case. Leaphorn never talked to me about how he solved it. Except to say he didn't understand the white culture's fixation on revenge, getting even."

"Wasn't that right after Emma died?" Bernie always wished she'd had a chance to meet Leaphorn's wife.

"Yes," Chee said. "He put in for retirement after that, but changed his mind. I think finding Ellie gave him a reason to stay with police work for a few more years."

"Are you surprised he and Louisa haven't gotten married?"

"I asked him about that once." Chee chuckled. "He told me he'd proposed to her and she turned him down. She said she'd already been married and it didn't agree with her."

Bernie leaned toward the windshield. "I think I saw something big out there."

"Yeah," Chee said. "I got a glimpse of it, too."

"Makes me edgy," Bernie said. She had grown up with stories of skinwalkers, the legendary Navajo shape shifters who assumed various animal forms and roamed in the darkness looking for and causing trouble. She vividly recalled the hair-raising tales her grandmother told of the evil they created. The unexpected motion on this still, moon-filled night made her feel like a nervous five-year-old.

"Elk have come back to this area," Chee said. "Maybe some cougar or even a Mexican gray wolf is following them."

"I just hope all critters stay out of the road."

"Oh, no," Chee said. "What about the cat? We won't be home to feed her."

"You fed her this morning," she said. "She had a full bowl of water, too. You can feed her first thing when we get home."

"Yeah, I know. But still. Poor little thing."

Bernie kept the truck at a brisk forty-five miles an hour to smooth out the washboards. Around the next curve the headlights bounced off the red coats of three lean Herefords, a small herd in the center of the road. She took her foot off the gas and with both hands on the wheel tapped the brake. She steered to the right, and the lights hit a fourth cow, this one walking toward its companions, sauntering toward the spot the truck would have hit if Bernie had not corrected again, moving farther to the right. She felt a front tire against the soft sand at the edge of the road. The cows looked up and took an interest in the approaching truck.

Bernie thought: Truck, don't roll. Cow, stand still, be calm. All cows, be calm.

She steered farther off the clay washboard, the tires sinking into the deep ridge of sand at the edge of the hard pack. The truck jolted and slowed, and then the back tires found the solid surface below. She gave it a bit of gas and brought it back to the road.

She heard Chee exhale. The headlights flashed on a road sign, a yellow triangle with a black drawing of a cow.

"Thank goodness that sign is there," he said. "Good driving. Let me take it awhile."

She stopped the truck, and they both climbed out. Even though the temperature had probably reached the nineties here during the day, the night air felt cool, pleasant, perfect against her sweaty back. Overhead, despite the brightness of the moon, she could see hundreds of stars. Thousands. Argo Navis, Coyote Star in the southern sky, glittering with a whisper of red and orange. The North Star, or Central Fire, Nahookos Baka'. The music of crickets and other creatures, sounds she didn't recognize, animated the evening.

"My grandmother never liked any of us to be out at night," she said. "*Chindi* roaming around, sniffing out trouble."

Chee stood next to her, studying the stars. "Mine was the same. It took me years to be comfortable in the dark. I still have my moments."

"That's just your good cop sense. And who is to say that those grandmothers were wrong?"

They bounced along for another twenty minutes, grateful for lunar illumination and the lack of cattle, elk, feral horses, or even another vehicle on the road. They could see the iconic bulk of Fajada Butte rising in the distance.

"I've never seen this place at night," Chee said. "It's even more deserted, lonelier, mysterious."

"Is the mystery still where the people went?"

"That one has been pretty much solved," he said. "It used to be said that they disappeared. Better research showed that they moved on when conditions here got too hard. No one yet really knows why they settled here in the first place, built these huge structures and miles of wide roadway to connect them. And of course we don't know what went on in their kivas."

"I remember my uncle telling me stories about our people and the old ones who lived here," she said. "How they were related to us Navajos, especially to the Kiiyaa'áanii."

"I heard how that clan was named for a stone tower somewhere out here. Or was that in Canyon de Chelly? Did your uncle tell you about Pueblo Pintado?" Chee said.

"Probably. I'm sorry I don't remember everything he said. But I know he told me that without the Diné, there would have been no civilization here."

They felt and heard the difference as the truck's tires rolled from dirt to pavement. Bernie noticed a sign: "Chaco Canyon

Visitor Center .5 mile." It would be good to stretch out and get to sleep.

Then she saw something move. "In the road."

Chee braked.

Large black shapes loomed ahead. The glare from the truck's headlights flashed in their eyes. Unlike the sleepy cattle, the elk bounded off the roadway and kept going.

"They're huge," she said.

"Yeah," Chee said. "They get bigger here at lower altitude. The ones you're used to are up in the Chuskas. Smaller there."

She laughed. "So that's why the trout swim in mountain streams and whales live in the ocean?"

"Exactly," he said. "I always knew you were a quick study."

They pulled into the campground, and Chee switched to parking lights. They passed domed tents next to picnic tables and grills on stands, camping trailers and the boxy shapes of RVs. It took a few minutes to find the first empty spot. They pulled the tarps and sleeping bags from the trunk, trying to be quiet, and spread them out on sandy earth still warm from the June day.

They moved their sleeping bags close together and started to take off their shoes.

"What's that noise?" Chee kept his voice low.

"Sounds like a cross between a gurgle and sandpaper. I bet it's frogs or toads or something."

"I thought they needed water."

"There must have been some rain here," Bernie said. The desert was wonderful, she thought, packed full of life waiting quietly under the earth's surface. Waiting for a drop of moisture to inspire it to spring forth. "I bet we'll see wildflowers in bloom tomorrow."

Chee walked to the truck. He returned with their water bottles and handed her hers. "You made me thirsty."

They climbed into the sleeping bags, and he pulled her close.

They watched the moon move across the endless New Mexico night sky until they fell asleep.

Bernie awoke to pearly predawn light. She looked at Chee, his dark eyes open to the sky. "Come run with me," she whispered. They pulled on their shoes and went to welcome the day. They ran through the campground, where blue, gray, and green nylon tents sprouted like mushrooms, jogging toward the main road beneath the weathered sandstone cliffs. The cool air reverberated with bird calls.

They ran until the sun rose, then circled back and found the campground coming to life. They heard muffled conversations and smelled bacon and coffee. A slot over from where they camped, a woman in a plaid shirt tended a fire beneath a grill. "Good morning, neighbors," she said as she saw them approach. She picked up the coffeepot by its handle, using a towel as a hot pad. "I've got some extra. Join me?"

"Sounds great," Bernie said. "How kind of you."

The woman gave Bernie a cup that matched the blue camping pot and poured Chee's into a red mug and offered them milk and sugar.

"I don't care where I am," she said. "I can't start the day without a hit of this."

Bernie tried a sip. It was tea, not the coffee she expected. She should have known from the smell. At least it was hot.

"Enjoying the ruins?" Chee asked.

"I come every few years," the woman said. "My husband used to come with me, always complaining about how far it was from Denver. Now he's with his new wife, complaining about something else, no doubt." She chuckled, refilled her own cup. "I'm Karen."

"I'm Jim. This is Bernie."

Bernie noticed a pad of paper open to sketches.

"You an artist?"

"Sort of. I make drawings of places I like, a visual journal. Chaco is still my favorite. I did the major ruins a few years ago with Mr. Complainer. Now I'm exploring sites farther out."

"Are you hiking by yourself?" Chee asked.

Karen nodded.

"Be careful," he said.

"I was." She sipped her tea. "I'd offer you breakfast, but I'm not cooking this morning. Packing up and heading for home."

Bernie said, "We're off to see the ruins, then we have to get this guy to work."

"So you live around here? I'm jealous. What do you do?" Karen asked.

"I'm a cop," Chee said. He turned his head toward Bernie. "She is, too. We're based in Shiprock."

"Well, you might find this interesting," Karen said. "Earlier this week, I was sketching on the trail out at Pueblo Alto. When I parked, there was one other car there. I hiked up, went off to find a place with a view of Pueblo del Arroyo—that's the ruin closest to the parking lot. I walked up a dry wash and set up in the shade at a great vista point. I lose track of time when I work, so I'm not sure how long I'd been there, but I heard a commotion. It sounded like people arguing. I noticed a couple of hikers on the rim trail. A woman in a long-sleeved shirt, you know, one of those expensive ones to keep out the UV rays? The other one had one of those khaki hats that tie on with a string. The dorky-looking ones that old people wear?"

Chee nodded. Karen continued. "The dorky-hat person was twisting the other person's arm, kind of pulling her. The woman was resisting, but Dorky Hat seemed to overpower her. Or she just gave in. They moved out of sight, but I could hear them arguing for a while longer. I didn't think much more about it. I went back to sketching. The light was just right, you know? Well, I stopped to get out my water bottle, and I noticed Dorky Hat down below, running. I thought at the time it was too hot to be running. I finished, packed up, ambled down to my car. The other car—I assume it was theirs—was gone."

Karen put her mug down. "I figured the woman must have hiked out earlier or later or something, and I'd missed seeing her. But it stuck with me."

"Did you mention it at the park headquarters?"

"No," she said. "I didn't want the rangers to think I was a deranged artist. I decided I'd go in this morning and report it, but the office isn't open yet and I have to get on the road."

"We'll tell them about it," Bernie said. "We're heading down there in a few minutes anyway. Anything else about that incident you think we ought to mention?"

Karen said, "I heard a loud noise while I was working. I thought it was a car backfiring, or someone setting off a firecracker out here. But now that I'm thinking about it and talking to you guys, it could have been a gunshot."

Bernie and Chee drove to the visitor center and went to the information desk. They identified themselves to the gray-haired ranger, Andrew Stephen, as police officers with the Navajo Nation. "Is Joe Wakara here today?"

"No. I'm in charge today. Can I help you with something?"

"So even that old geezer gets a day off," Chee said.

Stephen laughed. "You know him, huh?"

Wakara, a friend of Leaphorn's, had been head of security at the park for as long as Chee could remember.

Chee mentioned the conversation about the quarreling hikers.

"We haven't had any reports of anyone missing," Stephen said. "I'll ask our guy who makes the rounds to hike up that trail a ways this afternoon. Just in case."

"Where is Pueblo Alto, anyway?" Bernie asked.

Stephen showed her on the map.

"I haven't been to Chaco for a while," Chee said. "Isn't this a new visitor center?"

"It opened a few years ago. The old building you remember had to be razed."

"Old? Wasn't it built in the late nineteen-fifties?"

"Ironic, isn't it. Modern America couldn't build a visitor center to last seventy years," Stephen said. "These Pueblo buildings still stand after more than a thousand. But this time we did it right. We brought in an Indian to bless the site."

He smiled at Chee. "Policeman, huh? You're the one I call if someone gets nervous about livestock on the Navajo Nation part of the road?"

"Depends on if the cows want to file a complaint about the traffic harassing them. You worked here long?"

"Fifteen years," Stephen said. "I love it. Except for the road."

"Did you know a woman named Eleanor Friedman-Bernal who used to do research here?" Bernie asked.

"Ellie? A bit. I got hired on a few months before she nearly got killed. She called here last month, all excited. Said she'd left her college job and was moving back to New Mexico. Said she'd come see the ruins and that she'd stop in and say hi."

Bernie said, "I'm doing some work for the AIRC. I'd love to talk to her about some Chaco pots."

"She knows a lot about them," Stephen said. "That's her specialty. Absolutely passionate about it. Do you know her?"

"I met her," Chee said. "I worked on that case where she nearly died. So she has been back here?"

"Not yet. Not that I know of. I guess her plans changed. They say she always was a little flaky. I heard she planned to start up that appraisal business again, now that she's not teaching anymore. That must be keeping her busy."

Stephen smiled at Bernie. "If you're interested in pottery, we've got some books on it over there. Some hard-to-find reference stuff that focuses mostly on pots from here."

They wandered over to a section of the room that served as the bookstore, then spent a few minutes with the exhibits. Since most of the material found at Chaco Canyon had been shipped elsewhere a long time ago, the exhibit items were on loan. The Maxwell Museum at the University of New Mexico had provided the artifacts, examples of jewelry, animal carvings, bits of worked turquoise, stone tools, black-and-white potshards, part of a long and close association between the two institutions.

A group of Navajo kids, six- and seven-year-olds, swarmed into the visitor center. In addition to two women, obviously teachers, Bernie noticed a tall young man with the little people. Stoop Boy. She watched him intervene with two boys who had been pushing each other, put a hand on each one's arm and squat down to talk to them at eye level. Interesting, she thought. She'd assumed he didn't have a job.

Stoop Boy noticed Bernie and smiled. She never saw him smile when he was with Darleen. He walked over to her, bringing the kids along.

"Yá'át'ééh," he said.

She couldn't remember his name, and he seemed to sense that and let her off the hook. He looked at Chee, said, "I'm Charley Zah," and introduced himself Navajo style. "I'm a friend of Officer Manuelito's sister."

Chee reciprocated with his own introduction. The urchins in Zah's grasp squirmed. "You've got your hands full."

"Literally." Zah laughed. "We bring the kids here a couple times with the summer program. We tell Chaco stories on the bus, talk about the ones who lived here. Then we let them see the ruins, get some sunlight, watch the ravens soar.

"Are you here on business?" Zah asked. "I understand they found a few bodies out there. And then there's the question of what happened to all the other bodies they didn't find here. Alien abductions?"

Chee laughed. "We don't get to handle those cold cases. We leave that to the archaeologists. They are puzzling over how a place so big would have so few burials."

The restless youngsters pulled on Stoop Boy's hands. "We're starting our tour at Pueblo Bonito, in case you want to tag along, or avoid us. But the first stop is out there." He pointed toward the restroom with his chin and let the boys lead him away. "Nice to meet you," he said to Chee, and, "Nice to see you again," to Bernie.

"So that's the guy leading Darleen into trouble?"

"I may have pegged him wrong," Bernie said. "He sure seems different here."

"It must be what they call the Chaco Phenomenon."

"You know everything?"

Chee grinned. "And what I don't know, I make up."

They left the visitor center for the trail to Una Vida, a structure archaeologists call a great house, a towering ruin of hand-carved stone partly buried beneath eons of blowing sand and a thin layer of tough vegetation. The trail through what was left of the rooms took them to petroglyphs, ancient artists' depictions of animals, spirals, lightning, and perhaps divine beings.

Bernie paused near a section of wall that differed from the rest of the stone masonry. "This could have been an old sheep camp."

Chee trotted up with the tour pamphlet. "That's right. Evidently Navajo sheep corrals were here around eighteen hundred."

"With a touch of water this would be good sheep country," Bernie said.

They walked back toward the visitor center and the truck, aware of the growing heat.

"In a couple of weeks, this place will be full of people who come for the solstice," Chee said.

"All those spiritual seekers and wannabe Indians make my head spin," she said.

"I can't blame them for wanting to be here. There's no place in the world quite like this. And to think that the ones who lived here were so wise that we can still use their solar markers ten centuries later. That's impressive."

"I love the way the architecture blends into the landscape," Bernie said. "I wonder what brought the people here?"

Chee walked ahead to open the truck. "They came on foot, honey. The pickup hadn't been invented yet."

They didn't have time for more hiking, but they explored the paved loop trail with views of the remains of more massive ruins of a culture that rose and fell over the course of three centuries. Then they headed out of the park, driving past the Fajada Butte overlook and the junction for the Wijiji ruins. Bernie said, "Seeing this place makes me more curious about the pottery that came from here, the things the lieutenant was working on. And about Ellie."

Chee slowed as they left the pavement for the dirt road. "Interesting that the ranger said Ellie planned to come back to visit."

"That's probably why she had Pueblo Alto on her calendar," Bernie said. "Maybe she decided to shoot the lieutenant and go into hiding first."

"We'll ask her when we find her. Or when the feds bring her in."

Bernie said, "She sounds like a cool character. Focused on her job. I guess spending all that time with old pots would tend to make you, well, detached."

"Or not liking people much in the first place gives you the perfect personality for that."

"Sounds like Dr. Davis, too. Maybe pot people are all introverts."

They bounced along in silence for a while. The washboards they encountered on the way out had a pattern that denied the truck a comfortable ride at any speed. Fast or slow, the road threatened to shake the bolts loose. Bernie saw a lean coyote, its tan coat the same color as the sandy earth, a contrast to the gray of the sage. She watched a trio of turkey vultures soar against the vivid blue sky. No clouds yet.

Chee said, "Davis lied about not remembering me. I could tell by the way she looked at me that she knew who I was. I thought she seemed familiar. But when I met her she had long, curly red hair."

"When did you meet her?"

"Years ago. It was here at Chaco, working the missing Ellie case with the lieutenant. We interviewed her as part of the investigation. Most folks don't have that many encounters with the police. They remember them."

"Maybe she's trying to forget that whole phase of her life," Bernie said.

"Maybe. But she and Ellie lived in employee housing. It seems odd that she wouldn't have recognized EFB either."

"She might not have known what Ellie called her business," Bernie said. "You saw her check the database."

Bernie noticed a car approaching them, bouncing along the washboard barely under control. "You know, the other thing that's wrong here is this Leonard Nez. Jackson being so closemouthed about him and about what they were doing that day, if they didn't shoot the lieutenant. The Nez guy must have some pull with Jackson, holding something over him, threatening him."

"Yeah," Chee said. "I don't buy the story of an unnamed uncle who lives down a road Zuni way. Whatever it is, it's big enough that Jackson was willing to spend a night in jail rather than share it."

Chee pulled out to pass a king cab truck hauling a camping trailer, moving away from the cloud of dust it generated and into the clear air. "You know the ranch where Jackson said he works?"

"I've heard of it," Bernie said. "The Jacobs family has been out there for generations."

"I think the number Jackson gave you is the same number Ellie jotted down on her desk pad next to 'SJ,' " he said. "I remembered the Colorado area code."

Bernie checked her notes from the visit to EFB and took out her cell phone. When she finally had reception, she called. No answer, but the recording told her she'd reached the Double X Ranch.

"You were right," she said. "That ties Ellie and Jackson and the car."

She opened the glove box, extracted a map, and spread it across her lap.

"I think I've got this down," Chee said. "I stay on the highway until we reach Farmington. Or until I pull over for you to drive. Correct me if I'm wrong. But I guess I don't even need to say that anymore, do I, sweetheart?"

She punched him in the arm. Not hard, but hard enough.

"I'm looking for the shortest way to get from Shiprock to the Double X Ranch," she said.

"You could use the GPS in your phone."

"Right," Bernie said. "I love the way that computer voice twists up Navajo place names. Can I use the truck?"

"Sorry. While you're finding SJ this afternoon, I've got to get to Window Rock. I wonder what new torture Largo has dreamed up for me?"

15

While Chee showered, Bernie called the Double X Ranch again. Owner/manager Slim Jacobs answered, and she identified herself as a Navajo cop. Yes, he said, he'd talk to her about EFB, even though his ranch was not on Navajo land, and, he said, he didn't think she had any jurisdiction. And yes, he knew Jackson Benally. It was a slow day. Come on over. He gave her better directions than she'd been able to get from the map.

Bernie made a couple of peanut butter sandwiches and a pot of coffee and got out her traveling cup.

Chee looked at the counter. "So you're outa here?"

She noticed that he smelled like soap and sunshine. "If Slim Jacobs can help us track down Ellie, that's well worth the trip. I can finish the appraisal work and you can follow up with her, find out about that meeting she set up with the lieutenant," she said. "And who knows, maybe Slim can tell us something about Lizard Nez, too."

"Why didn't you just ask him about Nez over the phone?" Chee said.

"He doesn't know me, and he sounded prickly. Face-to-face is better. By the way, Largo called while you were cleaning up. Mrs.

Benally is waiting for you. She has info about Nez, but she'll only talk to you."

"I was right about torture."

Bernie poured coffee into her travel cup and handed it to him along with a sandwich. "I couldn't find your mug. Take this."

He kissed her. "What about you?"

"I'll drink my coffee here, take a Coke along instead."

"See you tonight," he said. "Don't forget to call Darleen."

The drive to the Double X Ranch took her an hour. Usually driving relaxed her, but not today. Odd, she thought. Alone in the Toyota, she remembered the percussion of the gunshot and the startled look on Leaphorn's face as he slipped to the ground. The roar of the sedan speeding off. The warm blood growing sticky on her hands. The dark eyes staring blankly from a face growing paler. The smell of the hot asphalt. The wail of the ambulance.

She lifted a hand from the steering wheel to wipe away the tears. Pay attention to the traffic, she told herself. You have a job to finish. You don't have anything to cry about.

She passed the sign that marked the boundary of the Navajo Reservation. Sleeping Ute Mountain, a special place to the Ute bands, rose to the northwest. To some, the bulky blue shape resembled a reclining man in a feather headdress; others saw a busty woman. The Ute Mountain Casino sat in its shadow, complete with blinking lights, neon signs, and a packed parking lot.

Someone had marked the turnoff to the Double X with an old tire hung on a fence post. She left the pavement of US 491, clumped over a cattle guard and onto the dirt. A horse picked through the scant vegetation. From the bony looks of it, a feral pony. Picturesque, the tourists called them. A nuisance for ranchers. She tapped the brakes as a lean brown dog trotted in front of her car, moving right to left. It stopped on the top of an earthen berm to watch her bounce past.

Double X Ranch was a first-rate operation with a reputation for respecting the land and treating workers well. Lots of room out here, Bernie thought. A maze of shallow arroyos, dirt tracks heading out into the mesas, stone outcroppings. Colorado plateau country, where coyotes and ravens ruled. It reminded her of the landscape that had been part of a huge manhunt for fugitives who robbed a casino years ago. Despite the best efforts of combined law enforcement, those bad guys evaporated into the dry landscape.

After about a mile, she noticed a line of pickup trucks and battered sedans—classic rez cars—parked along the road. She drove past them to encounter a backhoe partly obstructing the way around the next curve.

"I'll be working on and off all day," the driver said. "Best to leave your car back there so you don't get blocked in."

She made a U-turn, parked at the head of the line facing toward the blacktop, and walked toward the ranch house with the low growl of the backhoe's engine as background music. Most of the vehicles had their windows open, keys in the ignition, as Jackson had said.

A shaggy, oversize dog barked at her from the shade of the porch. It rose stiffly and didn't bother to move closer. The front door stood ajar, but the screen was shut.

"Hello in there," she called. The dog kept barking. "I'm here to see Mr. Jacobs."

The screen door opened, and a paunchy man in a gray checked shirt and jeans stepped onto the porch. "Princess, enough. Quiet down now." The dog hushed, keeping an eye on Bernie. "Just doing her job," the man said.

He smiled, a flash of crooked teeth. "Come on in. I'm Slim Jacobs. You must be Officer Manuelito."

"That's me," Bernie said. She wiped the soles of her Nikes on the doormat, which read "Howdy Pardner."

"Can I get you some water, Officer? I might have a soda some-wheres."

"Thank you, sir," she said. "Water would be great. Call me Bernie."

"Call me Slim," he said. "Or whatever you want. Just don't call me late for supper." He motioned her to a seat at a large wooden table covered with piles of bills, catalogs, correspondence. She saw a well-used Stetson on the hat rack.

"I heard about the old policeman who got shot in Window Rock," he said. "Terrible thing. Any idea who did it?"

"We're working on it," Bernie said. "That's why I wanted to talk to you about Ms. Friedman. She had an appointment with the po-liceman before he was shot. I've been looking for her to talk about that, and an old appraisal she did."

"I'm afraid you drove all the way out here for nothing, missy," he said. "I never got to see Ms. Friedman last week. That Ellie stood me up. No call to say she wasn't comin'. No call afterwards to explain about it. Of course, she always was a little scatterbrained. I tried callin' her to reschedule and tell her now she owed me a lunch. Left messages. Never heard back."

"It's odd," Bernie said.

"Especially for someone startin' up a business again. She came right out the first time I called, a couple weeks ago. She seemed real interested in the work, so we set the date. I got everything ready, even fixed us some lunch."

"I'm working for a museum in Santa Fe," Bernie said. "I'd like to track her down so I can finish an assignment. Sounds like you know her pretty well."

Slim grinned. "Oh, we had a thing goin' back when she worked at Chaco, before that jerk tried to kill her and she started teaching at ASU. She told me she got laid off there and decided to come back to New Mexico. Cooler here. Nice gal."

He stopped and seemed to be waiting for a question.

"How did you meet her?"

Slim said, "I hired her on to do an appraisal back when she was still wet behind the ears. I saw her little card on the bulletin board at the Laundromat in Cuba. She was just appraising part-time then, squeezin' in some evaluations along with studying old pots for her research. And I was workin' on a ranch near Cuba, takin' a break from this place and my old man."

Princess whined at the door, and Slim rose to let her in. She walked over to Bernie. When Bernie ignored her, the dog sauntered to Slim and put her head in his lap. He rubbed her ears absentmindedly as he spoke.

"I had some things I'd collected, mostly from guys who worked on the ranch and needed a few bucks for gas money. I wondered if any of the pots were worth a nickel. Coulda used the cash. She came out, we had a beer or two, got to talkin', hit it off. Besides whatever she did at Chaco, she told me she was gettin' her appraisal business started, workin' with a pardner. She landed a job to put the values on a big collection of Anasazi stuff headed off to Japland. Guess they call those old pots something else now, not Anasazi."

Slim stopped. "You part Pueblo?"

"No," Bernie said. "Navajo on all sides as far back as anyone remembers."

"Since Ellie lived in the employee housing there in the Chaco park, we used to meet up in Cuba. She had a storage locker out that way for some furniture, a bunch of books, boxes of potshards for her research, stuff like that. She had room in there to make pots, and she set up a little desk and files to do her paperwork for the business.

"Anyways, we'd dance at the bar, get a bottle of Cold Duck or Blue Nun, maybe a joint, and go back to the locker for some private time. We'd see the trailers and RVs and boats stored there and pretend we was on our way someplace exotic. We'd get to laughin' at those old silver Airstreams. Suppositories on wheels."

He paused. "That was more than you needed to know, right?"

Bernie sipped the cold water and glanced at the clutter of bachelordom intermixed with some Indian baskets, rocks, books, yellowed receipts, a few small but nice Navajo rugs. She waited for more of the story to unfold.

"Anyways," Slim said, "that Jap deal was the only time I saw her get riled up, seriously rubbed the wrong way."

"Why?" Bernie asked. "It seems that she would have appreciated the work because she was new in the business."

He chuckled. "I asked her that very thing. The guy wanted the values because he was sellin' the whole kit and caboodle to some rich Tokyo joker. I told her, 'Hell, Ellie, there's thousands of old pots around here. What do you care?' Lordy, I can still see her standin' there. She let me have it."

Slim pitched his voice a little higher. " 'America's patrimony!' 'Leaving forever!' 'Irreplaceable.' 'Unconscionable!' She would have bought those old pots herself just to keep 'em here if she'd had the moola."

He leaned away from the table, balancing the chair on its two back legs, causing Princess to wander off. Signaling, it seemed to Bernie, the end of his diatribe.

"It sounds like she knew quite a bit about Chaco Canyon pottery," Bernie said.

"It was her favorite thing in the whole wide world. She was especially partial to pottery that the Indians who lived right in the canyon made. She liked that better than what came in through trade or however else from other Indians or from the outliers on those big wide roads. You know about all that?"

"A little," Bernie said. "It's interesting to think of those roads, wide enough for a truck to drive on. I wonder why the old ones took the time and put in the effort to build them."

"Ellie and I talked about all that. I always figured folks came to Chaco to party, visit their kinfolks, maybe try to hook up with a wife. Pray a little, trade a little, then head on back home."

He stopped, grinned at her. "You're a pretty girl. Married?"

"Yes," she said. "You started telling me about Ellie not showing up for the appraisal last week."

"Not much else to say about that." Slim stopped talking. Readjusted his chair. Sipped his drink.

"That collection you mentioned, the one going to Japan. That might be the appraisal I need to ask her about," Bernie said. "Some pots she evaluated are coming to a museum in Santa Fe."

"Home again? That will make her happy. Ellie especially liked those tall pots. Cylinders, she called them, and they looked like that, too. She talked about them a lot, how rare they were. How pretty. She showed me a photo of one. It was kinda nice, I guess, but I just figured it was another skinny old pot."

He pushed his chair back and stood up. "Hold on a minute, missy. I'll be right back."

Princess looked after him, then crept beneath the table and put her chin on Bernie's knee. Bernie wasn't used to dogs in the house, but she gave her a few pats.

Slim returned with a photo. "I found this again last week. Jackson and I were goin' through stuff, gettin' ready for the appraisal when she didn't show up. This is the kind of pot she loves."

He handed Bernie a photo, probably taken twenty years ago. "Ellie's the gal with the pot."

A young woman, pale with light hair, held a cylindrical jar in front of her. Bernie noticed a triangle pattern that reminded her of the lieutenant's sketch. A second woman stood next to Ellie. She looked vaguely familiar.

Slim sat back down. "I'm kinda glad to hear you haven't had any luck finding Ellie. I thought she might be avoiding me."

"Do you have time for a couple more questions?"

"Ask away," Slim said. "I've got all day."

"Did Ellie mention going out of town, taking a trip to visit friends, anything like that?"

"No, ma'am. She sounded eager to do the job and kinda glad to come see me again, too."

"Did she ever talk about a man named Joe Leaphorn to you?"

"Not that I can remember, but I can't remember as good as I used to."

Bernie said, "You mention that you knew Jackson Benally. Have you ever had a problem with him?"

Slim hesitated. "Jack? He's a good man. Kinda young for his age because Mama won't let him sow any wild oats." He raised his eyebrows. "I've been around the block a time or two, missy. I can see where this is leading. Don't you be thinkin' that Jackson shot that policeman. He doesn't even like to kill rattlesnakes that get in the way of building a fence. Why did you ask me 'bout him?"

"Jackson's car may have been involved. He disappeared right after the shooting, and he lied to the investigator about being in class. He said he was with a friend, but the guy he says was with him is missing still."

"Friend? Who's that?"

"A young man named Leonard Nez," Bernie said.

"The Lizard?"

"You know him?" Jacobs, she realized, was a man of surprises.

"Lizard Nez? That guy is hot in rodeo. He hasn't gone missing. Check to see who's offering what prize money this month for bronc riding, and you'll him find there."

"Why wouldn't Jackson tell us that?"

Slim chuckled. "I imagine it has somethin' to do with his ferocious mama not likin' rodeo one little bit. Not wanting her precious son in any way, shape, or form involved in cowboyin'. As I see it,

Jackson's not especially interested in gettin' tossed in the dirt and stepped on. He goes with Lizard as sort of his manager. And to meet girls."

Bernie thought about that. A possibility.

"Did you ever have trouble with Jackson?"

Slim chuckled. "You asked me that already. You know how kids are. Jack has a touch of what I call attitude. Some growin' up ahead of him. But no. As long as he knows what I expect, he delivers."

Bernie thought of Darleen. The description would fit her, too.

Slim rose, took her water glass and his. Refilled them both from the tap. Added a single ice cube from the freezer to each. Sat down again. Princess angled up and waddled toward the front porch, pushing the door open with her nose.

"What does Jackson do here?"

"I guess you could call him an apprentice or assistant or some- thin'," Slim said. "He's good with numbers, helps with the taxes and government red tape. He works hard outside if I need that. Besides helpin' me, he goes out to a little dig once in a while." He glanced to the right, out past the fence, toward the horizon. "It's all on the up and up. My own land. Jackson works those jobs with Maxie on his own time, as long as no burials are involved. He tells me he likes learnin' a little about archaeology, but I think he knows a handsome woman when one comes his way."

"Maxie Davis? Is she the other woman in the picture?"

Slim said, "Yeah. Maxie calls herself Dr. Davis. You know her?"

Bernie nodded. "What kind of work is she doing out here?"

Slim said, "Well, that's a story. One of those roads from Chaco Canyon we were jawin' about earlier, turns out it went right through the ranch, or where the ranch would have been if I'd been around a thousand years ago. Maxie told me all that. She wanted to do some diggin' here, research. Called me out of the blue. I told her go ahead. She found a little compound. Some kind of settlement."

"That's interesting."

"They've got all sorts of high-tech stuff now to find ruins underground," Slim said. "But Dr. Davis—hell, I used to just call her Maxie, but now she's Dr. Davis. She didn't need any of that fancy stuff. She remembered seeing some of the pieces of pots out here and just followed her intuition. Bingo."

"So I guess from the photo you knew her in the old days, too?"

"Maxie's not the kinda gal a cowboy forgets, even though I was partial to Ellie. When Maxie came out to talk about the dig, she remembered me taking that photo of her and Ellie together, asked if I still had it. I told her no; I'd forgotten all about it. Then she asked if I had any of the photos she took when she worked with Ellie. I told her no, again."

Slim shook his head. "Ellie holds on to all that old stuff. That Ellie's a free spirit, but she kept an eye on her business records. She told me if she came across somethin' similar for a new appraisal, she could cross-check. Save herself a bunch of time."

"Did Davis say why she wanted a photo of the two of them?"

"I asked her. She said those were hard times for her and she didn't want a record of them. Next time she came out, she asked about the photo again. I told her I'd given it to Ellie just to shut her up."

Bernie sipped her water. Thought it over. "How did Davis help with the appraisals?

"Maxie took the pictures. Left Ellie to do the real work. I remember that on my job they came twice, first to look at the stuff. Ellie would take notes and Maxie snapped the pictures. Then they'd come back with the report. Ellie would sit out on the porch and we'd talk about the values, or just shoot the breeze, while Maxie would get new photos. Always seemed like some of hers would be fuzzy or something."

Bernie said, "Sounds like a good team."

Slim said, "That's what I thought, too. But when Maxie was out just lately to work on her dig, she started askin' me questions about

Ellie's records. Did I know where she kept 'em, things like that. I figured if Ellie hadn't kept her up to speed, it wasn't my place to do it. Told her to ask Ellie."

Princess stayed fast asleep on the porch, not even raising her head for a last bark, as Bernie left. When she got back to her car, she called Chee about the Davis/Ellie connection and the mysterious Leonard Nez, rodeo star in the making. She reminded him to run a background check on Ellie, and to add Davis to the assignment.

"And Collingsworth, too?" Chee asked.

"Why not?" Then she found a spot of shade and ate her sandwich before she drove out to Mama's house.

16

Chee checked in at the Shiprock station, learned nothing new, and was headed out the door for the Window Rock meeting with Mrs. Benally and Largo when his intercom buzzed. A call from Largo on line one.

"What the bejesus were you doing out at Chaco Canyon?" Captain Largo did not sound happy.

Chee bristled. Largo had no right to pry into his personal life.

"We went to Santa Fe to see Leaphorn. Bernie hadn't been to Chaco since high school, so we stopped there on the way back."

"And got wrapped up in a potential homicide?"

"Homicide?"

"Park personnel found a body off the trail. The trail where you sent them," Largo said.

"We met a woman who had seen something odd. It didn't seem like anything much. We reported it to a ranger."

"Yeah. That's always how this stuff starts out." Largo sighed. "Cordova wants to talk to you. Out there. He's on his way now."

"I already told the ranger, a guy named Stephen, everything the woman told us. What about Mrs. Benally and the meeting?"

Largo said, "You know how this all works with the feds. I'll ask Wheeler to talk to Mrs. Benally."

"It's a long drive out there," Chee said.

"Use the time to think about the Leaphorn case." Largo paused, and Chee heard the change in his tone of voice. "How is he doing?"

Chee thought about what to say. "He's on a bunch of machines and a lot of drugs to keep him quiet. The surgeon removed part of his skull for the swelling. Even with all that, I think he might have recognized us."

"Did he tell you who did it? Who shot him?"

"He can't talk yet," Chee said. "We asked him if he knew the shooter, and Bernie could tell he wanted to write a message. But he wasn't strong enough."

"Damn," Largo said.

As Chee headed out to Chaco, he reviewed what he knew about the Leaphorn shooting. The obvious suspect, Jackson Benally, didn't fit the profile of a killer. Leonard Nez didn't have a record of violence or any connection to the lieutenant as far as Chee could find. Garrison Tsosie? A whisper of a motive and a solid alibi.

Louisa? That was a different story. No reports of her Jeep showing up anywhere. Largo told him the feds had checked with the personnel office at Northern Arizona University and with her colleagues there. No record of any conferences she'd planned to attend that month. Not much in her file other than academic records. She listed Leaphorn as her emergency contact.

After that, the list was as broad as the lieutenant's long career, the legwork intense, and the trail getting cold. Ellie, who rudely left Leaphorn to have lunch by himself? Some ex-con with a grudge? A random cop hater who stole the Benally car, put it back, and disappeared?

Chee pulled his police unit into the left lane, glanced at the drivers, all cruising along at the speed limit with both hands on the wheel. No doubt with their cell phones on their laps, waiting for him to pass to go back to texting while sipping their coffee, eating a sweet roll, and applying makeup or shaving. Traffic was light, the sky cloudless and blue as a pale white man's eyes.

As he drove, Chee thought about Louisa's account of the lieutenant and a ghost from the past. He thought about Eleanor Friedman–Bernal and what Bernie had learned about her lowball appraisals. From what Davis said, Ellie was a shifty character. Chee remembered meeting the man who nearly killed her, Randall Elliot. He had seemed civil, smart, concerned that Ellie was missing.

Chee wondered, again, what motivated a man to commit a serious crime to cover up a lesser crime. To his Navajo Police way of thinking, illegal excavation for academic prestige wasn't much of an offense compared to battery with deadly intentions. Something else about Elliot and the case snagged at the edge of his memory. If only he could ask the lieutenant.

Chee flashed back to the visit to the hospital and thought about Bernie. He found himself continually amazed and delighted by her savvy. Bernie had great instincts, good intuition, a wonderful way of dealing with people. She would find out all about Ellie at the Double X Ranch with no problem. Then Bernie could contact her, put Leaphorn's AIRC job to rest. She might come up with something that would raise Ellie to legitimate suspect level or, more likely, eliminate her from the suspect pool.

Chee passed the little settlement of Nageezi and turned off toward Chaco. He cruised past the few dry homesteads, a handful of bored cows standing in the sun. He thought about the lieutenant, remembering the American Automobile Association map of the Navajo Nation that hung on his wall. The lieutenant marked each type of crime with a different colored pushpin, and used the map to discover patterns. He wondered what sort of tracking Leaphorn would do to solve his own case.

Bouncing along the empty road, Chee remembered how green the lieutenant had looked on the helicopter flight back to civilization after they had rescued Ellie. That was one of the first and only times he'd sensed that his occasional boss and frequent critic had some human weakness. During that turbulent trip, Leaphorn had honored him by asking him to do a Blessing Way ceremony. He never knew what fierce evil the lieutenant had encountered in that ruin-filled canyon, and never asked.

After the death of his uncle and teacher Hosteen Nakai, Chee had discontinued his studies to become a *hataalii*. Now, he couldn't do a traditional healing ceremony for the lieutenant, complete with sacred songs and sand paintings. But he could arrange it, make some calls today, get to work on that project. The lieutenant's interest in the ritual had surprised him, but the man had always kept Chee off guard.

When the road forked, Chee turned onto the main branch toward the visitor center, the route he and Bernie had driven yesterday. His police unit, a heavy-duty SUV, handled the washboard, sand traps, and potholes about as well, or as poorly, as his truck had. When it rained, this road became treacherously slick. Campers, SUVs, minivans full of hapless tourists had slipped off and gotten stuck out here. That was when the visitors realized cell phones aren't as smart as the commercials claim.

He thought about the dead woman up ahead. What would the people Karen heard have been arguing about? What if this wasn't murder, but a hiking accident? Chee mulled it over as he pulled out to pass a white Honda with Texas plates. What if Long Sleeves had talked about suicide, and Dorky Hat invited her out here to cheer her up? The cheering-up doesn't work. Dorky Hat gets annoyed that Long Sleeves won't listen to reason. They argue, and Long Sleeves pulls the trigger, shoots herself.

He rejected it even before he got to the end of the scenario. If a person really wanted to kill herself, why would she agree to come

here in the first place? And what kind of person runs off and aban-
dons a suicidal friend who has a gun? Or, after the gunshot, leaves
the dead or maybe just injured friend behind without calling for
help?

Murder, cold-blooded assault or a shooting sparked by anger,
seemed to be the only scenario that made sense. The crime would
have gone undiscovered longer if it hadn't been for Karen's inad-
vertent eavesdropping and the coincidence of their meeting in the
campground.

Chee noticed a dust plume rising on the road ahead and switched
his air conditioner to recirculate. He caught up with a black van with
New Mexico plates, passed it, and drove into the park, finally on
pavement again. Just beyond Pueblo Bonito, someone had placed a
Road Closed notice over the Park Service's descriptive sign. A Chaco ranger had blocked the end of the loop with his truck to keep out
the tourists. He motioned Chee's SUV through with a wave.

Chee cruised past the empty parking lot toward two sets of stone
ruins. The gate that kept visitors from driving any farther than the
picnic table and trail registry stood open, and a San Juan County
sheriff's car waited there. He recognized the deputy, Tim Morris,
an officer he'd worked with on a child custody case that involved a
Navajo mother and an oil field father from Shiprock.

Chee rolled down the window to greet Morris. "So you're the
lucky guy who got the call?"

"That's me," Morris said. "How you doing? Haven't seen you
since you tied the knot. How's married life working out?"

"Luckiest man in the world. Where's Agent Cordova?"

Morris pointed to the mesa top. "Up that way."

"You're kidding."

The deputy shook his head. "There's a trail on the other side of
those ruins that leads up the cliff side. Cordova said to tell you he'd
meet you on top. Did you see the Omega van?"

"Black, big, someone's idea of anonymous? Yeah, behind me," Chee said. "Must be somebody new coming for the body. He's taking those washboards too slow."

Chee drove through. He parked next to the Crown Victoria and climbed out, slapped by the dry, penetrating heat. He found the trail that led to the Pueblo de Arroyo ruins, old stone walls that had once been buildings, up ahead. He walked for fifteen minutes, searching for the trail to Pueblo Alto, another set of ruins off the beaten path in a place that was off the beaten path to start with. He stuck to a narrow route that ascended into the boulders above the Pueblo de Arroyo ruins, startling a pair of brown snakes beautifully camouflaged to blend in to the rocks. He followed a series of little brown signs that read "Trail."

Finally, he saw "Trail" with an arrow pointing toward the sky and noticed part of a footprint in the sand. An interesting impression, he thought, a swirly design.

Hiking turned to climbing now and involved using his hands for balance and to pull himself through the first section of the steep ascent. After that, the route required squeezing forward through a narrow slot. He paused a moment in the shade of the sandstone crevice, enjoying the coolness. If he had been wearing something other than his boots, Chee thought, the climb would have been much easier. He should have brought some water. Why is it the feds never tell you anything?

He emerged from the slot onto the mesa top to discover a flatter trail and a view that included Pueblo Arroyo, the deputy's car, and the fed-mobile. He trotted along the path, noticing the gray rock that resembled petrified mud. The vista opened to a panorama of sun-dried country divided by the curving dry Chaco Wash. He saw a rust-colored spot on a giant piece of eroded sandstone and, when he looked at it closely, realized he was seeing fossilized shrimp. The mesa ascended gently to his left in a series of dry washes and ledges.

Hiking to the top would be easier than the hike he had just made. He couldn't see the Pueblo Alto ruins yet; that involved another span of hiking. Why had Cordova wanted him up here?

He found the FBI agent crouched near a big circle of rocks, taking pictures. Chee hailed him.

"That's quite a climb."

"It is," Cordova said. "Glad you got here before the Omega team."

"I passed them on the washboards," Chee said. "They are at least twenty minutes out. What's up?"

"I understand you were the one who reported something suspicious out here," Cordova said. "You and your cute wife."

Chee said, "A woman we met at the campground had heard something that bothered her." He retold the story, searching his memory for Karen's exact words against the current of jealousy Cordova raised in him. "Karen's driving a white Camry, probably 2012. Colorado plate. She's the one you guys need to talk to."

Cordova asked questions about the argument story, focusing on descriptions. Chee remembered Karen describing a person in a hat running along the trail after the gunshot.

"Did she know if the person who left was a woman?"

Chee said, "I think she figured they were both women. But from her description, it could have been a boy. No deep voices involved."

Cordova laughed. "For once, we get a break. Ever notice how some women blame all the evils of the world on men? At least, my wife does.

"Karen Dundee is your witness's full name," Cordova continued. "We tracked her from her campground registration and eventually found her son in Denver, who said she was planning to go to Grand Canyon next. Evidently she's the only person in America without a cell phone. The highway patrol is tracking down the car."

"Why did you call me out here? We could have talked about all this on the radio."

"Two reasons." Cordova took in the view. Put his hands in his pockets and took them out again. "The bureau is trying to be more sensitive to Native American issues, to work with the Navajo Police and other tribal law enforcement more closely. Chaco is surrounded by the reservation. Since you two called the body to our attention, it made sense for you to be the liaison in case any Native jurisdictional issues are involved."

He smiled at Chee. "I hear you're a good tracker. That could help here, too. And since we're both working that Leaphorn case, I figured we could get better acquainted."

Cordova gestured toward the spot where Chee had seen him crouching. "I noticed some footprints in the sand here. Snapped a photo of them. I've seen others like them up here, too. Take a look."

Chee squatted close to the print. Different from the swirly one. Of course, he thought, this is a hiking trail. If he searched hard enough he could probably find dozens of different prints, an encyclopedia of shoe soles. Should he be grumpy about being stereotyped as an Indian scout, or complimented that the FBI was asking for his help?

Cordova gazed south toward the vast country, dotted with un-excavated ruins. "When the office got the call from park security that they'd found the body, the ranger here suggested that it might be suicide. What do you think?"

"I don't think this was suicide. Maybe Dorky Hat . . . " Chee paused. "Karen gave the women nicknames, and Bernie and I kept them. Anyway, maybe the one in the hat was trying to talk the other woman, Long Sleeves we called her, out of killing herself. Or during the argument Dorky Hat killed Long Sleeves, but not on purpose. Long Sleeves is ready to pull the trigger, Dorky Hat struggles to get the gun. It goes off, and Dorky Hat gets scared and runs. But I don't think it was suicide."

"All right, then." The way Cordova said it, Chee knew that it meant *Discussion closed.* Cordova led the way to the cliff side, careful to walk only on the rock. He had on dress shoes, Chee noticed, also bad for hiking.

Cordova stopped. "Take a look at this."

Chee followed his gaze to the edge of the sandstone cliff. He noticed a fenced area beyond it, below on the canyon floor.

"That's Richard Wetherill's grave. Have you heard of him?"

"Probably," Cordova said. "Remind me."

"He was the first person who did any excavations here. Had a trading post at Chaco, too." Chee could see the grave marker for Wetherill inside the fence and a simple unpaved trail from the parking lot to the burial site.

He told Cordova more about Wetherill and his wife Marietta, and about the controversy around his murder by a Navajo employee.

When he was done, Cordova nodded. "That's not what I wanted you to see. Notice those rocks?"

Chee examined the honey-colored cliffs, scanning the ledges and the boulders and vertical sandstone slabs that had broken free and tumbled down centuries ago, or maybe only decades ago. Behind the cliff that created a towering natural wall for the cemetery, he saw a body wedged in the rock. "Have you been down there?"

"Yes. She fell from up here."

Chee thought about how to ask what he needed to know. "You worked many suicides?"

"I was a beat cop before I joined the feds." Cordova's tone was cold. "I know the difference. Animals have been at her, but this was a gunshot to the chest. Women don't usually off themselves that way. "

So, Chee thought, the questions about suicide were a test. He didn't regret showing off about Richard Wetherill as much as he had a few minutes ago.

"Any ID?"

"Not that I found. No suicide note either. If she had anything, the killer may have taken it. The Omega crew gets paid to deal with maggots and body parts. They might find something. But feel free to look before they get here."

"Why climb all the way up here to murder somebody?"

"I've been considering that," Cordova said. "Maybe these two were partners. Lovers. Long Sleeves tells Dorky Hat it's over while they're hiking. She has a gun because they're camping. Spontaneous crime of passion."

"I like the crime-of-passion aspect," Chee said. "There are lots of places to kill somebody out here where a body could stay for years before somebody found it. This isn't one of them. That supports the impulsive aspect."

"It seems isolated enough to me," Cordova said. "She could have been out here for months without being discovered."

Chee looked at the cliff side, tracing the trajectory of the fall in his mind. He saw the ledges and outcroppings where the victim's body would have hit, bounced to hit again, and finally stopped. Cordova was right: the woman had fallen from around the place where they now stood. And he doubted the positioning was accidental. If the shooting had been elsewhere, the body would have needed a push to fall from the mesa top. At this overlook, the percussion from the chest blast would have sent it flying backward.

"Did you notice these swirl tracks anywhere else?" Chee pointed to a track in a place where sand had blown into a slight flat place on the rock.

"No. To tell you the truth, I didn't see those down there."

"Do you remember the victim's boots?"

"Hikers. Leather-and-fabric combination. Smallish. I didn't see the brand."

"The soles?"

"Hmmm. I don't recall."

Chee glanced down at Cordova's dusty shoes. Expensive. The FBI paid well.

"I'm going to snoop around a little," he said. Chee walked along the mesa top, looking for more hollows carved out by wind and water that might hold tracks. The surface was mostly rock. He found nothing at first, then a cigarette butt, which called his attention to a small patch of sand with a partial impression of swirled sole. Then a slightly larger print, waffle sole. Then a trace of a smooth sole from a larger shoe—Cordova, not watching where he stepped.

Chee squatted down and motioned Cordova over to the next shallow sandy basin. "You might want to get a photo of these prints, the swirl and the waffle track. The cigarette butt over there might be part of this, too."

"Unfiltered," Cordova said. "Like the Camels I used to smoke." He pointed at the swirly print. "You think this might be Dorky Hat?"

"Could be."

"Interesting that little bowl is perfectly round," Cordova said.

"Man-made," Chee said. "They call these pecked basins. Water collectors. They are up here because of the stone circles." Chee moved next to some large stones. "Look for more rocks like these, and you'll begin to see a pattern."

"Hmmm," Cordova said.

"When I was at UNM, the archaeology department was doing all sorts of work here. They think these circles had ceremonial uses. The catchment basins were for water for the people who came up here for ceremonies. Or for a ceremony that needed water."

Cordova said, "I think we're done. Let me know if you have any insights."

A raven glided over the cliff side, and Chee watched it settle on the rocks next to where the dead woman lay. "I'll check around down there before they move her. Keep the birds from doing any more damage."

Cordova said, "Make sure I didn't miss anything."

Chee nodded, not sure if Cordova was joking. "Is that trail we took the only way down?"

"That's what park security told me."

As he headed off, Chee smiled at the change in his mood. Without Cordova's summons, he never would have climbed up here. It was beautiful. Sensational. He had read that farther along, past where they had stopped to look down on the body, you could see the wide roadbeds the people of Chaco built and some of the steps they'd carved into the rock. He'd have to bring Bernie here.

After he climbed down, Chee crept along the base of the cliff face, moving toward the body, hunting for places a gun might have lodged itself. Discovering black-and-white potshards, lizard tracks, elk droppings. Even having seen the woman from the mesa, he had trouble finding her until he drew close enough for the unforgettable smell of death to lead the way. He heard a vehicle on the road and saw the black SUV parking near the Wetherill cemetery. Chee hurried.

His approach up into the boulder field scared the raven onto a pile of rocks. It perched, keeping an eye on him, biding its time. Chee neared the body, hoping for tracks and finding a few spots that held the three-toed impressions left by ravens, some coyote paw prints, and the ropelike path of a snake. He saw no shoe or boot tracks, no sign that whoever killed her had climbed down to make sure she was dead.

The victim would have been about five foot three, Chee figured. And as well as he could determine, she was dead when she fell.

He filled his lungs with fresh air and pulled his shirt over his nose to help with the smell. He walked to where the victim's cheeks, eyes, lips, and nose would have been. Predators love soft tissue. He noticed brown hair with gray at the temples. A glint of light caught his eye, something on the wrist reflecting the sun. He pushed the shirtsleeve away with the toe of his boot. Beneath it, a wide silver bracelet. Sand-cast with a heart design. He bent over the corpse to see the bottom of her boots. Waffle soles. A common pattern, but her feet seemed to be the right size to match the tracks on the mesa top.

He straightened up, took several long strides away from the body. Grabbed a breath of fresher air as he scanned the area, surveying the slope that angled below her. No backpack or wallet had worked its way loose during the flight down the cliff face. No weapon.

Chee took the trail back the way he had come, feeling the heat of the sun through his shirt and the sweat beneath his hat. He tried to calm his roiling stomach, forget the sight of what had once been a human face. The old ones advised staying away from the dead, and he agreed with the soundness of this ancient wisdom every time the job brought him together with someone like Long Sleeves.

Chee heard the voices and saw the hazard jackets of the Omega crew. As they came closer, he noticed a familiar face, a retired cop he knew from Farmington.

"Hey, Jim Chee," the man said. "Hot day for a hike."

"Right," Chee said. "Bad place for a body."

"Is there a good place?"

Back at the parking lot he found Cordova sitting in his car, engine running. Chee felt the cool rush of his air-conditioning when the FBI man rolled down the window.

"Anything else?"

"You might want to check in those rocks a bit to the right, up from the body," he said. "One of those fancy water bottles. Hasn't been there long enough to get sunburned. Might help with the ID."

"Okay," Cordova said.

"Her boots probably made the waffle prints you photographed."

"Anything else I should know?"

"She's wearing a bracelet." Chee described it.

"Like the one Bernie saw?"

"Seems like it."

"Thanks for coming out today," Cordova said. "This gal might have been the one who shot Leaphorn."

Chee's Navajo Police unit was stifling, hotter even than the air outside. He left the doors open a minute, then climbed onto the scorching seat, started the engine, turned the air-con up full blast, and rolled down the windows. He drove with the wind blowing away recollections of the rancid odor of death. He stopped at the visitor center for a drink of water and to say hello to Wakara, the park's head of security, a Ute from near Cortez, and tell him what he'd learned.

Wakara said, "The drought has meant more dead elk around here. Without you and Bernie, we might have figured that was drawing the birds. Not a dead person."

Chee called Largo from Wakara's office.

"So, all the feds need to do is ID the body and then figure out why this white woman would want to shoot Leaphorn," Largo said.

"That's what Wakara said, too," Chee told him. "Piece of cake."

"Tell him hello for me," Largo said. "By the way, we got the results of two of those background checks you wanted. Collingsworth and Friedman or Friedman-Bernal?"

"Yeah?"

"Both clean, as far as we can tell," Largo said. "Still working on Davis. Evidently Maxie is a nickname. You don't know her real first name, do you?"

"Never heard it."

"Never mind," Largo said. "You need to get back to the Shiprock office. Mrs. Benally wants to talk to you about Leonard Nez."

"She's coming to Shiprock?"

"Yeah," Largo said. "You're in luck. She has a sister who lives there." Largo told him the time Mrs. Benally expected to arrive. "Good luck with that."

As he got close to home, Chee remembered the cat. He'd stop at the house quickly since it was on the way to the station and leave it some food, make sure it had water. When he climbed out of his unit, he noticed the dirt on the floor mat. He had a little time before Mrs. Benally was due, so he looked unsuccessfully in the logical places for the vacuum. It had been a wedding gift from some of his relatives, presented with much joking about how he would be the one to use it.

He called Bernie on her cell. From the TV in the background, he knew she was at her mother's house.

"You're vacuuming?"

"Don't get your hopes up," he said. "I was out at Chaco again today. Now my unit is full of sand."

She told him where to find it. "While you're at it, the house could use some attention, too. Cat hair. What were you doing back at Chaco?"

"I got called to help Cordova." He told about the bracelet.

"If that woman is the one who shot Leaphorn, why is she dead? How did she get the Benally car? And who is she?"

"Good questions," Chee said. 'I'm going to check with Cordova when I get to the office, see how the feds are doing on the answers."

17

Bernie hung up the phone and tried to push away her frustration. She ought to be helping Chee. Not with the vacuuming. With the case.

Mama had smiled when she drove up. "Oldest daughter, I was not expecting to see you today. You are a blessing." Then Mama went back to work sweeping the porch slowly, systematically. The paint had faded on her old broom, the straw worn down to six inches from the base.

Bernie said, "Is Sister here?"

"I don't think so."

"Do you know where she is?"

"She went somewhere in the car," Mama said. "Don't worry about her so much. Tell me what you've been doing."

Bernie moved a couple of kitchen chairs out to the porch, and she and Mama sat in the shade. She talked about meeting Slim Jacobs that morning and about her visit to Chaco Canyon.

"I have never been to that place," Mama said. "But I remember it from the old stories."

Bernie knew the stories, too. The story of the Great Gambler who enslaved the Pueblo people who lived there by winning their possessions, wives, children, and finally the men themselves. A Navajo man, with the help of the Holy People, beat the Gambler at his own games and freed the Pueblos. Bernie also remembered the story of how the fifth Diné clan joined with the four original clans at Chaco Canyon, moving with the People to the banks of the San Juan River.

They heard the car before they saw it, music blaring from the speakers through the open windows. Darleen pulled into the driveway, hit the brake, generated a cloud of dust.

"Hey, Sister," Darleen yelled at her. "You come around? Good fa you."

Bernie said, "I finished an interview and figured I'd stop by. You were driving pretty fast there, like one of those NASCAR guys."

Darleen stumbled as she climbed out of the car, leaving the door open, engine running. She leaned against the roof.

"I like fast," Darleen said.

Bernie jogged to the car, reached past Darleen, close enough to smell the alcohol, and turned off the ignition. She saw three crushed beer cans on the passenger floor.

"You shouldn't drive when you've been drinking. You could die. Die or kill somebody."

Darleen laughed. "I'm gonna die anyway. What sa difference? You're a cop. Arrest me." She moved away from the car, swaying, nearly losing her balance.

Bernie put her arms out to catch her if she fell. Darleen lurched away.

"Lee me alone," Darleen said. "Doan touch me. I'm none a your bidness."

Mama said, "Youngest daughter, are you sick?"

"Yeah." Darleen wiped at her mouth. "Sick a bein' trapped here wid you. Sick of Miz Law n Order who knows every single goddamn thing pickin' on me for everythin' I do."

Mama said something in Navajo, something harsh concerning Darleen's swearing.

Another car pulled up, a dust-colored Chevy. Bernie recognized the driver: Stoop Boy, Charley Zah. He yelled out the window at Darleen. "I've been looking everywhere for you. We're late. Get in." Darleen had started toward his car even before it stopped.

"She can't go anywhere with you," Bernie said. "She's drunk."

"What's new?" he said.

Darleen trotted over with a lopsided gait. Stoop Boy pushed open the passenger door, and she lurched in.

"I'll take care of her," Sloop Boy said. "Don't worry."

"Where are you going? When will you be back? It's not safe for her to be out like that." Bernie's words disappeared in the sound of tires crunching on the gravel, the rumble of the engine.

Mama made the clicking sound she did when things weren't right. "You should have made her stay here."

"How? She's a grown woman."

"You are her big sister," Mama said. "You have to take care of her. That is why we have families, relatives. We have to take care of each other."

"I'm doing the best I can," Bernie said.

Mama shook her head. "It's not enough. Your sister needs you. She is too young to be so angry."

Bernie felt grief settle in with the same precise efficiency as her mother's work with the broom on the porch. She had seen too much of the evil that alcohol brought. She didn't need to experience it again with her baby sister.

"I think she's beginning to hate me," Bernie said. "Every time I try to help, try to tell her what to do, she just gets mad."

"I know." Mama patted her hand. "You do what you can. These things take time."

It's not fair, Bernie thought. Why did she have to be the dependable one and Darleen always the problem child? "I wish Sister would live up to her responsibilities."

"Don't concern yourself about that today." Mama wrapped her bony fingers around Bernie's forearm. "Be happy. You and I can spend the day together, my daughter. I am hoping that you will find the book again with the picture of the rug about the Holy People."

"I'd like to see that again, too," Bernie said.

She helped Mama over the threshold and into the house and then to the bathroom. She went into the kitchen and poured them each a glass of water. Even though she seldom drank alcohol, a cold Bud would taste great. She smiled at the thought. Darleen's problem with alcohol inspiring her to want a beer?

Bernie found the book, and Mama sat with her at the kitchen table, carefully studying the photograph of Hosteen Klah and his rug. She would enjoy her mother, Bernie decided, and not let Darleen's craziness spoil that.

Bernie noticed some magazines and catalogs from an auction of Native American art and artifacts on the table. "These are interesting. Where did they come from?"

"Stella got them at the library, on that free shelf," Mama said. "She saw one of my old rugs in the catalog with the blue cover. Look how much they have for the starting bid." Bernie thumbed through to find the page. The full-color photograph showed the rug to good advantage.

"I remember watching you make that rug when I was a little girl. Then we drove it over to the Crownpoint auction."

Mama laughed. "Only rich people could buy it now. They could buy a refrigerator for that money. They could get a refrigerator, and have enough left for one of those rugs that look like Navajo. You know, the ones that they make in Mexico."

Bernie chuckled. "You did beautiful work, Mama. The world

doesn't have many women who know how to make something so fine. That rug is worth more than twenty refrigerators. It's priceless."

Mama glanced at her gnarled hands. "Are you weaving now?"

"Not yet," Bernie said.

"You have to practice," Mama said. "Every day, like you used to."

Bernie leafed through the catalog. "These pots remind me of the ones my friend was researching." Showing the pictures to Mama, she noticed that the starting bids for the cylinders were twice as high as those for the rounder bowls, even though the bowls were larger. Interesting, she thought.

"Your friend was the one who got shot?" Mama asked.

Bernie nodded. She handed the catalog, open to the pots, to Mama, who looked at the pictures closely. "Made by the old ones," she said. "Touched by their hands."

When Mama went into the bedroom for a nap, Bernie sat on the edge of the bed. Mama said, "I am thinking about Darleen. When she comes back, I will tell her she is not welcome in my house when she's drinking." And then, for the first time Bernie could remember since her father died, Mama started to cry.

After Mama fell asleep, Bernie thought about how to handle things if Mama actually did tell Darleen to stop drinking or leave—and Darleen left. She reviewed the mental list of relatives who might help, with no immediate candidates, then pushed the potential problem aside. Maybe Mama's threat would get Darleen to shape up—but she couldn't bring herself to believe it.

She found her old textbooks again, and after twenty minutes, she discovered the information she wanted. The cylindrical pots the AIRC was about to acquire, if they had been made at Pueblo Bonito or one of the other Great Houses rather than at an outlier, were very rare. The Pueblo ancestors made little pottery in the great stone settlements. Most of the pottery uncovered in the Chaco ruins had been created outside the canyon and hauled in over those mysterious ancient roadways. The rarity of the design, the scarcity of Chaco-made pots in general, and the fact that the pots would have survived intact for a thousand years meant that they were close to priceless. Why had the EFB appraisal valued them so low?

An idea flashed in her brain. What if the pots were not Chacoan, like the Navajo rugs made in Mexico that Mama mentioned? What if the low appraisal was actually correct?

The buzz of her cell phone broke her concentration. Chee, she thought. But the voice on the other end of the line belonged to Captain Largo. He got right to business.

"I'd like you back on Monday," he said. "Bigman's got vacation scheduled, so we'll be a little short otherwise at Shiprock. That work?"

That gave her four days to clear up the appraisal for the AIRC, find Ellie Friedman, find out who shot Leaphorn. And arrange a caregiver for Mama if Darleen got mad and left or kept drinking.

"That works for me," Bernie said.

"You doin' okay?"

Bernie said, "I'll be a whole lot better when we figure out who shot the lieutenant."

"Me too," Largo said. "By the way, Mrs. Benally seems to have tracked down Leonard Nez."

"That's good news. What did he say?"

"I don't know yet. Chee's on it. You'll probably hear before I do."

18

Chee had just pulled into the Shiprock substation parking lot when his cell phone vibrated. He looked at the number. Mrs. Benally. As usual, she got right to the point.

"I can't come to Shiprock today because my sister is sick," she said. "Remember I told you I'd bring in Lizard?"

"I remember. Captain Largo told me you wanted to talk to me about that."

"I know where he is," she said.

"Where?"

"Oh, no," she said. "First I get my car back, and Jackson comes home."

Jackson was still in jail as a "person of interest." Unless they came up with charges against him, which seemed unlikely, he would be freed in the morning.

"You know, sometimes people get arrested for withholding in-formation the police need," Chee said.

"You got no reason to put an old lady in jail. If you do, who will take you to Lizard?"

Chee told her he would check on the car, do what he could for Jackson, and call her back.

Luck was on his side. The crime lab had finished. Mrs. Benally's sedan could be released at 8:00 a.m. the next day. He called her back.

She said, "You give me a ride over there. We get the car. We get Jackson. Then we talk to Lizard." Before he could say anything, she hung up.

Inside the substation, he had a premonition of bad news. He felt sadness in the air.

The receptionist didn't wait for him to ask. "The hospital chaplain, a Reverend Rodriguez, called for you." She handed Chee a slip of paper. "He asked me to have you get in touch as soon as you could. He thinks you're Lieutenant Leaphorn's nephew or something."

She looked up, and he saw her tears. "I asked how he was coming along. At first he didn't say anything. Then he said now would be good to remember him in our prayers."

Chee went into his cubicle of an office, closed the door, and dialed.

Rodriguez got right to the point. "You mentioned your friend wanting a healing ceremony?"

"He does."

"I saw your note, and I was checking into my connections with the native community here in Santa Fe to see if someone could help you. Then I ran into Dr. Moxsley. He said he thinks it might be good to do it soon. He asked me to tell you and your wife that Mr. Leaphorn has developed pneumonia."

Chee realized he'd been holding his breath. Exhaled. Waited for Rodriguez to say something more. He knew about pneumonia in hospitals. That was what had killed his uncle. He remembered Bernie telling him that the lieutenant wanted him, Jim Chee himself, to do the praying.

The chaplain kept talking. "Because Mr. Leaphorn is in our critical care unit, there are more rules to follow than if he were on a regular floor, but I'll help you as much as I can." Rodriguez recited the litany: No smoke, fire, or smudge sticks, because most of the CCU patients were on oxygen. No drums. All chanting had to be quiet. The list went on.

"Fine," Chee said. "I can't get a singer on such short notice, but I've had some training, enough so I can improvise. I'll leave as soon as I can."

"I know you have a long drive," Rodriguez said. "Let me know when you get to Santa Fe, and I'll meet you at the hospital. I want to make sure you don't run into trouble with anybody in CCU. Call me. Don't worry about how late it is."

Chee contacted Largo, asked for the rest of the day off. Got it when he mentioned pneumonia. Then he called Bernie and told her what Rodriguez had said.

"I'm going home to do a sweat, get my thoughts together. And then we can head out." He paused. "That is, I'm hoping you'll go with me. It would mean a lot to have you there."

"I want to go. I have to take care of a few things here. I'll call you when I leave Mama."

"Thank you," he said. "I love you."

Because of his long apprenticeship with his uncle, Chee knew better than most the danger that could result from performing sacred rituals in a manner that was less than perfect. It was impossible and dangerous to do a traditional healing ceremony outside the embrace of Dinetah, trapped in a city hospital. Impossible to do the ceremony indoors, without contact with the earth and sky, without the person to be healed seated on the ground so the sacred sand painting would encircle him. Some hospitals on the reservation had hogans for the singers and their ceremonies. Santa Fe was far away from Dinetah, and the one who got shot depended on machines to keep him alive.

Chee made a call to the daughter of a singer who lived near Tsa-
lie. The woman, a clan sister, had heard about Leaphorn's shooting.
"He would like some prayers and he has asked me to help with this.
I need to speak to your mother's brother to ask his advice," Chee
said. "They say that the one in the hospital may die soon."

"I think the one who got shot is a good man," the woman said.
"And I remember when my Angela got in trouble with that boy
from Chinle. You gave her a talking-to. It helped." The singer lived
without a telephone, so she would drive to the old man's home and
then call him back.

He waited half an hour for her call.

"I found him tinkering with the tractor. I told him what you
wanted. The *hataalii* is with me now. I'm handing him the phone."

Chee listened to the gravelly old voice speaking Navajo. The
instructions ran long.

Then, with a sense of somber purpose, Chee prepared a sweat
bath in his special spot along the river. He thought of Hosteen Nakai, much-missed uncle and teacher, as he sang the songs of purifica-
tion he had learned. Healing concerned more than the body. Death
had its place. That's why the Hero Twins had saved Sa, the monster
who brought death to the world. Without Sa, the old ones who
were tired of life would get no relief. He'd learned about death, not
only from his wise uncle, who welcomed it with a peaceful heart,
but from his experience as a policeman. Death deserved respect, but
Chee had seen many things more frightening.

Mama glanced up from the book with the photographs of Hosteen
Klah's weavings.

"Was that the Cheeseburger?"

"Yes. He's going to say some prayers in the hospital for the one
who got shot. He wants to do it tonight, and he asked me to go
with him."

"That is good," Mama said. "He is a good man."

"I think so, too," Bernie said. "A very good man."

"You leave now. When Sister comes home, I will let her sleep here."

Mrs. Darkwater had gone to her daughter's house and wouldn't be home for another hour. Mr. Darkwater said he was sure his wife would be happy to stay with Mama. In the meantime, he would come over, but could he watch ESPN? The Darkwaters didn't have satellite TV like the setup Bernie and Chee had installed for Mama.

Mama didn't like sharing her house with someone else's husband, especially when the package included turning the TV to sports talk. "I'll do it so you won't be so concerned about me. But I'm not fixing dinner for that man."

"No. Of course not. I'll make something for both of you right now."

Bernie warmed up canned soup and found the makings for peanut butter sandwiches and an apple to slice on the side. Then she sat at the kitchen table and wrote a note to Darleen:

Sister,

I had to go to Santa Fe unexpectedly with my husband to visit our friend there. I'm sorry we can't talk tonight.

Your drinking is interfering with your agreement to help with Mama. I've watched too many lives ruined by alcohol, including our father's. I see pain in you. I don't want to argue anymore. Please think about how we can make this better. I love you very much.

She folded the note and put it on Darleen's pillow.

Bernie drove Chee's truck to Santa Fe, and the trip took forever. Chee, wearing a new white shirt with pearl buttons, his best jeans, and freshly polished boots, seemed relaxed and energized at the same time. Focused. Strong.

Once she'd passed Farmington and Bloomfield, the dark road grew quiet except for the whine of the boxlike semis. She drove through the evening at a steady nine miles over the speed limit without conversation or the chatter of the radio.

She thought about the lieutenant, placing him inside a circle of love and healing, remembering all the people she knew who knew and respected him and adding them to the circle. Largo, Bigman, Wheeler, her friends and colleagues on the Navajo force, the Border Patrol, where she'd worked briefly, other law enforcement officers. She widened it in her mind to include their families and those who cared about them. The exercise always helped her set aside negative feelings, restore her thoughts to peace.

She remembered her promise to the lieutenant and silently renewed it. Ellie looked like a viable suspect, if they could find her.

By the time she reached Cuba, the last of the long June sunset had faded. She noticed the cars and trucks under the lights in the parking lot at El Bruno's, and it reminded her that she should have fixed a sandwich for herself along with the ones she made for Mama and Mr. Darkwater. Chee, she knew, wouldn't eat until the ceremony was done. She stopped for gas, a Coke, and a bag of peanuts, noticing that the arrival of evening brought the expected cooler temperatures, one benefit of living at high elevation. Then Bernie continued through town, past a block of timeworn storage lockers behind a chain link fence. She noticed a scattering of boats and RVs parked there, too. She imagined Slim Jacobs and Ellie Friedman nestled together in one of the little rooms on a mattress, candles and a joint or two adding to the experience. The image made her chuckle.

"What are you so tickled about?" Chee asked.

"I just pictured our mysterious appraiser and that old cowboy together in their little storage-locker love nest. A redneck version of John Lennon and Yoko Ono. Incense swirling around, Slim naked except for his boots and that battered old hat. The garage door stands open, and they're enjoying the view of rusting camping trailers instead of New York City."

Chee laughed. "Cowboy hippie lovebirds." He reached over and squeezed her hand. "I'm glad you came with me."

Bernie squeezed back. "You'll do fine. Your heart and mind are on the right path. You are helping someone who has asked for prayers for all the right reasons."

She glanced at the darkness outside the windows for a few moments, then told him about showing her mother the photos of the Hosteen Klah weavings.

"They mesmerized her," Bernie said. "I would love to show her the rug at the AIRC, but I'm not sure she can sit in the car long enough to get to Santa Fe anymore. I wonder if they'd let me take a photo of it—then I could make a big print and give it to Mama. She'd like that."

They stayed on NM 550, driving through land belonging to the Jicarilla Apache, Jemez Pueblo, and Zia Pueblo. They entered the edge of suburban sprawl outside Rio Rancho. They sped past the junction for the Santa Ana Casino and Tamaya Resort, headed through the outskirts of Bernalillo, over the Rio Grande, and onto I-25 north for another forty minutes. When they saw the glitter of Santa Fe from La Bajada, Chee called Rev. Rodriguez. He met them outside the CCU.

"You made good time," Rodriguez said. He had talked about the ceremony with the staff. There should be no problem. They would have as much privacy as possible with a minimum of interference, as long as Leaphorn remained stable.

"You're welcome to stay, to add your prayers," Chee said.

Rodriguez said, "I will. Let me know what I should do, or not do. I don't want to be in the way."

Chee nodded. Bernie said, "Stand quietly. Send up your healing thoughts."

Rodriguez said, "I have been praying for your friend there. I pray for everyone here and their families."

"That's good," Chee said. "Every prayer is a blessing."

Their favorite nurse was on duty in the ward. "He's been restless all day," she said. "I'll check on him now, before you get started. Are you ready to walk down to his room?"

The lieutenant's skin had a gray pallor. His eyes were closed, with dark circles beneath them, his breathing shallow. His body looked even smaller, shrunken in the bed as though the life force that plumped him up had leaked away. The displays on the machines in the little room moved to a steady, mechanical beat.

"Mr. Leaphorn, your relatives are here," the nurse said. Bernie noticed that the lieutenant didn't seem to hear her. The nurse checked the monitors and showed Bernie the call button. "Use this if you need me. I'll be right outside at the desk. I've asked the aides to stay away until you're done."

"Thank you," Chee said. "You're welcome to be here with us."

"I'd like to, but we're shorthanded tonight." Her eyes scanned the room with its expensive technology. "I've seen miracles that had nothing to do with medicine or our fancy machinery."

Bernie, Chee, and Rodriguez stood next to the bed, surrounded by stands and equipment. Chee put his leather bag with the sacred items for the ceremony on a chair. He leaned toward the lieutenant and spoke softly in Navajo. "The people at this hospital told me it would be wise to come and see you now. Bernie is with me, and a good man who has helped us. I've come as you asked to sing for you. To ask for you to be restored to harmony, for your spirit to go once more in beauty."

Leaphorn's eyes stayed closed. Bernie reached for his hand, cool and bony.

Then, when the time was right, Chee began to chant in Navajo, softly at first and then with more energy.

Bernie listened to the old songs. They reminded her of songs she had heard as a girl at the ceremonies for her grandmother, her great-aunt, and, last year, for her mother's oldest brother. The steady, gentle rhythm, the repetition, the beauty of the Navajo words that related the stories of the Holy People, soothed and transformed her. After a while, her chest felt lighter, her breathing deeper, more regular. Rodriguez moved subtly to the rhythm of Chee's chanting. The chaplain had closed his eyes, and she saw tears that ran beneath his eyelids, over his cheeks, dropping gently on his shirt. In her own prayers she now included him, all the people at the hospital and their families, all the people in hospitals everywhere, all the ones who were sick, and all the people who loved them. Most of all, she sent her healing thoughts to the lieutenant and to Chee.

She knew he had made whatever changes the *hataalii* he talked to instructed him to make. She also knew Diné who would criticize Chee for praying this way, without the sand paintings, without the other parts of the ceremony as prescribed by the Holy People. But times had changed. How could anyone with an open heart judge him harshly for bringing solace to a much-respected mentor, colleague, dying friend?

When it was finished, the lieutenant seemed more peaceful. His legs had stopped twitching. He lay quietly. Then he opened his eyes. He gazed at Chee, then at Bernie. He raised his right hand off the bed, his thumb and forefinger together, moving them from left to right.

They looked at each other, puzzled. Leaphorn moved his hand again, a subtle circular motion.

Bernie remembered. "Would you like to write something?"

The lieutenant nodded. She took her notebook and a pencil from her backpack. She put the pencil between the thumb and middle finger of his right hand. She opened the book to a blank page and held it steady for him. The lieutenant lifted his bandaged head an inch or two from the pillow, then drew two sharp peaks with a narrow valley between. He let his head drop, and the pencil rolled out of his hand.

They studied the mark.

"Is this a clue to who shot you?" Chee said.

Leaphorn moved his chin up and down ever so slightly.

"We will use this to solve the case," she said. "Remember? I promised you I'd find out who shot you, and why."

Leaphorn seemed to nod once more, and his eyelids fell shut.

Rodriguez asked if they would like coffee, a milkshake, something to eat from the cafeteria. Chee shook his head and put his hand lightly on Leaphorn's shoulder. "I want to sit with him until the sun comes up."

Chee looked at Bernie. "All those years, I thought this one was judging me, critical of me. I thought I never lived up to his expectations, never was good enough. Now I know that he was meant to be my teacher. I fell short only because of what I expected of myself." She saw both exhaustion and peace in his eyes.

"I'd like some water," Bernie said. "I'll be back in a while."

She and Rodriguez left together. In the lounge, a gray-haired woman snoozed in a chair with a book on her lap. The rest of the room was empty.

Rodriguez handed her a bottle of water from the little refrigerator and took one himself.

"You can rest here." He indicated an empty couch with a swoop of his arm. "No one minds if people sleep. I can find a pillow and a blanket for you. Sure you don't want something to eat?"

"I'm going back to sit with the lieutenant for a while, too. I'm not hungry. Even though I'm tired, I feel better than I have since the lieutenant was shot."

"Thank your husband for letting me stay," he said. "That was strong praying."

"I'll tell him," Bernie said.

But first she walked out onto the patio, appreciating the 2:00 a.m. stillness, the clear night sky, the beauty of people like Rodriguez and the hospital staff. Interesting, she thought. The bad thing that happened to the lieutenant had changed her opinion of Santa Fe from a stuck-up rich person's town to a place with a heart.

She carried the bottle of water back to Leaphorn's tiny room to share with Chee. He had pulled the chair next to the hospital bed and sat quietly, eyes closed. Leaphorn seemed to be asleep. Fatigue swept over her like soft fog. The nurse had left some pillows on the second chair. She curled up there and closed her eyes.

Chee awoke, stiff but clearheaded. He watched dawn's faint, soft pink tinge the sky. He saw Leaphorn lying still except for a slight rise and fall of his chest with his breath. And Bernie, her feet drawn up under her like their visiting cat, her straight, coal-black hair falling over one side of her face, eyes closed. Beautiful. He rose as quietly as he could and left the room.

He noticed new nurses on duty now, told them good morning. He walked through the empty hallways to the lobby and outside into the parking lot to greet the sunrise. It was good to be alive, he thought. Good to be breathing the fresh morning air, watching the wispy clouds grow brilliant against the sky's blue expanse. The volcanic Jemez Mountains, home to Los Alamos National Laboratory and dozens of archaeological sites, spread broad and tall on the western horizon, their navy blue peaks catching the early light. To the east, a sprinkling of houses as brown as the soil, rolling foothills dotted with native piñon and juniper and, beyond that, the slopes of the Sangre de Cristos.

It was rare that he rose before Bernie. He had never seen her as tired as she had been in the days since the attack on the lieutenant. He doubted that she'd had a full night's sleep since she witnessed the shooting. Chee thought about the shape Leaphorn had drawn, wondering how it could be a clue. It could be a symbol for something or someone. Maybe he was drawing the valley in between, not the peaks, after all.

And then, for some reason, he remembered Mrs. Benally. Remembered that he had promised to take her to pick up Jackson in exchange for an interview with Leonard Nez. And he had to be at the Window Rock office by noon to meet with Agent Cordova, Captain Largo, and the delegates from the Arizona Highway Patrol who were working the Leaphorn case. If they left now, he and Bernie would have time for a nice breakfast somewhere.

He trotted back to the hospital room to tell her of the plan, thinking of hotcakes and bacon. His stomach growled with anticipation. He expected to find Bernie awake, perhaps absorbed in a book, but she was exactly where he'd left her, asleep in the chair. Leaphorn seemed to be sleeping, too, despite the noise of the machines. Then he noticed Louisa, sitting next to Leaphorn and holding the lieutenant's hand through the hospital rail.

She noticed Chee, put a finger on her lips, and pointed to the door. She gently placed Leaphorn's hand on the bed without waking him, and crept out to where Chee stood.

"I didn't expect to see you," Chee said.

Louisa hugged him. She was a little taller than Bernie and considerably softer. "I got here as soon as I could," she said. "Life has been crazy, but I'm here now. Here to stay."

"Do you know you're still a suspect in the shooting?"

Louisa nodded. "I finally felt well enough to talk to that FBI guy on the phone yesterday. I told him I'd be at the Santa Fe hospital until Joe left, and that he could find me here if he wanted to talk more and that he could arrest me if he needed to after Joe got better or . . . or left us." She stopped, and Chee saw her eyes glisten. "I would chop off my right arm before I'd do any harm to Joe. But you know that. They're checking my alibi."

Chee saw the exhaustion in her face, the yellow hue to her skin. She looked years older than the last time he'd seen her.

"Why did they have such trouble finding you? They even checked the flights to Houston."

"I never bothered to legally change my name from when I was married a million years ago. I use my maiden name, Bourebonette, professionally. It's just when I fly that I have to book tickets as L. A. Tyler so the name matches my driver's license."

"L. A. Tyler? That's pretty Hollywood."

"Louisa Ann," she said.

"The feds want to grill you about the message you left on the answering machine and why you disappeared," Chee said. "You really need to take care of that."

"I'll tell them, you, anybody who wants to know, what happened between Joe and me and why I couldn't get here sooner. That can wait. I want to save my energy for him."

She paused, glancing back at the hospital bed. "Will you and Bernie be here all day?"

"I have to get back to Window Rock for a big police meeting. Bernie's on leave because she witnessed the shooting, but we drove out together."

"You go on, then," Louisa said. "That's a long drive. Bernie must be worn out. She didn't even stir when I came in. When she wakes up, I need to talk to her, to apologize for acting so odd. Then I might go to the lounge for a nap, let Bernie sit with Joe."

Chee remembered what Bernie had said about how she thought someone ought to be with the lieutenant while he was in the hospital. But he'd miss her company on the drive back to the Four Corners.

Louisa said, "I'll loan her my car if I need to stay longer than she can. She and I can work that out later when we see how Joe's doing." Her eyes brimmed with tears again. "I watched both my parents die. They were lucky enough to die at home. I am here for Joe for the duration. When Bernie wakes up, she can decide what to do. You go on. You've got to find out who did this to him. You know better than to argue with a fierce old woman."

"Tell Bernie I'll call her," Chee said.

"I'll tell her you love her, too. I'm sorry I didn't tell Joe that more often."

"Do that for me."

As he drove out of the hospital parking lot onto St. Michael's Drive, Chee thought about the way Bernie's eyes had lit up when she saw the Klah weaving. Instead of stopping for breakfast, he'd get a photo for her with the camera on his phone on his way out of town. He could print it and surprise her with it. She could show it to her mother—even give it to her, if she liked. The detour shouldn't take long. He'd pick up coffee afterward.

Chee noticed just one vehicle in the AIRC lot, an old red pickup with a faded bumper sticker: "America: Love It or Give It Back." Rakes, hoes, and shovels poked their heads over the sides of the truck bed. Chee parked next to it, in front of the visitor center. It was early, he realized. The campus wasn't officially open.

Chee snapped a few photos of flowers, including large bright red peony blossoms that had been buds when he and Bernie had visited before. He photographed the little cemetery the couple who originally owned the property had built for their pets: cats, dogs, even a parrot. Another indication that white people lived in an altered universe. He sent the flowers and a couple of other shots to Bernie with a text: *Guess where I am?* He knew her phone was on mute from last night, so the chirp of an arriving message wouldn't wake her.

A black garden hose stretched along the flagstones. Chee followed it to find Mark Yazzie offering water to daylilies.

"Yá'át'ééh," Chee called to him.

"Yá'át'ééh." Yazzie gave Chee a snaggletoothed grin. "What happened to your uniform? Did you go undercover to arrest me?"

Chee said, "Your luck holds. I'm off duty. I was at the hospital with a friend. I came to get some photos of this place for Bernie. Then I head home."

"Go ahead. All these flowers look pretty good today."

"I'd like to get a picture inside the museum, too," Chee said.

"I can't help you there. Ask Dr. Davis about that."

"When will she be here?" Chee asked. "I didn't see another car."

"Oh, she parks over at the museum. She's been putting in a lot of hours getting ready for the new collection." Mark Yazzie pointed with his lips. "You know how to walk there?"

"One foot in front of the other. Thanks. *Ahééhee' shínaí.*"

The museum's front door was locked. Chee walked to the rear of the building and saw Davis's Lexus in the loading zone. Through the tinted windows, he noticed a stack of boxes and a small navy duffel. The back seats were folded flat.

He found the building's back door propped open with a rock.

"Dr. Davis? Are you here?"

Inside, it took a moment for his eyes to adjust to the dim light. The only noise was the whirl of what he assumed was the ventilation system. Other than the red EXIT signs, illumination came from a single source, a room at the end of the corridor.

Chee headed in that direction, his steps reverberating against the cement floor of the museum's inner sanctum. Unlike the fancy public area, this was a basic, utilitarian work space, with simple metal shelves for open storage and a few plain tables. The environment reminded him of his brief stint as a hotel desk clerk in Albuquerque during his university days. In contrast to the opulent lobby, the staff offices were tiny windowless spaces furnished with castoffs and crammed with excess equipment.

He turned when he heard the thud of a heavy door close behind him. In the dim light, he could barely see Davis standing in the hallway with a gun in her hand, the muzzle pointed squarely at Chee's midsection.

19

"Hey, there. It's Jim Chee. Don't shoot. I just came for a photo."

She angled the muzzle to the floor. "Hi. What a surprise."

"I guess."

"I get a little jumpy here alone," Davis said. "The security guys hate me for disabling the alarm. Even Yazzie tells me to keep the door locked, but that's a pain when I'm going in and out for a smoke. You, Mr. Handsome, are the first person who has ever come visiting before official working hours."

"I didn't mean to bother you. Are you always here this early?"

"Come on down. I'll show you what I'm doing." She gave him a smile that made him keenly aware he was a man in the prime of life alone in the building with a dangerously attractive woman.

Chee followed her to a back room with shelves stacked deep with ceramics. Boxes, bubble wrap, and rolls of tape sat on the table.

"I need to move some of these pots from our collection out of here so we'll have room for the new ones we'll be receiving from the McManus gift. Some of these old beauties have to go into off-site storage. Out with the old, in with the older."

"How do you decide which ones to box up? Couldn't you get somebody else to do this for you?"

"Some of these are similar to the ones included in the gift. It takes an expert like me to know the difference. These are my babies."

She perched on the edge of the table where she'd been organizing the pots and set her gun down next to her leg. It reminded Chee that his weapon was locked in his truck.

"You know, I'm almost sure you and I have met before," he said. "With Leaphorn at Chaco Canyon, when you were a researcher."

"I wondered how long it would take you to put that together," she said. "Chaco. Place of mystery and magic. These rare beauties are from Chaco, too." Her perfect lips moved to the hint of a grin. Davis picked up a tall, slender pot painted with vertical lines, perhaps to make it look taller. It reminded Chee of the urn in her office. She wore black cotton gloves. "A masterpiece, isn't it? Dates to about 1200. Not brought in from an outlier but created in the canyon itself. Among the McManus pots we'll be getting are a few more of these. So very, very special."

"I don't know much about pottery," he said. "Why the gloves?"

Davis put the pot down and began to wrap it. "They prevent oil from my hands from adhering to the surface. Now, tell me, why are you here? I'd like to think it's because you knew you'd find me alone."

"Nothing like that. I was hoping to get a picture of the Klah blanket for Bernie. The gardener told me you'd come in early. I thought you might bend the no-photography rules an inch or two."

"Where is your wife? Waiting in the truck?"

"She's at the hospital with Leaphorn."

"He's not dead yet?"

Chee let the comment hang, wondering what she'd say next.

"No photos allowed in here, but let me think about it, since you're so cute.

"You know, each pot tells a story. Even after years of working with them, pieces like this take my breath away." Davis picked up some bubble wrap and the tape gun and began to create a transparent cocoon for the pot she'd shown him. "Every time I stand here, I think of the women who made these, mothers and daughters, aunts and grandmothers, old and young. The hours they spent digging clay, cleaning it, tempering it, shaping the pots, painting on the slip. Firing them, decorating them. It humbles me to think that my hands touch what those women's hands made."

Chee caught a glimpse of silver on her right arm. "I bet a man made your pretty watchband."

"You're right about that, but it's a bracelet." She put the pot in a box and moved closer to him, close enough that he smelled perfume intermixed with cigarettes. She pulled up her sleeve so he could see the piece. He noticed the way the silver seemed to flow around the procession of open hearts.

"A jeweler in Gallup, a Navajo, made it," Davis said. "Tsosie. Maybe you know him?"

"I met a guy who sells at Earl's—you mean Garrison Tsosie?"

"That might be his brother. Notah Tsosie made this. My fiancé asked him to come up with a broader, more masculine one for himself, this for me, and an identical one for Ellie—Eleanor Friedman, used to be Friedman-Bernal. You remember her from those days?"

"What does she look like?"

"Oh, a little shorter than I am. Mousy brown hair." Davis pushed a strand of her own blond hair behind her ear. "I'm not surprised she didn't make an impression."

"I remember her," Chee said. "She got in some trouble a long time ago, right?"

"She was trouble," Davis said. "She told some terrible lies about my boyfriend, my Randall. She claimed he falsified his research data. She meddled where she shouldn't have, creating a situation that would have ended Randall's career. Ellie had a bad accident at the ruins where she'd gone to spy on him. She moved to Arizona after that. I lost contact with her, but I never forgot what she did either."

Chee felt cold sweat on the back of his neck. This woman made him uncomfortable. "When we asked you about EFB, you said you hadn't heard of it. But that was Ellie's business."

Davis laughed. "If you remember correctly, I said EFB wasn't in the AIRC records. It wasn't, because her startup was older than our files. And she hasn't applied to do appraisals with us or our donors since she's set up shop in Santa Fe."

"I was called out to Chaco Canyon yesterday. A park worker discovered a woman's body. She seems to have died of a gunshot. The feds think it might have been Ellie."

"Really?" Chee noticed the way she asked it, her slight change in tone.

"No ID, but she'd been reported missing and the body fits her description," he said. "The animals had been at her, so it's hard to say how long she's been dead."

"Did she kill herself?"

The question caught him off guard. "We don't know for sure yet. Why do you ask?"

"She was moody. She had a gun. And she probably had a guilty conscience. I think she was the one who shot Leaphorn."

"Leaphorn saved her life. Why would she shoot him?"

Davis picked up a grapefruit-size bowl decorated with black lines and angles on a white background. She began to wrap it. "It goes back to the job Leaphorn had working for Collingsworth, checking on the McManus appraisal. Did Bernie talk to you much about that?"

She wrapped the bowl as she talked. "Ellie did the evaluations Leaphorn questioned. She told me she was scared that he'd expose her shady appraisal business."

"So you talked to her?" Chee swallowed his surprise.

"She called me when she found out the AIRC had acquired the McManus collection. She knew some of those pots were not what the McManuses had assumed they were. She thought Leaphorn would find out."

"Why would she fake the appraisal?"

Davis chucked. "You're cute. You don't understand how evil works."

"I guess I don't."

"Usually, people fake appraisals to get more money," Davis said. "But Ellie hated the idea of Indian pots going outside the country, and she especially detested the fact that her favorite rare pots from Chaco Canyon would be exiled to some rich guy's house in Asia. After she'd had a few drinks, she'd get maudlin about it and say idiotic things like 'The poor Anasazi clay babies, forever refugees.' So she liberated the ancient pots and sent substitutes to take their places."

"Where did she get fake pots?"

"They weren't fake pots." Davis had one of those disdainful expressions Chee had observed on people who considered themselves smarter than average. "They were exact replicas Ellie made using photos from the appraisal material. She shaped them by hand in her little apartment, so she could honestly say they were created at Chaco Canyon."

"That's complicated," Chee said.

Davis smiled. "Not for Ellie. She'd started making pots in high school, before she became an archaeologist. She'd studied Anasazi technique in grad school. Ellie found a source in the canyon for good clay and ground shards as the temper, to give hers aged authenticity."

She winked at Chee. "I know you're thinking destroying those old shards, that's illegal. It wasn't as suspect as it sounds. Ellie had a huge collection of broken pieces, authorized for the work she was doing, tracking a certain family of Chaco potters. She only destroyed the ones she didn't need, and I had already helped her photograph and document them. We could argue the morality of destroying those shards, but Ellie had a greater purpose in mind."

"And you approved?"

Davis ignored the question. "We used to joke that Ellie was part Anasazi, the way she could copy the old designs, the details. She was a whiz at the painting, too."

"So she stole the real pots, substituted hers in the McManus collection. The lieutenant figured this out—"

" 'Stole' sounds too harsh. I called it rescue," Davis said. "The McManus collection set her off because it had rare cylindrical jars. Pots like this one." Davis held up a jar painted with linked rectangles over a white base. It reminding Chee of one of the sketches he'd seen in the lieutenant's little notebook.

"Making the substitutions hadn't occurred to Ellie before she encountered these and fell in love with them," Davis said. "But the good-girl part of her got nervous about the values, so she lowered them in the appraisal to what the pots she made would have been worth. The McManuses had so many items, they never noticed. Or if they did, they were glad to pay lower insurance. Ellie thought everything was fine until Leaphorn started nosing around."

"And that's why she tried to kill him," Chee said. "Do I have that straight?"

"Kill him, then kill herself. The world of Native American art appraisers is a small, closed circle. Word gets out that her evaluations can't be trusted, and it's over. The problems with that old job would have ruined her future. She was done either way."

Chee thought about it. "Ellie probably did the same with other appraisals, too. Why didn't she just take the proceeds from selling the stuff and disappear, move to an island somewhere? Why come back here?"

Davis put the wrapped cylinder in a box. "She kept the pots, never sold any of them. After the McManus collection, she never agreed to another job that involved Indian art if it was being sold outside the United States. She said the intrigue made her too nervous."

"So the McManus pots were the only ones she switched? You believe that?"

Davis smiled. "I hated her for the lies she told about my Randall. But she didn't lie about that."

Chee took a breath. "So Ellie has a secret stash of rare pots, and she shoots the man who saved her life to preserve her business reputation?"

"You got it."

"Why didn't she just talk to Leaphorn, explain what happened? If she still had the pots—"

"Actually, she made an appointment to have lunch with him. Then she got cold feet."

"You know a lot about this," Chee said.

"We used to be friends."

Chee nodded. "The FBI will need to talk to you."

Davis looked surprised. "You take care of it. You're a cop. You do your job."

Chee shook his head. "I'm not convinced that a few old pots gave her enough motive to try to kill a good man who had saved her life."

Davis stared at him. "You don't understand a thing. That Leaphorn is pure evil. He left my Randall on that mesa. Left his body for the coyotes."

"You're wrong about Leaphorn," Chee said. And you're wrong about Ellie, he thought. "I should let you focus on your work. I've got to get back to Bernie. We have a long drive home."

"Which way do you go?"

"Through Cuba."

"Cuba? Someone was recommending a restaurant to me there. El Bruno's? Ever heard of it?" Davis asked.

"It's on the main street, down from a rent-a-garage place, commercial storage units."

"Storage units? I didn't know Cuba had a business like that."

"It's been there as long as I can remember," Chee said. "They've got a big yard for RVs and camping trailers there because it's not that far from Chaco."

Davis picked up another bowl. "I'll have to let you out. The back door locked when I closed it. Give me a minute to finish these last pots. You mentioned a photo of the Klah tapestry? You know where the rug room is. Go get your picture. Enjoy it. I'll find you there."

As soon as he reached the hallway, Chee took out his phone. No signal, probably because of the building. He texted Cordova: *asap re Leaphorn*. He quietly tried the back door. Locked, as Davis had said.

He found the rug room unlocked, and the light came on automatically when he entered. He closed the door behind him and tried his cell again, same result.

He looked at the Klah rug, took some photos for Bernie, a long view and then close-ups of the various design elements. He told himself to enjoy the moment. If Davis tried anything, he could overpower her, keep her there until Cordova sent backup.

When he tried to open the rug room door, the handle wouldn't budge, and he recalled Marjorie punching a code into the keypad next to it. He unsuccessfully entered the most common combinations of numbers, then several variations.

Through the window he saw her approach, pushing a dolly. In one smooth move she opened the door, stationed the dolly to block his exit, and pointed a weapon at him.

"Thanks for telling me about the storage lockers," she said. "Let's go see what's in Ellie's."

"Wait," he said.

She fired, and as the pain from the Taser hit, he realized he had given her the information to get away with murder.

Bernie opened her eyes, saw the white ceiling, heard the rhythmic sounds of the equipment monitoring breathing and heartbeat. Were they keeping the lieutenant alive, or was it his own deep resilience? She felt another presence in the hospital room, someone at the bed looking at the man, not the machines.

"Louisa! When did you get here?"

"A while ago." Her normally plump face was drawn, her skin sallow. "I told the hospital admissions people I was his wife. I guess I am, unofficially at least. They told me my niece and nephew were here. I guess that's you and Jim?"

Bernie nodded. "Largo asked me to track down his family. I only found one man, Austin Lee, and I haven't been able to talk to him directly."

"Joe never mentions relatives." Louisa took a breath in and released it slowly. "You and Chee and me and the Navajo Police Department. We're his family."

Louisa eased herself from standing into the bedside chair with a grimace.

"Are you feeling well?" Bernie asked.

"Better now that I'm here with him, not in Houston."

"You look tired. Are you sure you're okay?"

Louisa nodded. "I'm fine. I was at MD Anderson, you know, the big hospital in Houston. They don't let you go until they've checked every inch inside and out."

"I didn't realize that's where you were. You told me you were at a conference." Bernie knew MD Anderson specialized in cancer.

"It was a sort of conference. Lots of conferring with doctors. I needed some tests, consultations, more tests, experts. I didn't tell

Joe, didn't want him to worry after what he'd been through with Emma. That's what the argument was about."

Emma, much cherished, who'd died from an infection following surgery for a brain tumor before Bernie ever met her.

"It's enough having one woman you love die," Louisa said. "I didn't want to talk to him about it, at least not until I knew what we were dealing with."

"What are you dealing with?" Bernie asked. "Cancer?"

"No. It's one of those autoimmune problems no one hears about until they get it. The doctors say I'll probably die of something else before it can kill me. That's the good thing about being old. Less to worry about."

"That's still a lot to handle on your own."

Louisa said, "I left a message that I had something important to tell you, but I know it was hard for you to reach me at Anderson." She glanced at Leaphorn. "I'm sure he thought I was mad at him because of the way I left. I was ill-tempered, tense, argumentative. I hope I'll have a chance to explain. I left without telling him I loved him. I never expected to find him like this."

Bernie said, "Every couple gets crossways once in a while. He knows you love him."

"That reminds me. Jim left early to get back to Window Rock. I told him we could drive back together, or you could take my car if I wanted to stay. He said to tell you he loves you."

Bernie said, "I don't envy him his morning. That Mrs. Benally he has to deal with is a tiger."

Leaphorn stirred, moaned. Louisa went to the bedside.

"I'm going for a little run to shake out the cobwebs," Bernie said.

She wandered past the cafeteria, noticing the tables of aides and volunteers chatting over breakfast, and a few people who could have been visitors waiting for news, taking a break from bedside vigils.

The tantalizing smell of fresh coffee wafted into the lobby. She'd get a cup on her way back.

She walked through the big doors, past the landscaped patio with its curving benches. She strolled into the sun, enjoying the warmth on her skin, the breeze, the enticing aroma of green from the hospital's landscaping.

She turned on her phone and saw messages. Darleen. Slim Jacobs. Some photos from Chee. She'd deal with all that later.

She jogged across busy St. Michael's Drive and ran past United Church of Santa Fe and down a dirt road. It felt wonderful to be outside, to be alive. She savored the sight of Santa Fe's piñon-dotted foothills rising to the east.

Why would the lieutenant spend precious energy to draw them a picture as a clue? She thought about it, reached no conclusion except that she'd look at the picture again when she got back to the hospital. Maybe she'd see something else in it this morning.

She timed herself, then circled back after twenty minutes. She stopped outside the entrance to catch her breath, noticing a statue of a smiling Saint Francis, the patron of Santa Fe and, she knew, of animals. She was heading toward the big glass entrance doors when her phone rang. She figured it was her husband, but heard another male voice.

"Hi, there," Cordova said. "Do you know where Chee is? I've been trying to reach him, just got his message."

"He's on the road back to Window Rock to meet with you and Largo and the Arizona guys," Bernie said. "He probably has his phone on mute from the hospital last night."

"You're not with him?"

"No, I'm still in Santa Fe. We came to be with Leaphorn."

"How is he, anyway?"

"He's peaceful," Bernie said.

"Is that Indian for dead?"

Bernie sighed. "No. I wouldn't joke about that."

"Could you ask Chee to call me ASAP? I have to cancel the meeting. That dead woman at Chaco was your missing appraiser, Eleanor Friedman."

"Wow," Bernie said. "What happened?"

"Shot in the chest, same caliber bullet as Leaphorn. We found that Karen gal you talked to. She didn't have much to add, but you can tell Chee he did a good job finding her swirly sole prints."

"What else did you find out?"

"That Davis woman Chee asked for the background on?" he continued. "Turns out your associate director had a husband who filed for divorce and then filed domestic violence charges against her."

"Wait, I thought that archaeologist was her fiancé?"

"I don't know anything about that," Cordova said. "This all happened when she was in her twenties, living in the midwest."

"Are you sure it wasn't the other way around, her filing against him?"

"Oh, she had a restraining order against him, too," Cordova said. "What's interesting is that the ex, a former cop, disappeared. Three years later someone discovered his bones off a backcountry trail. At that point, no one could tell what happened, but they found a bullet hole in the skull."

"This is the same associate director, Dr. Davis?"

Cordova said. "Maxie Davis. Same gal. She spent some time in the National Guard. Got good grades for marksmanship."

"Did anyone find the bullet that did in her ex?"

"I like the way you think," Cordova said. "We're checking on that now."

When Cordova hung up, Bernie called Chee and got no answer. She called Largo. No, he hadn't heard from Chee that morning, or from Cordova. Bernie filled him in.

"Have Chee call Cordova as soon as you hear from him," Bernie said.

"I thought you were off the case, not in charge of it," Largo said.

"Sorry, sir. I didn't mean to sound so bossy."

"It's okay, Manuelito. It's just the way you are. How's Leaphorn? How did it go last night?"

Bernie told him a little about the ceremony. "Louisa is here now, too."

"I'm glad about that," Largo said. "Tell the old guy I'm on his team."

"I will, Captain. But I think he knows that already."

20

Bernie thought about Chee and the photos as she walked to the lieutenant's room. Louisa sat resting her head in her hands. Bernie touched her gently, and she startled awake.

"I'm happy to sit here awhile if you'd like to get some coffee or something to eat," Bernie said. "Or if you want to stay here, I can bring you something and you can eat in the CCU lounge or out on the deck."

"I'm fine for now," Louisa said. She handed Bernie the drawing the lieutenant had made last night. "What's this?"

"Earlier, we asked the lieutenant if he knew who shot him. Yesterday he made these marks. As a clue I guess."

Louisa frowned. "*W* for *white man*? Or maybe it's an *M* for *mystery*. Or a mountain with a deep valley? Did it help?"

"I'm trying to decipher it," she said. "I promised the lieutenant I'd figure out who shot him."

Bernie remembered Chee's photo message and saw "Guess where I am." She opened it to find a beautiful red peony in full bloom. Lovely, she thought. Why had he sent it? Then she remembered seeing the plant when it was in bud. How nice of him.

She turned to Louisa. "Do you have a car I could borrow? Chee turned his phone off. I just got some important information he needs."

Louisa extracted a set of keys from her purse. "My Jeep is in the front row. There's a handicapped placard hanging from the mirror. And a loaded pistol in the glove box."

Bernie gave her a questioning look.

"Is that for the placard or the gun?"

"Both," Bernie said. "The FBI searched the airport for your Jeep. Did you hide it somewhere?"

Louisa smiled. "A friend let me leave it at her house. Took me to the airport and picked me up yesterday. I didn't know how long I'd have to stay at Anderson, and parking at the airport gets expensive."

"I'll be back soon," Bernie said.

"You better be," Louisa said. "We've got a lot to talk about."

The Jeep started right up and drove smoothly. Bernie turned on the air-conditioning, even though it wasn't hot yet, just because she could.

Bernie saw Chee's truck near the visitor center. He'd proba-bly gone to the museum, she thought. Got absorbed in the collec-tions, forgot that he'd silenced his phone during the ceremony for Leaphorn.

But the museum was closed, lights off, not even a cleaning per-son. Bernie walked around to the back door. Locked. No cars. She saw a large dolly at the loading dock, deep tracks in the gravel, some cigarette butts.

She walked the grounds, searching for Chee, trying to keep worry at bay. She found Mark Yazzie near the administration build-ing, rolling up the hoses. "My lucky morning," he said. "Two offi-cers of the law, and I'm still a free man."

"So you saw Chee?"

"Fine-looking man," Mark Yazzie said. "Even out of uniform."

"I'm trying to find him."

"Last I heard, he was headed to the museum."

"I was just up there," Bernie said. "It's closed."

"I told him to use the back door."

"I tried that, too, but it was locked."

"Guess she must have left already," Yazzie said.

"She?"

"Dr. Davis. If I see Officer Chee, I'll tell him you're after him."

Bernie walked to Davis's office, noticing that her SUV wasn't there. Knocked and got no response. She called Chee's phone again. No answer.

She went to the administration building, where she found Marjorie watering the plants in the big office. Collingsworth had joined potential donors for breakfast, the secretary told her, and ought to be in around ten. Bernie was welcome to wait, have some coffee. And, no, she hadn't seen Chee.

"What about Dr. Davis?" Bernie asked.

"Oh, she works off-site today. I can give her a message. She's got a research project out on some ranch in southern Colorado."

"The Double X Ranch?"

"Usually that's where she is. Sometimes she goes to Chaco Canyon."

Bernie said, "I need you to call campus security. I found my husband's truck in the lot, but he's missing. Doesn't answer his phone. I'm afraid something has happened to him. The gardener said he went to the museum, but it's dark and locked over there."

"Why would he be here so early? It doesn't seem likely—"

The expression on Bernie's face stopped the monologue. Marjorie dialed, said a few words, hung up. "The guard will be here in a minute."

Bernie sat still on a bench outside the administrative offices as she waited, repositioning pieces of the puzzle, remembering the lieutenant's mantra: Nothing is a coincidence. A *W* for *woman*? Did a woman shoot him? Was it Ellie? If so, who killed her? Or an *M*, she thought, an *M* for *Maxie*? When she found Chee, she'd bounce that theory off him, after she teased him for getting locked up with the artifacts.

It was fifteen minutes before Security Man arrived, well-built, steel-haired, with the presence of a retired marine and a gun in his holster. From the tightness in his shoulders and the dour expression on his face, Bernie expected conflict.

"What can I do for you?" he asked.

"I think my husband is locked in the museum. I need your help to—"

He cut her off. "No, ma'am. That can't be. The alarm is on, and the motion detectors show there's no sign of anybody there. I checked just before I walked over here."

"What if he's unconscious?"

Security Man made a clucking noise with his tongue. "Well, unless he's on staff, he shouldn't be there in the first place. The museum personnel will be here in another hour or so. I'm sure they'll—"

She felt her anger rising. She took her wallet out of her backpack, showed him her official Navajo Police ID.

"My husband is a Navajo Police officer, too," she said. "I'm here working on a case for Dr. Collingsworth, and he's helping me. I don't want to involve outsiders in this, but if I need to call the Santa Fe Police Department or the State Police, I'm sure they'll respond."

"Point made," he said.

"Tell me about the alarm system," Bernie said as they walked.

He explained that complicated electronics kept track of every building on campus, monitoring exterior doors and windows, with motion detectors in crucial areas. Key staff who had reason to work late or come in early knew the code to disable the system and reinstate it when they left.

"It works great," Security Man said. "Hardly any false alarms. The only problem is human error, when people forget to activate it when they leave."

He wanted to amble, but when she broke into a jog, Security Man kept pace. They reached the swipe box near the front door, and he slid a card in to open it.

"Wait here while I take a look."

"I'm going with you," Bernie said. "You know, two sets of eyes . . ."

She saw his face harden.

"Come on," she said. "What's the big deal? If he's isn't in there, I'll buy you a cup of coffee."

"It's not . . . but what the hell?" he said. "I like pushy broads. Be my guest."

They entered the empty reception area, with its deserted research tables.

"Chee," she called. "Chee? You locked in here?"

They walked through the lobby to the research rooms, storage and office areas, places Bernie hadn't visited on her first tour. In the pottery vault, she noticed the empty boxes, tape, the bubble wrap.

Security Man said, "Usually this room is perfect. Dr. Davis loves these old things like a family, more than some families I know. I've never seen her leave it disorganized, but she's been working hard, packing up all this old stuff for storage so that fancy new collection can come in."

"Was she here this morning?"

"Yeah. She disabled the alarm and then reset it when she left, half an hour ago. Maybe she let your hubby in and then they went out for breakfast or something. Seen enough? Do I get my coffee?"

"One more stop," Bernie said.

The overhead lights came on automatically in the rug room, but in the split second before they did, Bernie noticed a little green flash blinking beneath the table.

"What's that?" she asked.

Security Man retrieved it. "Looks like someone dropped a phone." It came alive at his touch, showing a photo of Bernie and Chee in traditional Navajo dress. Their wedding picture.

Bernie squatted down, examining the carpet. She noticed a few spots of blood. The blood was damp.

"Can you check the surveillance cameras?"

He looked up at the video camera aimed at the rug room and shook his head. "This one isn't taping. On my to-do list for today."

"Call the police right now," Bernie said. "Don't let anyone in here, or in Dr. Davis's office." She raced out the front door, running back to Louisa's car. She called Cordova as she drove, explained what she'd found.

"The security guard here is calling the local cops," she said. "But I think we're too late for that."

"You're sure she kidnapped him? From what I hear, she's an attractive—"

Bernie cut him off. "I found blood close to where he dropped his phone."

Cordova would alert the rangers at Chaco Canyon in case Davis was headed there, and put the New Mexico and Colorado State Police on alert for her car. The Colorado cops would also check the Double X, Davis's other probable location. He would also call Largo with an update.

"Where are you going?"

"I'm headed toward Chaco, and if they aren't there, then to Double X," she said. "I can't just—"

He interrupted. "Don't be a hero. Don't do anything stupid."

Louisa's Jeep surprised her with its responsiveness. It also, unfortunately, had less than a quarter tank of gas. That ought to get her to Cuba, Bernie thought, and that service station would be a fast in-and-gone. She turned off the air-con to save fuel.

Bernie drove south in traffic that grew lighter once she got past the La Cienega exit. Most vehicles were pointed toward Santa Fe, traveling the opposite direction. She concentrated on the road, kept the speedometer at 85, scanned her memory for every detail she could muster about Davis. Focused on staying calm. They'd found Chee's phone in the rug room. Davis must have let him in, and before that, they probably chatted about the pots she was boxing up. Chee must have said something that made her feel threatened. But what? Davis was a smart woman. She wouldn't risk abducting a cop unless there was a lot at stake, and unless she thought she could get away with it.

Bernie reviewed her impression of the woman. She loved her job. She'd loved her boyfriend, who had died mysteriously, kept his ashes on her desk in that cookie jar urn. She probably loved the pot he was in as much as she'd loved him.

Pots. Pot. Bernie flashed on Ellie and Slim smoking pot in their hippie hideaway, surrounded by Ellie's boxes of potshards and junk.

She remembered the photo Slim had shown her. Remembered Slim saying Davis had taken the pictures for Ellie during her early appraisal work. Davis must have known about Ellie falsifying the values. In fact, Ellie probably used Davis's photos to make the fakes. Leaphorn's calling attention to the phony appraisals would have raised questions about a scam, implicated Davis. Chee must have figured this out, and Davis somehow knew that he knew.

Bernie thought about the scene at Ellie's office and at her apartment. She'd assumed that Ellie was messy, was leaving town in a hurry, or had been looking for something. But what if Davis had been there, tearing the place apart, looking for the incriminating pictures?

The Jeep's orange gasoline warning light began to glow beyond San Ysidro, catching her attention briefly. She drove on, trying to ignore it and the E on the gauge, because there was no place to stop for fuel. She rolled on fumes for the last ten miles, hoping, hoping,

hoping the Jeep would make it into the gas station. She exhaled a percentage of the built-up tension when she saw buildings along the highway, the storage complex, and, finally, the Conoco station in the next block. She'd fill up and be on her way.

As she was about to pull up to the pumps, she remembered that Chee and she had decided that the rent-a-garage compound would have been the place for Ellie's love nest and original office. Davis desperately wanted the pictures. Would she think to look for them here? What better place to dispose of Chee?

Bernie turned and drove to the storage yard entrance.

She parked, took Louisa's gun from the glove box, and put it in her backpack. She shoved the car keys into her pants pocket. She hurried to the office, a small building just outside the fenced entrance. A ten-foot cinder-block wall topped with concertina wire surrounded the complex.

The young man at the desk turned his attention away from a handheld video game. The console behind him had four screens, three of which offered black-and-white views of the storage yard—toward the entrance, toward the highway, toward an empty field. One screen was black.

"Interested in a rental? We've got both sizes available, and a special deal through the end of the month."

"No. I'm a Navajo Police officer, and I need your help," Bernie said.

"Really?"

Bernie kept talking as she pulled her ID out of her backpack. "I'm tracking a missing woman who may have a locker here. Ellie Friedman, or perhaps she registered as Eleanor Friedman-Bernal or EFB Appraisals. Please check."

"I don't need to check," he said. "You just missed her. She couldn't remember the locker number. No wonder. She hadn't been here for years. Pays the rent, though."

"She's here? You're sure?"

"She showed me her ID," the man said. "She's a blonde now and used to be a brunette in the photo. You know how women are."

He gave Bernie the number, told her where to find it.

Where did Davis get Ellie's ID? she wondered. The obvious way would have been murder. Chee must have figured out that Davis killed Ellie. She'd learn the reason later. That was why Davis needed him out of the picture.

Bernie said, "She was driving an SUV, right?"

"Right," he said. "Silver Lexus. Nice car."

Bernie said, "You're sure she hasn't left already?"

"She's here. Everyone has to go out the back. That gate sets off a noise up here. Drives me crazy."

Bernie took the gun from the backpack and put it in her pocket. "I need you to call the local police. Tell them they need to provide assistance to me right now. You got it?"

"Wow," he said. "But the phone—"

His words hung in space. Bernie left at a dead run.

The storage yard consisted of six long pods of lockers, each composed of smaller units with metal doors and larger units with garage-style access. Trailers and RVs had their own section on the north end of the lot; the entrance to Ellie's locker would open to face them.

She slowed to a jog as she approached the lockers with the lovebird view. She'd seen other cars and a few people as she raced by, but no sign of Davis's car, Davis, or Chee.

She reached the end of the row, flattened herself against the wall, and peered around the corner, searching for the Lexus. Bingo. Davis had parked the vehicle with its silver nose outward, driving about halfway into the garage-size locker.

Bernie felt the weight of Louisa's pistol in her pocket, tried not to consider the idea that she might be depending on a gun she had never fired before to save her life and Chee's. She crept along the wall toward the SUV, sticking as close to it as she could, skirting plastic bags and faded fast food wrappers that had drifted in against the doors. She heard the wind, the occasional rumble of distant traffic, and finally the high-pitched clatter of a radio coming from Ellie's open garage door. She reached the edge of the open doorway and crouched beside the car, listening for signs of Chee or Davis. She slipped off her backpack and set it down in a pile of weeds, noticing the electrical outlet on the wall above. In case the worst happened, the backpack could be a sign to someone that something was wrong.

The clatter was classical music, violins broadcast over tinny speakers. She heard no talking or arguing, no moaning. She stood up slowly and peered in the car's darkened windows. On the front passenger seat was a big turquoise purse, clearly not Davis's style. A navy duffel sat on the floor. The rear seats lay flat, and the back hatch was open.

She squatted down again and moved enough to bring part of the garage into view—a long row of dark filing cabinets along the rear wall, brown cardboard boxes neatly stacked on top. A table covered with clear plastic held rags and a pile of loose papers. She found the source of the music, a small black cassette player. On the cement floor beneath the table were several buckets and boxes with dirt inside. Not dirt, she thought. Clay. A setup for pottery making.

Davis's voice startled her. "I'm almost finished here, Handsome." The woman herself came into view, a cigarette dangling from plump, lipstick-red lips. She had an armful of manila folders. She flipped the folders upside down, letting the paper flutter out and pile onto the worktable. "A few more of these. Ellie saved everything. Then I'll box up the clay babies and we'll be on our way." She laughed. "Except, of course, we're not going to the same place. You, my dear, are going to hell. What a waste of a sexy man."

Bernie pulled Louisa's pistol from her pocket and released the safety.

"I should have put you to work, big guy. Next time, I'll have to think about that. Not that I plan a next time." Davis glanced toward the car. Bernie froze. Then Davis turned her attention back to the table.

Bernie shifted, straining to find Chee. If Davis was talking to him, he must be alive. She saw a galvanized bucket full of broken bits of pottery. Green garden hoses neatly rolled. A black guitar case. An old sled with rusty runners. Two red gasoline cans in a corner. A yellow kayak. She moved farther from the car to take in more of the room. Now she could see the edge of a mattress and a boot and the shape of a leg in blue jeans. She shifted again and saw Chee on top of the mattress, lying on his back. A wide piece of black duct tape covered his mouth. Davis had wrapped more tape around his ankles. His arms were pinned behind him, fastened at the wrists. She noticed a bloody place on his left forearm. She willed him to open his eyes and look at her.

"Ah, Officer Manuelito." Davis's voice came from behind her about the same time Bernie felt something hard press against her ribs. "I have a weapon. Drop yours and walk ahead of me into the garage. Do it now."

In one quick motion, Bernie turned toward Davis. But before she could shoot, Davis jumped back. Then hot pain knocked Bernie to her knees. She felt liquid fire spreading from her shoulder to her scalp and then to every molecule of her body. She recognized the Taser experience before she collapsed: she'd been shocked to a lesser degree in police training.

She heard Louisa's gun skid across the concrete floor behind her, out the open garage door. Bernie's nervous system, on overload from the electricity, ignored the command to rise and fight for her life.

Davis stood over her, pointing the weapon at Bernie's chest.

"My ex loved this new three-shot Taser. One of the few good things that came from that relationship."

Bernie heard the squeal of violins and willed her brain to focus on anything except the clamoring noise and the wave of raw pain. She knew she had to relax. Relax and wait for her nervous system to straighten out.

Davis walked closer, keeping the Taser pointed at Bernie's chest. She grabbed Bernie's left arm and then the right and began to drag her farther into the garage.

"You're lighter than I thought you'd be," Davis said. "Just a slip of a girl. It would have been easier to shoot you, but I don't want to disturb the neighbors."

Bernie yanked her arms free from Davis's grip and rolled, ready to rise from the floor. Davis jumped like a panther.

This time, the Taser sucked the air from Bernie's lungs and every cell in her body, replacing it with sizzling agony, a searing river that started above her head and ran to below her feet. Bernie heard herself scream, then heard Chee moan. She willed the sound to stop, willed her eyes to open and stare at Davis.

"It took Handsome a while to understand the power of technology, too. Women's bodies have less capacity for this sort of thing."

Bernie felt a hard kick in the ribs, a new sensation of pain. "Roll over, facedown." Bernie forced herself onto her belly and felt Davis roughly grab her, wrenching her arms behind her back. Davis pressed her wrists together, binding them with duct tape. Bernie saw the empty tape roll bounce along the concrete floor.

"Tasers are handy little items. I kept this in my car along with my gun and the demolition kit for the happy day when I could make sure none of Ellie's phony appraisals were traced to me."

Bernie tried to think, ignoring the pain from her ribs piercing her chest each time she inhaled. Demolition kit?

"That Ellie. She had everything except an extra roll of tape. But this will do." Bernie stayed limp, nonresistant, as Davis looped a bungee cord around her ankles, pulling it tight.

"Roll over so I can see your face."

The weight of Bernie's body made the hands trapped behind her back hurt more than she imagined they could. She saw Davis walk to the improvised shelf and carefully peel back the tablecloth, rolling it to keep the dust from flying. Beneath it were four black-and-white pots, similar in style, different in decoration.

Davis stood admiring them as the violins wailed. She pulled a cigarette from her pack of Camels, lit it with a match from a paper book of matches, put the pack and matches back in her pocket.

"Beautiful," Bernie said. Talking above the clatter of the music took effort. She felt as if someone had parked a car on her forehead.

"These are the real thing, honey," Davis said. She looked down at Bernie, took a long draw on her cigarette. "Your lieutenant was the only one who realized there was a problem with how much Ellie thought the pots were worth. Her stupidity and his meddling gave me a chance to settle up with both of them for what he did to my Randall." She took another deep lungful of smoke. "And then your hunky husband helped me figure out where Ellie kept the photos I took. Nice!"

Davis put down the cigarette and pulled a pair of black cotton gloves from her pocket. She picked up a pot and held it toward Bernie. Bernie noticed the hearts on her bracelet. The black gloves. The final pieces of the puzzle.

"Take a look at this beauty. It was the first one Ellie copied." Davis laughed. "I haven't seen it for years. Look at these tiny black stripes inside the triangles. Perfect. But Ellie's copy was almost as good."

"Like Acoma?" Bernie's voice sounded far away. Speaking intensified her headache, but as long as Davis was talking about the pots, she wouldn't kill them.

"Right," Davis said. "I read once that some Indians consider pots living beings, the union of clay and water. The potter's hands provide the magic, transfer life into the vessel. The firing gives them birth, and when they break, they return to Mother Earth."

Davis carefully picked up the next pot.

"This dates to around 1100," she said. "You can see why those greedy bastards wanted this. Exquisite. Archaeologists used to believe that the Indians used these as drums. Now we know that the women made them for drinking chocolate, beans brought all the way from Mexico. Ellie did well to save it, to save them all. When Leaphorn came sniffing around, I told her to ignore him, that I could use my pull at the AIRC to fix things. Just give me the old pots. I would have put these in the McManus collection when it got to the museum, given her the copies. Simple. But she'd changed. She wanted to keep these. I took her to Chaco to talk some sense into her, hoping that seeing the place where the pots were born would change her mind. I tried to get her to tell me where they were and where all the photos were, too."

Davis looked at the pot. "I remember the day I met this one. It was the first time Ellie asked me to go along with her to take the pictures for the appraisal. It's always been one of my favorites."

Bernie forced herself to speak. "Bird?" She felt her stomach churning. If she had to throw up, she was glad Davis hadn't taped her mouth.

"What? Hard to hear with this music. Oh, this?" Davis moved her gloved finger above a design. "Ellie and I decided it was a macaw. They traded scarlet macaws up from Mexico, too, raised them for their feathers at Pueblo Bonito. Archaeologists found their hollow bones, but never found any signs that they reproduced."

Davis looked down at Bernie. "Even some of my colleagues argue against calling that design 'macaw.' Academics can be so closed-minded. But I don't care. Once it's in our collection, I can see it every day. Won't that be wonderful?"

Davis wrapped the pot and boxed it, handling it as gently as a mother would an infant.

Bernie realized that if she turned her neck all the way to the left, she could see Chee. His skin had a gray hue, and droplets of sweat glistened on his face. She scanned the floor, looking for a tool, an idea, some way to get out of this.

"This is one of my favorites," Davis said. She held the cylinder so Bernie could see the zigzags inside. "A classic rain design."

"Acoma?" Bernie said. How odd, she thought, to spend her last minutes of life talking about pottery.

Davis sat down in the folding chair. "You are a smart one. Acoma potters use this quite a bit, and their variation is closer to the ancient ones than those you see at other pueblos. Take a look at these beautiful little handles." She adjusted the pot so Bernie could see them. "Very rare. Ellie and I figured it must have been some sort of clan connection. Relatives teaching other relatives the technique. No way to prove it, but an interesting theory, isn't it?"

Bernie felt a firm nudge in the ribs from the toe of Davis's boot. The pain made it hard to speak, but she squeaked out, "Yes. Interesting." She thought of the message she had given the attendant. Had he called for help?

Bernie watched Davis pick up two cardboard boxes and heard the dull echo of her boots against the hard floor during a pause in the music. Ten steps away. She listened to the scraping of the boxes against rubber mats as Davis pushed them into the back of the car. Bernie felt her chest tighten and fought the rising panic, shifting her focus to the dead numbness in her hands and agony in her side. She heard Davis's footsteps again. Saw her gather up the final two boxes.

Bernie twisted to look at Chee. His eyes were open. He winked at her.

Davis returned with the turquoise purse and the duffel bag Bernie had noticed on the floor of the front seat. She put them down on the littered wooden table and picked up her Taser. "I'm glad I ran out of duct tape," she said. "I enjoyed your questions."

Bernie said, "Jackson's car?"

"What?"

"For shooting."

"Oh, that Benally guy with the sedan. Clever, wasn't I?" Davis smiled. "Jackson offered to let me use his car at the ranch in exchange for gas money. I hated to drive the Lexus over those terrible roads, so I used it for errands, always with my researcher gloves. I made a copy of the key. I drove to Bashas' on the day I knew he parked there. Left my SUV, borrowed Jackson's car, and brought it back to the same parking place. I knew Ellie had been at the ranch, too, so I figured she would have had the same access I did to make her a suspect."

Davis looked through some tools, placing a few in a box. She pushed a button to stop the screeching violins, put the cassette in a box, and examined the stack of tapes.

"By the way, letting Leaphorn suffer turned out to be better than killing him. Suitable punishment for what he did to Randall. Thanks for the updates on his condition, Bernie—you were a world of help." She poked Chee in the side with the toe of her boot. "Thanks to you, too, Handsome. Without our conversation about Cuba, I wouldn't have thought of this place. I wasted a lot of time looking at lockers in Farmington."

Davis walked away again, and Bernie heard the Lexus start up and the sound of tires on cement as the car moved out of the garage. When Davis came back, she unzipped the duffel and took out an orange extension cord, a brown electric cord, and a white box. The box was a timer, Bernie realized.

On one end of the box, Davis plugged in an electric cord that looked as if it had once belonged to an old lamp. She had stripped the wire covering off the end and twisted several small strands of copper together. She plugged the long orange cord into the other side.

"I knew someday I'd find Ellie again, and then I'd find her records. When that happened, I knew I'd need a way to destroy all the old paperwork. So I fixed up this little igniter, kept it and the extension cord in my car. You cops aren't the only smart ones."

Davis fiddled with the dial. Then she picked up the Taser again and aimed at Bernie.

"Move yourself over, next to Chee."

Bernie inched along on her back, noticing the way the bungee slipped slightly against her pants with the friction of the floor. She stopped at the edge of the mattress.

"Get up there." Davis nudged Bernie in the ribs with her boot, finding the spot that hurt the most. "Quickly now. You know I'll use this."

Bernie maneuvered to lie next to Chee. Her ribs burned.

"How sweet," Davis said.

She walked to the back of the garage, returned with the two red gas cans. Put them down.

"I could gag you, but you've been such a good girl, I'll put on this old Janis Joplin cassette in case you get an idea about screaming for help. It was one of Ellie's favorites from our Chaco days. Good music to die with."

Davis punched the button. The scratchy sound of Joplin's voice filled the room. She raised the volume until the music reverberated off the block walls and cement floor. Davis took a gas can to the table where she had piled up the papers, photos, old newspapers, and cardboard boxes. She put the turquoise purse in the middle of the paper pile, opened and poured gasoline inside, saturating the purse and the papers, letting the gasoline pool.

"Purse?" Bernie asked.

"You're a cop to the end, aren't you? I had Ellie leave her purse in my car when we got to Chaco. In case I had to kill her, I didn't want to make things too easy for the cops. Her ID came in handy, and she had the key to the unit's padlock on her key ring."

Davis began to pour gasoline from the second gas can onto the mattress, on Chee's and Bernie's jeans and shirts. Bernie felt the moisture on her skin. The fumes stung her eyes and expanded her headache.

"Don't do this," Bernie said.

"I've set the timer to let me get the pots out of here safely and to give you both a moment or two to think about the havoc you've wrought. Think about how my Randall must have suffered because of your fine lieutenant. Think of how he forced me to kill Ellie. Not that she didn't deserve it, too, for the lies she told about Randall hurting her."

"Wait," Bernie said. "Stop. Please."

Davis stretched the extension cord out the garage door as she walked. "All that's left to do is to plug in the cord and put on the padlock."

Davis lowered the sliding door. The room grew instantly dark. Against the din of the music, Bernie heard Davis's voice.

"Guess what, Bernie? Your backpack is out here. I'll put it in the Lexus for safekeeping. Gives me a place to put your gun."

Bernie listened to the car door slam and the tires rolling against the pavement.

"Use the toe of your boot to help get my legs out of the bungee. Then I can kill the timer." She yelled over the music as she moved her legs on top of Chee's, then scooted down. After three tries, she caught a loop of the bungee in the toe of his boot. As Chee pushed down, she felt him shudder with pain. The bungee moved, stopped. The cord tightened at the top, cutting into her calf like a tourniquet.

"Again," she said. "Again. Again."

She felt a loop slip off her shoe and the coils loosen. She squirmed her legs free.

Bernie lurched to standing, light-headed and queasy, hands still bound behind her back. She wished that Chee's mouth wasn't taped shut so he could speak, help her figure this out.

When the room stopped spinning, she moved through the darkness toward the timer. Something caught her right foot. As she fell, her shoulder hit the table and it crashed down on top of her. She landed sandwiched between it and the concrete, facedown. She tasted hot salty blood and the bitter gasoline, struggled to breathe.

Chee grunted.

"I'm okay." The hideous Joplin tape blared on. The fall had cost her valuable time. She used core muscles she didn't know she had to shrug the table off her back, then powered herself to sitting and, with more effort, maneuvered her aching body to standing again.

She remembered where the timer had been, but the fall had changed that. Where was it now? She would find the extension cord, let it lead her to the box, probably buried beneath gas-soaked debris.

Bernie tapped her feet, still numb from the bungee, like a blind person using a cane, feeling for the thick, rounded cord and wishing the soles of her shoes weren't so firm. She listened for the timer's ticking. Heard nothing over the whine of electric guitars and the pounding percussion.

She moved into the clutter that had crashed off the table. With her feet as probes, she discovered the box of clay, the bucket filled with potshards. The cloying, pungent smell of gas made her stomach churn. She pushed back against tightening terror.

Through the cacophony of the music, she heard something new, rhythmic bashing against the metal garage door. She couldn't see him, but she knew Chee had shifted himself to the back of the room, doing what he could to keep them from going up in flames.

Then she felt something roll against the bottom of her right shoe. Lost it, found it again. Pressed against it, felt it move. The extension cord. She slid her foot over it, moving toward the timer quickly. Felt her foot slip off and lost time finding the cord again.

She realized that her eyes had begun to adjust to the darkness. Despite tearing from the fumes, she could see the cord, an orange snake on the floor against the lighter newspapers. She followed it to the white box and found it. Facedown in the gasoline. She used her feet to push the soaked newspapers off the box. They might live! She let the thought hang a split second.

Now, to unplug the power cord. Bernie lowered herself to kneeling and reached for it with the dead fingers behind her back. She couldn't make them work. A third Joplin song had started. Eight minutes, more or less, since Davis left. Chee's banging forced her to think.

The old lamp cord at the other end of the timer was smaller, more impossible to disconnect. Could she stomp the timer out of commission? Doubtful, especially with her unsteady balance.

Something tickled the back of her brain. She pictured the timer as Davis had pulled it from the duffel. It had a dial, which she had set to start the fire, and a switch to turn it on or off. Instead of trying to break it, she could turn it off. Or, if she guessed wrong, she could turn it on, creating the spark to incinerate them.

She sat and scooted through the gasoline and rubble. Used her foot to flip the box faceup. She could hear the timer ticking now despite the music and Chee's racket. She moved her face close to the switch, straining to see if she should push up or down. But the writing was too small, her eyes too irritated by the fumes, the room too dark. The clicking had grown louder, as rapid as her heartbeat. Up or down? On or off?

The Joplin song blared toward its climax. She wrapped her lips over her teeth and grabbed the switch. She pulled down with all her strength.

21

The ticking stopped. She exhaled.

She hollered to Chee, "I did it. I'll get my hands loose and then I'll help you."

It took a lifetime to scrape enough of the duct tape from her wrists against the edge of the metal garage door frame to pull her hands free.

She punched the button to silence Janis Joplin's howling and found a sharp metal pottery tool in the rubble beneath the table.

"What first? Hands?"

He shook his head no.

"Mouth."

He nodded.

Her fingers had gone from numb to excruciating pain, but she pried enough tape off the skin at his upper lip to grab an edge. "This will hurt." She yanked hard, removing the tape as though it were a big, ultra-sticky Band-Aid.

She felt him flinch.

"Sorry. Are you okay?"

"I'll make it."

He kissed her, ever so gently. "Good thing I didn't have a mustache. Now I never will."

She cut the tape from his hands and left him with the tool to undo his legs while she looked for a stick or a pole to force up the garage door. She found Ellie's gasoline-soaked purse. Ellie's phone, in an outside pocket, still worked. Bernie called 911. Told the dispatcher to contact Agent Cordova, gave her their location. After that, she called Captain Largo.

Finally, Bernie heard a siren. The noise came close, closer, stopped. She heard a car door open, footsteps running toward the locker.

"Cuba police," a male voice yelled. "You okay in there?"

"Yeah, fine," Bernie shouted back. "Glad you made it."

"The manager is right behind me, and he'll have the lock off in a second. We'll get you out of there. Need an ambulance?"

She looked at Chee, and he shook his head. Several times.

"No ambulance. Be careful. This place is full of gasoline."

She heard the grate of metal on metal. A second siren. She heard more voices, probably the other renters, looky-loos attracted by the police commotion. Finally came the happy creaking of the garage door being raised.

The dry air had never smelled so fresh, or the sun's light seemed so wonderfully intense. She helped Chee stand up, swaying, and steady himself.

"The FBI crime scene folks are on the way," the deputy said. "I know they'll want to talk to you."

Bernie said, "The main thing is to catch the woman who did this."

"Everyone's looking for her," he said. "You can't shoot Joe Leaphorn and try to fry up a couple more cops without getting some attention."

"Not only that," Bernie said. "She stole my favorite backpack."

The manager looked at Bernie. "I never would have made you for a cop."

"Did you call for help?" she asked him. "It took long enough."

"That what I was trying to tell you when you ran off. The office phone doesn't work, so I had to go over to the gas station and have them call."

The deputy studied Bernie's wrists and Chee's pallor. Chee said, "I'm fine. Really. Just a little shaky."

Bernie said, "With all the times Davis must have Tasered you, it's a wonder your heart is still beating."

"You. That's why."

Cordova arrived within the next half hour, taking charge of the scene efficiently and, Bernie noticed, with a touch of humility. "Guess I was wrong about Jackson Benally and Leonard Nez," he said. "We found Nez at a rodeo in Crownpoint. He didn't even know we were looking for him. When we talked to him, it was clear he didn't know Louisa, Leaphorn, anything about the shooting. Or much else except bronc riding."

They walked through the gate, back to Louisa's Jeep. Bernie extracted the keys from her pocket and clicked the doors open. Chee climbed in the passenger side. She started the engine and rolled down the window. She drove across the street to the service station, pulled up in front of the closest pump. "I'll be right back," she said. "Need anything?"

"An aspirin or two would be good."

When she got back, Chee was standing next to the car, his hands on the roof, taking some deep breaths. "Those fumes," he said. "I never want to smell gasoline again. Or get Tasered, either."

He noticed that instead of the blouse she'd been wearing, Bernie had on a clean blue T-shirt with the yellow New Mexico state flag on the pocket.

She handed him a T-shirt and a package of baby wipes. "Those will help with the gas smell. No pants in there, but I got lucky on these shirts. On sale for five bucks."

"I got lucky," he said. "You saved my life. You solved the case."

"I should have figured it out sooner," she said. "All the clues were there."

He took off his white shirt and saw the bloody places where the Taser probes had penetrated his skin. "I loved this shirt," he said. "My best one. You think you can get it clean again?"

She looked at it. "Don't worry about that now."

When he was done, they climbed back into Louisa's Jeep and Bernie pulled out a big bottle of water, a bottle of extra-strength ibuprofen, and a package of beef jerky from the shopping bag. "Here, I brought you something else."

He took the pills and the water and gave her back the meat. "You have it," he said. "My stomach isn't there yet." He smiled at her. "Davis took your backpack. How did you buy all this? And the gas?"

"The guy who runs the store just gave it to us when I told him my wallet had been stolen with my backpack. He's the one who called for help. And I think he wanted me out of there quick because of the way I smelled."

Chee took a sip of water and closed his eyes.

How odd, Bernie thought, to have no electronic communication. No phones. No police radio. They were halfway back to Santa Fe to pick up Chee's truck and return Louisa's Jeep before she felt like talking. Chee stared out the open window at the Rio Puerco Valley, the sandstone cliffs, and then the flatter, more desolate landscape that framed the sprawling community of Rio Rancho.

"If you're up for it, we ought to make some notes about what happened back there," she said. "Cordova is bound to have more questions."

"I'll start with what a fool I was to let her overpower me with that Taser at the museum. I knew she was guilty of something, I just hadn't figured out what."

"And I thought she was concerned about Leaphorn when she asked how he was doing. She wanted to make sure he wasn't going to recover enough to tell us what had happened."

"Yeah," Chee said. "*M is for Maxie. M is for murder.*"

The nurse had messages for them on the way to Leaphorn's room.

"Officer Chee? Agent Cordova from the FBI has been trying to reach you. Needs you to call him. He said to tell you, 'We got her.' You know what that means?"

"Yes," Chee said. "It's good news."

"And here's another message. I wasn't sure I understood it, so I wrote it down." She handed Chee the slip of paper. "What happened to your face?"

"Long story," he said. "Nothing to worry about. I won't have to shave for a year."

The nurse looked at Bernie. "You look like you had a fall."

"Yeah, I tripped over something," Bernie said. "How's the lieutenant?"

The nurse paused. "Not much change from this morning."

In addition to Louisa, they found a middle-aged Navajo man in pressed jeans and a dress shirt in the lieutenant's room. He introduced himself as Austin Lee.

"I'm the one you called for in Farmington," he told Bernie. He pointed toward the hospital bed with his lips. "He's been good to me. I'll see if I can help him, working with his lady here."

Leaphorn seemed about the same, Bernie thought, tied to the maze of tubes, lying still as death on his back.

"You both look kind of tired," Louisa said.

Bernie said, "You look exhausted yourself." Bernie had never thought of Louisa as old, but she seemed ancient today, used up.

Louisa told them what the doctor had told her. Leaphorn's vital signs were slowly declining as a result of the pneumonia. Nothing dramatic or exciting, but a natural progression that often led to death. She started to cry. "I'm going to go outside for a minute or two, maybe get some soup or something."

Austin Lee joined her.

"Take your time," Bernie said. "We won't leave until you get back."

"I want to hear the details of where you've been and what happened," Louisa said. "But later, okay?"

After Louisa and Austin left, Chee took the lieutenant's hand and spoke in Navajo, telling Leaphorn how much he respected him, how much he had learned from him. "Not only about how to be a policeman. About how to be a man. How to walk in beauty despite the evil and disharmony that the world gives us. I thank you for all that."

Bernie listened. Her husband was more than her friend and lover. He was the man she needed to remind her of what life was about—how to make a difference in the world and how to live with honor.

Bernie stood across from Chee and put her hand on top of the lieutenant's chest. When Chee finished, she spoke. She called Leaphorn Uncle now, not Lieutenant. She told him she was grateful to him for encouraging her to follow her heart, and for somehow knowing that her heart would lead her to accept the love of Jim Chee.

She stopped talking and looked at Chee. The tears in his eyes matched her own.

Chee said, "I wanted you to know that Bernie found the woman who shot you. She found out why. It had to do with revenge and with greed."

The lieutenant opened his eyes and looked at Bernie, then at Chee, then back at her. He made the sign again for a pencil.

Bernie found one that Louisa had been using and a slip of paper.

This time the lieutenant drew more slowly. A smaller picture. This time, it looked exactly like a heart. Then he closed his eyes. They stood in silence for a while on each side of his bed, watching his chest move up and down in the struggle to breathe against the force of pneumonia.

Then Chee started to sing, softly at first. The Bluebird Song, the song that traditionally greeted the day, the song that mothers taught their little ones. Bernie sang, too, surprised her voice cooperated. They didn't care who heard them.

Leaphorn opened his eyes. He looked up at the ceiling and then to the left, toward Chee, and the right, toward Bernie. Then he gently closed them.

When she returned, Louisa said, "You two should get home. I'm staying here until, um, until it's time for me to leave. I'll call you with updates."

"I don't want to leave you alone here," Bernie said.

"I'm not alone," Louisa said. "Joe's here. Austin Lee will be back. I'm surrounded by the staff. And by all your love."

"Well, then," Bernie said. "We'll take care of your cat until you get back."

"She's not really our cat," Louisa said. "She's a stray. Joe started feeding her, then she figured out how to get in the house. Last week, he let her lick his bowl when we had vanilla pudding. That sealed the relationship."

Chee said, "I'm sure she's very annoyed at not being fed for twenty-four hours, but I left her plenty of water."

"Chee bought an ice cream maker," Bernie said. "He's been threatening to try it out on me. When he does, we'll invite you and the lieutenant and the cat to join us."

Bernie reached in her pocket and handed Louisa the Jeep keys.

"I parked it close to where you left it. I hung up that handicapped sign. I'm afraid I lost your gun, but we'll get it back."

"Don't worry about that. After everything you did for Joe when I . . ." Louisa's voice started to shake. "You'll never know how much . . ."

Chee put his finger on her lips. She was crying now, and he wrapped her in his strong arms.

The nurse let Chee use the hospital phone to call Cordova.

"We arrested Davis back at the AIRC," Cordova said. "Found the pots. Bernie's backpack was in the Dumpster behind the place. Davis seemed really surprised to see us."

"Did she resist?"

"We didn't give her much chance after what happened to you two," Cordova said. "Can I talk to Bernie a minute?"

Chee handed her the phone.

"John Collingsworth at the AIRC asked me to thank you," Cordova said. "And I want to say you did great. Both you and Chee. Tell Chee I said so."

"I will," she said.

"Take care of yourself. Be safe out there."

"Good advice," Bernie said. "Same to you."

Chee jiggled his truck keys. "Let's go home," he said.

"Your truck is still at the AIRC."

"Nope," he said. "I forgot to show you the message the nurse gave me."

Chee extracted the note and read it to her: "Mark Yazzie says west lot last row near Dumpster."

"What in the world?"

"I get it," Chee said. "It's a guy thing."

They found the truck where Yazzie had parked it with a note inside: "More police came to the AIRC. They didn't arrest me either. I saw your truck. Thought you might need it."

Bernie laughed. "How did he break into it to drive it over here?"

"That is one of the beauties of an old truck," Chee said. "Or one of the problems, depending on what side of the break-in you're on."

"One more question. What was that drawing about? The heart?"

"I think it was the bracelet," Chee said. "The matching heart bracelets that Davis and Ellie had. I think he'd noticed it on Davis when he visited the AIRC and then again when she shot him."

"Maybe," Bernie said. "Or maybe that's his way of saying he loves us."

"Not a chance," Chee said. "Well, maybe a tiny one."

22

Chee and Bernie arrived at the Navajo Inn in their best uniforms. The FBI had established a special award to honor Lieutenant Joe Leaphorn as he slowly recovered from his injuries, and decided to make the announcement in Leaphorn's home district with the Navajo Police in attendance.

Agent Cordova was there, along with other top-ranked FBI officials, all wearing dark suits. The Navajo Police, Arizona and New Mexico State Police, and assorted sheriff's departments, U.S. marshals, livestock inspectors, and other law enforcement personnel who had worked with Leaphorn over his many years as a policeman sat in the audience, along with civilian support staff. Even Joe Wakara showed up from Chaco Canyon.

"I hate stuff like this," Chee said. "Too much talking."

"Cheer up," Bernie said. "It's not every day we both get invited to a free breakfast."

It was her first visit to the restaurant since Leaphorn's shooting. Chee parked in the side lot near the adjoining motel, whether intentionally or by happenstance, and they walked in through the portal. When the meeting was over, she told herself, she'd go out the front door, look at the place where Leaphorn had fallen, release any hold that memory still had on her.

"It's nice for the feds to do this," Bernie said. "I guess whoever is in charge now doesn't know how much trouble the agency caused Leaphorn on so many cases."

"Forgive and forget," Chee said.

They assembled in the hotel's meeting room. A podium had been set up at one end, along with a buffet of scrambled eggs, bacon, pancakes, sweet rolls, and canned fruit mixed with cantaloupe and honeydew.

The waitress, Nellie Roanhorse, made sure they had hot coffee. "How's he doing, the one who got shot?"

"He's hanging in there," Bernie said. "A long road ahead of him."

Officers Bigman and Wheeler joined them at the table.

"What's your mother up to?" Bigman asked Bernie.

"She's well," Bernie said. "In fact, she's going to Santa Fe with us tomorrow to see an old rug she's been wanting to look at."

"That's great," he said. "The rug she made for my wife and me is on our bedroom floor."

Chee said, "Bernie got offered a research job at that place in Santa Fe where they have all the Indian stuff. The man there is willing to work around her police schedule. Wants her to help him find oral histories on some of the old weaving."

Wheeler said, "I heard there was some more trouble at that gas station down from there, the one on the corner of 491 where you turn off for Toadlena."

"I heard that, too," Bernie said. She wondered if Darleen had been involved. She knew she ought to invite Darleen to go with them to Santa Fe, but she dreaded the idea of a full day with her sister.

Chee said, "They had rain on Narbona Pass yesterday. The view must have been spectacular after that."

"I love it up there," Bigman said. "You can see the whole world. Or at least most of the whole Navajo world, when the dust settles."

Cordova had switched on the mic, thumping it with his thumb.

"We hear you," Wheeler yelled.

There was some noise in the back of the room, and Bernie saw Mrs. Benally and Jackson, all dressed up. They waved at her. Mrs. Benally made a sign to Wheeler that she wanted to talk to him afterward. Fudgsicles, Bernie thought.

Cordova welcomed everyone and introduced dignitaries, including a Navajo Council member, some FBI bigwigs, an Apache County commissioner, and a retired U.S. marshal.

Then he said a few words about Leaphorn and the award, which would be given annually to an outstanding officer working in the Southwest.

"And today, as a surprise, I'd like to announce that the first recipient of the Leaphorn Award of Valor is here with us. Officer Bernadette Manuelito, would you please step forward?"

Bernie sat back in her chair. Swallowed hard.

"Officer Manuelito is receiving the award for efforts that involve both mental strength and physical ability, for a cool head in the face of challenging circumstances, and for persistence despite many obstacles."

Bernie stopped listening. It wasn't right to be honored just for doing your job. It certainly wasn't the Navajo way. She stared at the table. Her skin felt hot and red.

Chee poked her and whispered. "Go up there and get the plaque and say thank you," he said. "You can argue with me later about why you don't deserve it."

And so she did.

Acknowledgments

With appreciation . . .

First of all, I have to thank my dad, Tony Hillerman, for, well, for everything. For writing the first book in the series, *The Blessing Way*, published in 1970. That book introduced Joe Leaphorn, Dad's original Navajo detective. Dad believed that interesting stories and good writing mattered and his passion for books inspired me from girlhood. I will be forever grateful to him for encouraging me to read and write, write, and write some more. Although we never talked directly about my taking on the series after his death, working with him on my previous book *Tony Hillerman's Landscape: On the Road with Chee and Leaphorn*, laid the groundwork for *Spider Woman's Daughter*. His example as a writer and his support as a father gave me the gumption to adopt Leaphorn, Chee, and especially Bernadette Manuelito, and make them my own. While I enjoyed all his books, his novel *A Thief of Time* with its wonderful plot and settings created the platform for *Spider Woman's Daughter*. If you haven't read it, or haven't read it lately, I encourage you to take a look.

Dad's longtime editor Carolyn Marino reacted with enthusiasm rather than skepticism when I mentioned my plan. Marino worked with Tony beginning in 1990 as coeditor with Larry Ashmead and then as Dad's main editor through the end of his series. She was also the editor of his memoir *Seldom Disappointed*. She gently prodded me out of my comfort zone as I moved from years of writing nonfiction to the challenge of writing fiction. I am thankful for my good luck in being the beneficiary of her long and skilled work as the editor of the Tony Hillerman mysteries. My gratitude extends to her associate, Amanda Bergeron, for her insights on *Spider Woman's Daughter*, and to my agent, Elizabeth Trupin-Pulli, for her business acumen.

I am more grateful than I can express to my colleagues, writers Margaret Coel and Sandi Ault, both of whom strongly and continually urged me to keep the stories of Leaphorn, Chee, and Manuelito alive. A tip of the hat to my Santa Fe writing partners Cindy Bellinger and Rebecca Carrier for their wise insights, skillful nagging, and refusal to let me take the easy way out. Special thanks to Jean Schaumberg, my business partner for Wordharvest Writers Workshops and the Tony Hillerman Conference, for doing more than her share while I worked on this book. And to Miranda Ottewell-Swartz for her assistance with Navajo star lore.

Rick Iannucci, a retired U.S. Marshal and former Green Beret, shared his knowledge of law enforcement procedures and the psychology of bad guys. Iannucci is executive director and an instructor with Horses For Heroes—New Mexico, Inc. You can learn more about the work his group does with returning veterans at http://horsesforheroes.org. David J. Greenberg, recently retired from the FBI, taught me about crime at Chaco Canyon National Historic Site and interagency cooperation in Indian Country. Both these gentlemen helped me learn what everyday law enforcement in the Southwest involves. Thanks to Santa Fe Police Officer Louis Montoya and his associates from the Santa Fe County Sheriff's Department and the New Mexico State Police for all the information they conveyed to me during the multiweek Citizens' Academy, a program that shows to the public the complications, dangers, and rewards involved in police work.

I drew on the research of fellow author Laurance D. Linford reflected in his book, *Tony Hillerman's Navajoland*, for insights into the real places that populate Dad's novels. I am grateful to Dr. Joe Shirley and all the generous and supportive Diné I met during my three years of research. I have nothing but respect and admiration for the hardworking men and women of the Navajo police force who risk their lives to keep the Navajo Nation safe.

My mother, Marie Hillerman, continually encouraged me to write about the characters Dad created, assuring me that Tony would be happy to see them live on. She read drafts, shared her astute insights, and worked with me on two bouts of end-of-project proofreading. Brandon Hillerman Strel did a fabulous job catching inconsistencies and raising questions that helped make the book better. My husband, Don, deserves a truckload of chocolate for all his assistance and for putting up with me on those days when writing the book became an obsession.

And, from head to toe, I appreciate the scores of my Dad's fans who asked if he had another manuscript stashed away somewhere (no, he didn't). Like me, they wanted more stories of Jim Chee and Joe Leaphorn, and Bernadette Manuelito. They urged me to jump into the job by sharing their own stories of affection for Dad, the characters he created, and the landscape in which they lived.

About the Author

ANNE HILLERMAN is an award-winning reporter, the author of several nonfiction books, and the daughter of *New York Times* best-selling mystery author Tony Hillerman. She lives in Santa Fe. This is her first novel.